THE CHANDELIER BALLROOM

A tale of heartache and drama with supernatural overtones.

When small-time crook Horace Butterfield buys an antique chandelier to enhance his brand-new ballroom at Crossway Lodge, little does he realize what's in store. For the chandelier is said to be haunted by the ghost of a young woman who hanged herself during the Wall Street Crash – and tragedy and heartbreak befall all those who move into the Lodge.

THE CHANDELIER BALLROOM

Elizabeth Lord

Severn House Large Print
London & New York

This first large print edition published 2015
in Great Britain and the USA by
SEVERN HOUSE PUBLISHERS LTD of
19 Cedar Road, Sutton, Surrey, England, SM2 5DA.
First world regular print edition published 2014 by
Severn House Publishers Ltd., London and New York.

British Library Cataloguing in Publication Data

Lord, Elizabeth, 1928- author.
  The chandelier ballroom.
  1. Haunted houses--England--Essex--Fiction. 2. Great
  Britain--History--George V, 1910-1936--Fiction. 3. Great
  Britain--History--George VI, 1936-1952--Fiction.
  4. Paranormal fiction. 5. Large type books.
  I. Title
  823.9'14-dc23

ISBN-13: 9780727897688

Severn House Publishers support the Forest Stewardship Council™
[FSC™], the leading international forest certification organisation. All
our titles that are printed on FSC certified paper carry the FSC logo.

MIX
Paper from
responsible sources
FSC
www.fsc.org   FSC® C013056

Printed and bound in Great Britain by
T J International, Padstow, Cornwall.

One

The letter had come from a solicitor he'd never heard of, scaring the living daylights out of him. Now that the initial shock had subsided, it lay open on the coffee table, with Horace Butterfield, known to most as Race, reading it through a second time with only one thought racing around in his head: someone had to be stitching him up.

Reading the letter over his shoulder, his wife Millicent was suspicious too.

'It's too bloody good to be true, Race. You're going to 'ave to phone these people, find out who they are, what they're up to, who they're working for.'

'If it *is* a catch,' he replied slowly, 'it's a damned silly one. What do they expect to gain?'

Seeing the name of an unknown law firm on the envelope, his first thought had been that Linkman, the little bastard, had gone to the police after all about the job they'd done just over a week ago. Or maybe he hadn't, because as yet no police had come nosing around. But you never could tell.

Last week he'd stood over the snivelling Linkman after Race and his two mates had given him a going over. Glaring down at the bruised and bloodied upturned features, he'd warned: 'You go bleating to the fuzz and it'll be the last thing you ever do.'

The job hadn't gone off well. They'd only just made it before the police arrived. Coshing the elderly night watchman on the bonce as he was making the phone call to them, they'd had to leg it quick, but Linkman had been terrified that they'd killed the old boy. He had been pretty ancient.

They hadn't. The local paper had reported him recovering in hospital. But it had been too much of a close shave. Robbery with violence, all four would have gone down for a long stretch. He was fifty-three. At his age the last thing he wanted was to end up doing fifteen years or more. It hadn't even been a big job. None of them were these days and he had this feeling he was getting past it.

All his life he'd been only slightly better than a petty thief, dreaming of becoming someone, carrying off the big heist, but somehow never rising very far up the rungs of the criminal world.

''Cos you're too bloody nice, tryin' ter act the bloody gentleman all the time!' That would come up every time, Millie scoffing at his efforts to improve himself from a hard upbringing. 'Yer can't be nice in your game,' she'd nag, her harsh Cockney tone grating on his nerves. 'You need to 'ave a bit more clout.'

He thought he did. Prone to a quick and vicious temper, he wasn't above giving someone a good hiding – like Linkman. As he'd ripped the letter open he had been sure Linkman had squealed despite his warning.

Now all that was flushed from his mind as he whispered, 'If this letter's genuine then it's a bloody fortune! It can't be true!'

Millie was gazing down at the legal wording. 'I ain't never 'eard of this Robert Sacker person. If this ain't a set-up then it's got to be a mistake.'

Race looked up at her with faint irritation. Her acid remarks never ceased, even with money like this staring them in the face. But the remark made him think clearer now that the initial fear had passed.

'Yes you have,' he said. 'He was my dad's brother. You only ever saw him the once. He turned up at the church at our wedding, right out of the blue, then left – didn't come back to the house, just left. Not set eyes on him from that day on.'

'That was twenty-eight years ago.' She sniffed. 'Bloody long time!'

It was. They'd married in 1901. Before that he'd only ever met his father's brother a couple of times as a kid. After the shock of seeing him at their wedding, he'd forgotten all about him until this letter arrived telling him his Uncle Robert was dead. As if he cared. Except that the letter named him as the man's only surviving relative.

It explained that he'd left no heir, made no will; that after his estate had been sold to settle the usual outgoings, Race himself had been found to be the sole surviving beneficiary. He still couldn't believe it.

'I 'ardly remember him,' he muttered. 'I only saw 'im a couple of times as a kid when my parents were alive. They died in 1888, leaving me to be shoved into an orphanage. Then he turns up at the church the day of our wedding. I certainly didn't invite him. I took it that he'd died years ago.' He gave a chuckle. 'Of course he is now!' Then he sobered. 'The letter says he never married or had any children. His only relative was my dad. Seems he was a bit of a recluse. But to be worth all this much – fifty-odd thousand quid! When most blokes earn, what, thirty bob a week, maybe two quid? There must be some catch somewhere. If there ain't, then we're bloody rich!'

He glanced around the untidy room: a pile of Millie's undies and other stuff on a chair still waiting to be ironed from last week, a stack of old newspapers that should have been thrown out ages ago, used plates left from last night's supper still on the dining table next to the remains of this morning's breakfast, the room undusted and badly in need of new wallpaper when he got around to it, the ceiling brown from years of cigarette smoke, the net curtains likewise.

Millie had never been one for extreme cleanliness, tidiness, elegance. She had been once. When they'd first met she'd been a real doll, but the sparkling blue eyes were now faded, the once platinum blonde hair now mousy grey, the slim, supple figure now thickened. She had turned many a man's head those days, but he'd been the one to claim her.

8

Even her attitude had changed since then – the scintillating young thing now a carping middle-aged nag. He'd altered too, of course, but not like her; he'd never put on weight or developed a pot belly, still had his looks to a certain degree. He flattered himself he still looked young, though lately there were times, becoming ever more frequent, when he felt old, past it, out of sorts.

She was looking at him. Now convinced of the validity of the letter, her pale eyes had lit up at the prospect of the life they could have from now on.

'What are you going to do with it all?' she asked in a whisper.

'Do with it?' he echoed, staring back at her.

All this time, fighting to make a buck or two, hoping to hit the jackpot. All his life dreaming of making it big! He could put it behind him now. Since leaving that orphanage, unequipped for the world, having hardly been taught to read or write, he'd found a natural grasp of figures and easier pickings helping himself to things belonging to others.

He'd learned to be sly, manipulative, and by the time he was in his twenties had a small following of like-minded mates whom he controlled. He was tough and quick tempered, brutal when need be. But luck had never been on his side and he'd done time, a couple of years here and there.

This last job was to have been big. But the business with the night watchman had been a bit too much for him, and that little crap Linkman had threatened to bleat to the police to save his own skin. He'd had the bugger cringing on the floor at his feet, face battered by the kicking he'd given him. Knowing there'd be a knife in his guts next, the snotty little sod had understood.

He wouldn't talk. Race knew that now. But the letter had frightened the life out of him and he suddenly realised how sick he was of it all, jumping at every knock on the door, plotting, planning, but never quite making the grade. He was a small-time crook, always would be, and getting too old – not exactly old, but his mind tiring of trying to achieve that big job that never came.

With this money he could become legit, live the life of a gent, looked upon as respectable. He knew how to pull the wool over people's eyes. He'd surround himself with fine friends instead of the crap he now went around with, leave behind the life he'd led all these years. He had visions of buying a nice large house not too far out of London, throwing huge parties for posh new friends, dabbling on the stock exchange, going to the races, taking trips abroad.

Filled with these dreams, he said brightly, 'I'm getting in touch with this solicitor right away – today!'

'Beats me 'ow yer uncle made enough fer you to spend on a place like this,' Millie said as they stood outside their new home.

'Probably doing the same thing I did.' He didn't smile as he said it. To make that much cash his uncle'd had to be up to some caper all his life. If so, he'd been a damn sight cleverer at it than Race had ever been. 'Well it's mine now,' he added gruffly. 'So shut up and appreciate it!'

She was starting to get on his nerves, standing here doing nothing but moan. A whole year it had taken to find a place he wanted. Maybe it was a bit of a way from London, too far as she insisted on pointing out, but far enough to stop those he'd known from popping down, trying to get him to do a job with them, feeling it would go smoother if planned by someone with the money to carry out something stylish. He was well out of it and intended to keep it that way. He had no need of more money, at least not by dishonest means.

He'd thought Millie would have been thrilled with this place. With the impressive name of Crossways Lodge, its imposing frontage set well back from the road behind a sturdy hedge, it was more like a mansion. Yet here she was, pulling a face at the place as if she'd just eaten a sour apple.

'What's it supposed ter be?'

'What d'you think it is?' he answered sarcastically. 'It's a house.'

'But it's miles from anywhere and it's far too big. What d'yer need one this big for, just us two?'

He fought to keep his temper. 'So as I can entertain people.'

'Who fer Gawd's sake? Them mates what you knock around with? Do a bit of showing off ter let 'em see 'ow bloody well off you are now?'

11

'No,' he said slowly, trying to curb his irritation at the way she spoke. Since finding this place in a village called Wadely, he'd continued to improve his speech. Not far from the Essex town of Brentwood, people here had money, spoke nicely, and the last thing he wanted was to be shown up. But she had made no effort to improve herself. The moment she opened her mouth she would let him down. 'I mean to find better friends here,' he went on. 'And if you don't like it, too bloody bad. You can like it or lump it!'

'Huh!' was her response as she followed him at a distance down the extensive gravel driveway. 'Stuck out 'ere in some old village, no wonder it was cheaper than you expected. What do we want with a place like this?'

He ignored her, in a world of his own now. To one used to a two-up-two-down terrace in Stepney Green, the frontage had taken his breath away, the eighteenth-century building having been tastefully added to at the rear in more recent years. There were three acres of grounds attached, but he was a Londoner, not interested in grounds. It was the house that drew him.

Three of the downstairs rooms facing front were absolutely huge, with high ceilings and tall, elegant, narrow windows, the room across the hall having a wider one with a spectacular bay. The moment he'd seen the place an idea had formed. A ballroom! The three rooms knocked into one and the wall of the hall demolished to make one large room, the stairs widened to a grand staircase descending spectacularly from the upper landing to the final result – maybe not as huge as some, but grand enough.

It had taken a lot of work, but the result was now big enough to hold parties and dances. He'd been a good dancer when young, so had Millie. They'd not danced in years, she grown broader and sloppier nowadays, had let herself go, and who'd want to take that dancing? Now he had his own ballroom, expensively papered in gold and blue, highly polished wood floor edged by soft blue carpet, two or three settees, elegant chairs, some small tables, a grand piano, space for a saxophone, double bass, set of drums – it would be a talking point among the fine friends he intended to make here.

Within weeks workmen had demolished the walls and made good, strengthened the ceiling, laid a new floor, the whole redecorated through-out. The narrow passage behind the room divid-ing the newer part of the house from the older had been renovated to include a cloakroom/toilet and had revealed a small sealed-up door, the handle long since lost.

He had prised it open to discover some four or five steps down to a small basement, dark and stuffy but dry. His first thought had been a priest hole, but there was no other way out, no window, nothing, just a few bits of rubbish, old cardboard boxes, revealed by the gleam of his torch – noth-ing of interest. Marks on the walls suggested racks had once stood there – an old wine cellar perhaps, but now unsavoury. The door resealed, papered over to hide its unsightliness, he had turned his mind to suitable lighting for his new ballroom. Something grand, spectacular was needed – a chandelier, the bigger the better, would make a huge impression on everyone who saw it, in addition to the expensive wall lights he'd had installed.

Today he'd found one in a London antique dealer's shop, just what he had been looking for. Now he stood admiring it, mesmerised.

'It is not exactly old,' the man was saying with a slight trace of an accent he couldn't place, probably Mediterranean or something. 'But it is of genuine crystal, not of common glass, and this is why it is just a little more expensive. But good quality always reveals itself, Mr Buttyfield.'

Yes it did. Huge, impressive, suspended above him, its many graceful arms of fine brass supporting a double tier of crystal shades and electrified candles half hidden by swathes of glittering crystal drops, he could see it in all its glory gracing the high ceiling with its moulded central rose which matched the room's elaborate cornice. Standing stock still, he continued to gaze up at it. It was absolute perfection.

The man was making an obvious effort to sell it as he beamed, 'There is too an interesting 'istory attached to it. I think you would like to 'ear, Mr Buttyfield?'

Recovering himself, Race overlooked the mispronunciation of his name, eager to glean anything of interest that he might pass on to guests.

'It is from a fine Knightsbridge apartment,' the man went on eagerly. 'It is said the owner, a wealthy middle-aged lady, lost all of her fortune in the very Black Thursday, the Wall Street Crash. At the time she is having a lover very much younger than she.'

He paused, waiting for Race to nod, then resumed, 'Her fortune lost, her lover forsaked her, poor lady, she so devastated wanting only to destroy herself and from this very chandelier she tried to hung her sad body.'

Race couldn't help half smirking. It was a lot of rot. 'I'd have thought it wouldn't have taken her weight,' he said, trying not to sound too amused.

'It did not,' the man supplied eagerly, his customer's scepticism going completely over his head. 'It is quite ironic, for having dragged an armchair on which to stand to do the deed, the chandelier did not take her weight and she fell back on to the armchair and it fell down on top of her, killing her, so the story is told. The chandelier was not damaged at all for the armchair cushioned its falling down, but it killed her.' He gave a small sympathetic sigh. 'The most strange of ironies – the poor lady trying to kill herself, using of this very chandelier, but it is this very chandelier killed her!'

Having ended his lengthy tale maybe with his favourite punchline, he lapsed into silence, awaiting Race's reaction.

For a moment Race gazed back at him then he broke into a loud guffaw. 'A great story if it's true. I could tell that to my guests. They'll be well impressed.'

The man didn't laugh. He looked hurt. 'I assure you, Mr Buttyfield, I swear by the Holy Virgin it is true story.'

The man breathed the name so reverently that Race's laugh of scorn died on his lips. He even felt goose bumps ripple along his arms and heard himself burst out impulsively, 'I believe you. Yeah, fine. I'll take it.'

The man knew his customer. As far as he was concerned, the story was true, but it did command a greater price by virtue of its very provenance. He grinned as his customer made no effort to bargain. 'I will have it delivered, Mr Buttyfield,' he said, quickly adding, 'there will of course have to be a small delivery charge I am afraid,' shrewd enough to know that not to charge for delivery would make him appear far too eager to sell and the customer feel he had been taken in by a glib tale.

But it *was* true. Even he had shuddered when he'd heard the story. Poor lady, looking for oblivion from loss and misery. Yet he wondered – had it been suicide she would have lingered in purgatory, never permitted into heaven. Instead the chandelier had killed her, but she had *attempted* to kill herself, so could it be deemed suicide? He hoped not. Sad lady, whoever she had been.

Two

The finished ballroom looked wonderful – more than that, a revelation, enough to draw a gasp of admiration from anyone who entered. Centre stage, the chandelier hung in all its glory, even dimming the added splendour of the wall lights. Here he'd watch the wonder in the eyes of his many guests.

While demolition of the walls and the supporting of the now extensive ceiling were going on, with all the accompanying dust and debris, Millie had kept to the master bedroom, chosen for its wide veranda at the other end of the house above the lounge. 'Away from all that bleedin' dirt and dust and noise and mess,' she'd said, though their old East End home had never been free of dirt and dust and noise and mess. Now she stood gazing around the new ballroom as he called it, the sneer on her face wiping the grin from his.

'Ballroom?' she spat. 'A few rooms knocked tergether! An' who d'yuh think's gonna come? You don't yet know that many around 'ere to ask.'

'You'll be surprised how many I know,' he hissed, walking off to leave her talking to herself, her words following him faintly: 'Bloody

17

old fool!'

In the small library he poured a neat whisky to calm himself, swigging it down in one gulp. There were times he hated her. She'd done nothing but moan since coming here.

He was making himself known to quite a few people in the area and they were responding to their new neighbour. He had charm, made friends easily, had recently sent out invitations, gold-edged, to the Christmas party he intended to give three weeks from now, though it wouldn't actually be on Christmas Day. People preferred to spend that with family. This year it fell on a Friday so the party would be Saturday, just when most were at a loose end, and he'd had more acceptances than he'd dared hope.

He intended to follow it the next week with a huge New Year's Eve party. 'And sod what she thinks!' he said aloud into his empty glass before refilling it to drink more slowly.

From the start she'd not shown one ounce of enthusiasm for this place, for all his hard work getting it just right, still going on about it being too rambling, she feeling lost in all this space, how she missed the old friends and neighbours she'd known.

'It's like the back of beyond 'ere. They'll never come 'ere and if I went back there they'd say that now we're in the money I'm just showing off.'

'If you feel that way,' he'd told her, 'you can always go back there to live on your own. I'll set you up in a two-up-two-down. It's up to you.'

But he knew that much as she moaned about their new wealth, she wouldn't go and leave it all behind. She wasn't that daft. But she refused to mix with those he was now getting to know. She seemed to enjoy being miserable, but it was embarrassing meeting men of some importance and their wives and her never with him.

This past six months he'd made it his business to acquaint himself with those that mattered. He was generous and they liked that. He'd learned to play golf and had got himself introduced into the golf club, and through it had met several local councillors and members of quite a few notable societies. He felt he was becoming respectable and respected – no one aware of his past, of course. He was starting to hold his head up in society, had improved his speech even more, though it had never been that bad. Millie of course persisted in remaining as Cockney as she'd always been.

'I ain't putting on no airs just to suit the toffee-nosed lot you like ter 'obnob with these days. I ain't ashamed of me roots. Nor should you be.'

'They're nice people,' he tried to tell her, but she wasn't listening.

'Bad enough living in this mausoleum of a place with no neighbours to talk to, at least none like I used ter feel comfortable with, without suckin' up to the likes of them you call nice. At least I ain't no hypocrite.'

No wonder she felt out of it, making not one move to improve herself since coming here. It irked. Here was he, needing to move on from his old life, and here she was, clinging like a leech to hers.

Wisdom told him not to drop his old mates too

soon in case they felt themselves snubbed, looking to pull him down a peg or two. Him now being in the money, there was always the chance someone might see him as a soft touch for a few quid. Eventually they'd forget him. He was never a big-time crook and hopefully wouldn't be missed.

Still prickled by Millie's attitude to all his efforts with their new house, he drained his second glass and, slinging on a warm coat and scarf, stalked out for a drive around in his new Rolls to get some of the anger out of him.

It was still fairly cold after a frosty morning, though mid-afternoon clouds had gathered to hang low with the promise of a bit of sleet to come. Slowly his aggression subsided. Wadely was a nice area, not too far from London to feel isolated, but far enough away for a man to breathe clean air.

He might have chosen the west of London, but here seemed more suitable to his temperament. The East End was in his blood and he felt comfortable with the people of Essex. And he was proud of the house he'd bought, shielded from the road by trees to give it privacy from most of the houses that dotted the area. These were occupied by business people, professional men, families of some wealth.

He was starting to move in good company if only Millie didn't hold him back. She'd been something of an obstacle for much of their marriage, apart from the first few years when she'd still been pretty and full of life. But by the time she'd reached thirty, her pretty looks had faded and she'd grown into a sour old nag.

Slowing the Rolls to a stop, he sat staring unseeing through the windscreen at the clustering trees of Wadely Woods while the car hummed gently. If they'd had children things would have been better. But she hadn't wanted children, said they'd ruin her slim body, take away her looks. She had no love of children or for them. Babies bored her. She never peered into prams and cooed like lots of women did. It would have been nice to have had a son though. But that was life.

He'd hoped that coming here, starting to live the high life, would give her a lift, but it hadn't and never would. He could see that now. He could see her being an utter wet blanket whenever he threw a party. He just hoped she wouldn't end up ruining the Christmas one for him. If she did he'd kill her!

Fiercely he let the brake off and, stamping on the accelerator, shot off towards home.

After he'd stalked out on her, Millie heard his swift, angry footsteps cross the rear passage, the bang of the library door echoing through the house. For mid-fifties he was still agile, and anger seemed to make him even more so. She felt sympathy for anyone he aimed it at. He could pack a punch when he wanted. Not at her though, never at her. As soon as he got angry with anything she said he'd turn away, just as he had today, and stalk off. Sometimes she wished he would stay and see out his argument, but with her he always left whatever was on his mind unsaid.

She herself got satisfaction from a good slanging match. When she lived back home – even after all these months she still thought of Mayfield Street as home, with its dingy houses and friendly people – she would often have it out with one of them who'd upset her, although the falling out never lasted long. It was like that. Neighbours would be there the moment you were in trouble. If you needed something repaired, there was always someone to give a hand. People would pop in for a chat over a cup of tea, or if the weather was nice bring a chair out and sit outside the front door and chat while taking in the sunshine.

That sociable habit dated from when the places had first been built, though in recent years it happened less and less, which was a shame. In Wadely it had never happened, the idea unthinkable, neighbours all separated by their front gardens, closeted behind their own front doors, hardly knowing each other. Maybe there'd be a polite nod if they passed in the street, and men doing their front gardens would sometimes pause for a chat – that's if they hadn't employed a gardener – but no one paused on a corner for a friendly gossip like they would in Mayfield Street. Maybe if they met in some grocery shop or other they might pass the time of day, but that was all. She hated this place, yearned for the friendliness of Mayfield Street.

All these months, she still didn't know anyone here, but then, she had no wish to. The moment she opened her mouth, she'd see their noses turn up, their eyes glaze over. In fact if she was to bother to pass the time of day with any one of them, she wouldn't be able to resist the impulse to come out with a nice string of ripe Cockney words just to see the looks on their faces. They could all sod off as far as she was concerned.

She felt only contempt for the way Race was behaving, talking like some toff, using his full name Horace. This inheritance of his had gone to his head, more a curse than a blessing. He'd started going off to the racetrack with his new friends, investing big money in companies, playing the stock market; it seemed he couldn't lose. But the amounts he invested only needed to go wrong a few times for it all to come tumbling down around him. Then where would they be?

Millie pulled a sour face. But what if it all went wrong? Look at the Wall Street Crash. Investments could suddenly be worth nothing and then having known what it was like to be in the money, he'd be devastated to have it disappear. It'd kill him to end up back in the East End feeling himself laughed at. But it wouldn't kill her. She'd be back where her heart was, head held high.

She heard him come back into the passage, heading for the rear door. The crash of it being viciously slammed behind him brought a grin to her face. He was in a fine old temper with her. Well, let him walk it off, though he'd no doubt take his precious Rolls for a spin. When he came back he'd be all mild and sweet again. Well, let him be sweet somewhere else for now, silly bugger, taking his temper out on a door.

She looked about the lavish room, its fancy

decor, its grand piano, the gilded doors at either end, the huge chandelier in the centre of the ornate ceiling, like some gorgeous goddess from the way he seemed to worship and adore it – in love with the damned thing!

Casting it a last contemptuous glance she went out, closing the door with a purposeful click. Say what he liked, she was her own mistress.

The Boxing Day party was a great success. It would have been even greater if he hadn't had to cover for his wife. He had told her that if she couldn't be bothered to put on the beautiful evening gown he'd bought her for the occasion, she needn't come down at all. She hadn't come down. After the last guest had departed he'd gone for her up in the bedroom.

'What the bloody hell do you think you were doing?' he stormed. 'Are you deliberately setting out to make a fool of me?'

'Do I need to?' had been the reply, making him lift a closed fist to shoulder height as if to hit her, letting it hover for a moment before dropping his arm to turn away and bash the door with the fist. It hurt and he drew in a sharp hiss of pain but she merely stood watching him without moving.

'I had a headache,' she said quietly.

'Sod you and your bloody headache!' he raged, nursing his hand then jerking the bedroom door open to leave. In the doorway he looked back at her, his tone now plaintive. 'If you'd just once try to be sociable. You said you liked the dress I got you. I buy you no end of stuff but you never wear any of it. It was a stunning dress.'

24

Yes it was, had cost a bomb: figure-hugging black rayon, ground-length, fluted from mid-calf down, fashionably sleeveless and backless – she still had a decent back – but with a bolero to conceal her slightly saggy upper arms. She had tried it on in the fitting room of the fancy Bond Street boutique and for a moment had experienced a deep thrill, but only for a moment, as, looking at herself in the mirror, the thickening waist, the widened hips, the sagging shoulders and now stubby neck spoiled the creation entirely, despite the outfit being her size. She'd said nothing and let him buy it for her as willingly as if she was still the slender young girl he had once known, and for once she'd felt sorry for him, felt a moment of nostalgia for those days. But on leaving the boutique she'd caught something like a pained look on his face as he stared solidly ahead of him. That was when she'd vowed not to go down to his stupid party, to have herself belittled by all those stuck-up wives in their fine gowns. No one was going to laugh at her

She wondered if they weren't secretly laughing at him, an oaf trying to be one of them. Knowing him, it wouldn't even dawn on him.

'Won't you just try to mix, if only for my sake?' he was pleading from the door, and a wave of pity washed over her.

'Alright, I'll try,' she said, and saw him nod, unconvinced.

She was trying. There'd been several parties this past year and she was beginning to feel more at ease. Maybe she was settling in at last, now and again finding a few wives there stouter than her. On occasion Race would install a couple of roulette tables that turned out to be even more of a draw. Even without them, every party was a success. The house bore the air of a small country estate, Race seemingly acquiring some status at last.

They were beginning to live the life of the better off, too. Last spring they'd taken their first ever foreign holiday, flying Imperial Airways to Paris. Her first time on a plane, a bit scary but thrilling, and Paris was wonderful, the only other city she'd ever seen outside London. This year, following the trend for steamer cruises, they were sailing down to the Med. The weather so far had been wonderfully calm. She'd not been a bit seasick, which she'd dreaded when Race spoke of doing a cruise.

Having called in at Gibraltar, it was on to Morocco where they took a trip on a single-line railway into the desert before returning to the ship to sail even deeper into the soothing warmth of the Med, relaxing on a sun bed, drinking cool glasses of lemonade. At last she had begun to feel at ease, noting quite a few matronly wives on board. In fact, against some of them she was starting to feel quite slim. She'd even made friends with one or two. Sailing quietly along, her world began to take on new meaning. This was the life.

The ship was the new Italian vessel, *REX*, the two of them going first class with money no object. She felt pampered, fortunate, special. Their fine suite was delightful. The décor of the main ballroom and vast dining area, art deco to the highest degree, overawed her. Their own home had been done out mostly art deco, but none of it came up to this.

It was nice to sit in the comfortable and peaceful lounge, enjoy deck games or relax in a deck-chair in the sunshine, and she took full advantage of it. Race was mostly in the casino but she was quite happy taking a turn around the decks on her own. She was acquiring a tan and sometimes was sure he was looking at her like she was a new woman. Dancing every night, she and Race were picking up on their old steps. At mealtimes, sharing tables with others, her accent was fading a little – which she'd never intended it to – as they slowly sailed for home.

Tonight, the ballroom crowded, everyone making the most of it before docking in two days' time, the only table they could find already had four young people sitting there who readily made room for them. But she couldn't help feeling just a little uncomfortable beside their collected youth.

As she whispered to Race, 'I think I need to pop off to the ladies,' one of the two girls there, who had been introduced as Sally, leapt up exclaiming, 'Mind if I come with you, darling? I certainly do need to pee!' Turning to the other girl while the men rose courteously to their feet, she twittered, 'You coming, Cee?' her voice bright and cultured.

Cee, or Celia as she had been introduced, shook her head. 'Not just yet. I'm quite comfortable.'

'Okay!' chirped Sally, promptly linking an arm through Millie's as if they'd been friends for years. She was a pretty enough girl, but Celia was simply ravishing, and knew it.

Millie estimated Celia to be around twenty, twenty-two, but she was no innocent, she was sure of that. There was a manner about her that to Millie's mind said she knew how to use her looks to full advantage. More than once Race's eyes had swivelled towards her, and even when he'd nodded in reply to her need to pop off to the toilet, his gaze had flicked back yet again to the girl.

Returning to the table with Sally close behind, she saw that Cee was now sitting next to Race. Both were smoking, the girl's cigarette in a long ivory holder which she held delicately between thumb and forefinger, the other three fingers held daintily upwards.

Millie let out a somewhat audible sigh of exasperation as she sat on the other side of Race, but the girl didn't seem to hear, just leant forward to peek across Race at her and said, 'Feel better now, dear?'

Maybe meant as a joke, Millie took it as derogatory and looked away without replying. Race, however, had noticed her pique and turned to her almost guiltily.

'Want to dance, love?' he asked.

'No thank you,' she returned curtly.

'I'd like to,' Cee offered promptly, already on her feet, stubbing her cigarette out, still in its holder, and taking hold of Race's hand before Millie could react. 'I bet you're a smashing dancer,' she said as she pulled him to his feet.

He was making a play of reluctance, shaking his head and saying he wasn't that good, flapping his free hand in protest, but Millie felt certain he was thoroughly flattered at being led out onto the small dance floor by this young thing. He glanced back at her, saying, 'You don't mind, do you, Mill?'

Millie didn't answer, merely picking up and sipping at her wine while she stared ahead. If he couldn't read her thoughts into that gesture he had to be blind.

Daft old fool came the thought as, sipping steadily, she surreptitiously watched their gyrations to the beat of a quickstep, the girl in her backless, sleeveless, midnight blue gown that set off the wavy blonde hair, writhing and swaying in his arms, he trying to do the same, old enough to be her father but suddenly thinking himself as some youngster and looking a proper idiot.

The other two had also got up to dance, leaving the one young man who might have been Cee's escort. Having found himself sitting alone at the table with one middle-aged woman, he perched himself sideways-on in his chair with one leg crossed over the other and pointing away from her, staring blankly and perhaps even a little desperately about the room.

Millie knew just how he felt and continued to sip her wine as she watched her husband's antics.

Three

It was a relief to be home, if one could call it that. It would never be home to her, still a mausoleum of a place, isolated, the long views across empty fields offering no close comfort of streets and cheek-to-jowl neighbours.

These last two days sailing back to Southampton had taken forever, with that girl Celia Howard ignoring her to a point of rudeness while hanging around Race like a leech. And him, the daft old fool, revelling in her attention and her fluttering eyelashes, her pursed red lips, acting as if he was nearer twenty-five then fifty-five years old. Perhaps, she told herself while he brought the cases into the hallway, things could now get back to normal. At least he'd acted his age driving back from Southampton, talking of the Halloween party he would be holding six weeks from now.

'People don't seem to want to bother with it here. In the USA they celebrate it in a big way. We should do it here. I'll put on a show anyway.'

Any excuse for inviting a crowd, having them admire his beloved ballroom and its great glittering centrepiece, Millie thought a little sourly. But at least the idea seemed to have swept all thoughts of Celia from his mind.

* * *

As usual, the weeks leading up to the Halloween event seethed with preparation – caterers to do the buffet, champagne arriving by the bucket-load, people being hired to serve drinks, a small dance band with a female vocalist engaged, an army of cleaners to get the place spotless even though a woman from the domestic agency came twice a week to clean and tidy. Decorations were hung, coloured lights installed outside front and back.

Millie kept out of the way, not wanting any part of his preparations.

'Promise to try and make yourself presentable, won't you?' he said to her. 'I want you to look your best for this one, like you did on the cruise.'

'I'll be as presentable as you want,' she said, and she meant it.

'And come down to meet everyone?' he went on beseechingly.

She melted. ''Course!' At least until bored by all that high-blown chatter when she'd return to the privacy of her bedroom and her radio instead.

She'd taken no part in the sending out of invitations and had no interest in who he'd in-vited. Now she was home, the social niceties she'd developed during the cruise had faded and once again she looked on the friends he'd made here with some disdain, seeing no reason to suck up to them as he did. Holiday friends were dif-ferent; when the holiday is over, you can put them all behind you.

The party was in full swing before she bother-ed coming down. She felt a bit put out that he hadn't come rushing upstairs to remind her. If he had no intention of pleading with her, she wouldn't go down at all. But as the music, sounds of laughter and squeals of excitement mounted, most likely at the variety of Halloween costumes Race's guests had come in, curiosity got the better of her.

Putting on one of the evening dresses she'd worn on the cruise – she was blowed if she was going to make a fool of herself in fancy dress – she applied a dusting of face powder, a trace of lipstick and, combing her short, faintly greying hair, ventured as far as the top of the stairs. The small band was playing a quickstep, a favourite of hers from years ago.

Keeping out of sight behind the door to the upper landing, she could just glimpse couples whirling around to the beat, each seen for one brief moment before they swept on, to be replaced by other couples. Race too was dancing, a young woman in his arms. In the second that they passed her sight, it felt as if her heart had missed a beat. The girl was Celia Howard.

Clad in next to nothing, her brief top seemed to be made of dried grass. She wore a grass skirt, a garland of paper flowers, the same flowers around each slim bare wrist, in her blonde hair a red hibiscus. All glimpsed in that one split second, it felt as if the moment hung suspended for an age before the two moved out of sight.

Millie turned and fled back along the short landing and through the door to the passage behind. The way Celia had practically hung in his arms, he gazing at her with that silly grin on his face. In her bedroom, a demented wave of fury hitting her, Millie tore off the lovely evening dress. Hearing the seams rip prompted her to help the ruin along, screaming abuse at the top of her voice as she continued to rip. 'Damn 'im! The bastard! Asking that bitch 'ere into me own 'ome, right 'ere in front of me. Bastard! And 'er ... smarmy little cow ... I'll kill 'er ... I'll kill 'im ... I will ... I'll kill 'em both...'

Hoarse from screeching, her voice finally giving way, she sank onto her knees in misery amid the shreds of her beautiful gown.

In bed she lay staring up at the ceiling, ready to go for him the second he came up to find her. But he didn't come up. That made it even worse, the waiting. Later she heard the departure of the guests, voices calling goodnight and thank you, laughter, cars revving up and departing. She waited.

Ages passed and he still didn't come up to bed.

Thoughts were playing around inside her sleepless mind, ears keen to the slightest sound from downstairs. The bitch hadn't left with the others, she was sure of it. She imagined him having drawn her back into the house, or perhaps she had persuaded him to let her stay a little longer.

There was no sound at all from downstairs. Had he got into his own car amid the hubbub of people leaving, the two of them driving off into the dark, enjoying each other in some quiet country lane, he satisfying a longing she now guessed he'd been harbouring ever since meeting that hussy? They should never have gone on

33

that damned cruise, but she knew that if it hadn't been Celia Howard it would have been someone else in time. He with all his money beginning to fancy his luck, seeing himself as something of a blooming God's gift to women.

Yet why ask Millie to come downstairs to the party if he'd intended that girl to be there? Or had she turned up uninvited? Then how had she heard about the party? Perhaps he'd spoken about it on the cruise. Like a sleuth, Millie turned the questions over and over in her brain, feeling worse and worse the more she thought.

She lost track of time, how long she lay awake, until startled by the bedroom door opening and him entering the room. She'd heard no car door click shut, no cautious closing of the front door, but suddenly he was staring down at her in the dim light through the half-closed curtains.

'You didn't come down,' he said slightly accusingly as he bent and switched on the small lamp on his side of the bed.

'I didn't feel up to it,' she said tersely.

'I meant to come up and see if you were all right, but there was so much going on. Lots of fun.'

She couldn't help herself. 'Like entertaining a bit of skirt or two! That Celia Howard, for instance?'

She could have laughed at his stunned expression had she not been so livid.

'How did you know she was here,' he blurted, 'if ... if you didn't come down?' The words made him sound even guiltier.

'I did. I saw you dancing with her. I was standing on the stairs.'

'I didn't realise.'

'No, 'course you didn't. You was too tied up with 'er!'

'What I mean is you should've come and joined us all.'

'You was doing well enough wiv 'er.' Since the shock of seeing him with that woman, her improved diction had gone out of the window. She didn't care.

He was staring at her in righteous indignation. 'All I did was dance with her. She came with that Cyril Oliver we met on the boat. You remember, one of those chaps Celia and her friend were with. I got on well with him so I asked him and Celia to our party.'

Millie ignored the *our* bit. 'This bloke's 'er fiancé then?' she asked.

'I don't think so,' he muttered, calmer now as he began to undress for bed. 'They were all just friends as far as I know, all four, just a small crowd of friends.'

'And they all came 'ere?'

'The other two couldn't come.'

'And did this Cyril dance with 'er?'

'He don't dance.' Race heaved a weary sigh. 'Look, it's late. I'm tired and I need to get a bit of sleep. It'll be light in a couple of hours.'

'I thought everyone left ages ago,' she persisted. 'What've you been doing all this time?'

He paused in buttoning up his pyjama top. His expression in the light of the table lamp had tightened. 'What's the matter? Why the third degree?'

'No reason,' she said, and turned over on her pillow away from him.

'You should have come down,' he said, but she didn't reply. She felt his side of the bed press down, movement as he turned off the lamp. ''Night,' he whispered, but again she didn't reply. For a while all was silent. She heard his breathing deepen, then jerky snoring. But she didn't sleep until the first glimmer of morning stole into the room.

He was up before her, saying he had to go out, wouldn't be back until sometime late afternoon. The catering staff and cleaners would be coming in to clear up the debris from the party, so she'd have to get up and let them in.

'Where you off to?' she asked, ignoring his instructions, her mind still thrashing over last night's events, full of suspicion and accusation.

'Just into town,' he answered as he dressed. 'Some business I need to do – a meeting of sorts.'

She sat up to look at him. He was putting on one of his really good suits. Instantly her mind came alive. 'Who're you meeting?'

'Just some people – a bit of business I'm after, that's all.'

'What business?'

He turned to her, his expression annoyed and impatient, his tone sharp. 'What does it matter what business?'

She didn't reply. Why had he become so suddenly angry? He was a man of quick temper, but why get angry at such an apparently innocent question? Or maybe it was the tone she'd used to ask it, or more to the point maybe she'd touched a raw spot, filling him full of guilt.

'I won't wait for you to get up,' he said, his tone still sharp. 'I'll get me own breakfast and be off. See you later!'

It was late when he came back. He didn't say much and she didn't ask. Usually he was full of his day, especially if he had achieved results from any deal, and if things hadn't gone right for him there would be a string of complaints, everyone else in the wrong but himself. But there was nothing.

When she asked him how his day had gone, all he said was, 'It went alright. Why?'

'No reason,' was all she said and left it at that, but she knew well enough now that there'd been no business meeting.

Nor was this the only time; it seemed that almost every day he was having to go up to London.

'I'll be holding another party soon,' he told her, 'something really big. It needs a lot of planning, a lot of sorting out.'

It was a poor excuse. He'd never before had to spend time in London just to throw a party. But by now she knew why he was there, though she said nothing in case she was wrong.

Then two days before the planned party, Millie saw him through the wide lounge window, getting out of his car and moving round to open the passenger door.

It was Celia Howard who got out, sliding her long legs forward to reveal slim calves, trim

37

knees, high-heel shoes. She stood up, her beige suit and blouse perfection, a dainty little matching hat perched on the side of her head, her make-up immaculate, her red lips smiling at him as he took her arm to lead her to the front door. She seemed to lean against him as they came, far closer than mere acquaintances.

Millie shot out of the lounge and up the stairs, in no way prepared to welcome the girl in. With two days still to go before the party, why was she here so early?

Something didn't sit right, but it was hours before she could bring herself to ask, 'Why's *she* here?' knowing she sounded huffy.

'Had a row with the bloke she was living with, Cyril Oliver,' Race told her, not the least bit ruffled by her demanding tone. 'He got stroppy with her so she walked out. I don't believe there was anything there between them.'

Why should that last bit need to be said, came the thought, but Race was still talking. 'She needs to find other digs but until she can I suggested she could stay here with us for a while.'

Cosy, a second thought came, but all she said was, 'Until the party then and that's it!' stalking away before she betrayed herself further.

But Race followed her, he himself growing angry. Catching her up, he put a rough hand on her shoulder, swinging her round to face him. Ever a man of quick and sudden temper, he glared at her, his voice raised.

'What's the matter with you, Millie? Can't I ask a friend of ours to stay a few days? The place is big enough. We've five bedrooms – five bloody bedrooms – four of 'em never used!'

'*Our* friends!' she blazed back at him, her own anger rising. 'Not our friend, y*ours*! You're the one what likes to dance with 'er. You're the one what's asked 'er 'ere, not me. If you want the truth, I don't like 'er. And if you want 'er to stay, for God knows 'ow long, because that's the way I can see it turning out, then she won't be the only one to walk out on someone.'

'What d'you mean by that?' he shot at her.

'I mean you seem ter fancy 'er, the way you looked at 'er when she got out of the car, the way you put yer arm through 'er's walking 'er to the front door, gazing into 'er face. You ain't done that ter me fer years.'

'Why should I? We've bin married for years!' It was such a stupid answer that Millie burst into bitter laughter, but he seemed to take it differently.

'Look,' he said, 'she's a friend, that's all. She's a nice, friendly girl. You were okay about her during our cruise. Why've you changed?'

She could find nothing to retort. It now seemed so silly getting upset over one dance. Him putting an arm through Celia's today, maybe it *was* just friendliness, yet she couldn't bring herself to see it that way. Fear and jealousy bit into her like the taste of a sour lemon as she gave a sigh of capitulation and walked off before she said anything else to make matters worse. But a barrier had come down between them; she could feel it, though nothing more was said.

Race was hardly talking to her, nor she to him.

But she watched when he thought she wasn't looking, and yes, he was making too much of Celia, far too much. They seemed to be together all the time, she hanging around him, and him lapping it up.

Just now she'd come in on them in the lounge in time to catch the sudden movement of two people springing urgently apart, Celia staring innocently down at a newspaper on the coffee table, he looking into the fire in the grate. But that hasty movement, to her, spoke louder than words.

In that split second Millie had backed out of the room in one smooth and swift movement. Now she tapped on the door before re-entering to find them on opposite sides of the room. It looked so obvious. Celia had already regained her composure as she turned from the window through which she'd apparently been staring at the cold grey sky with its fine drizzle, her greeting far too bright to be convincing.

'Oh, hello there, dear! What a terrible day. I do hope it won't be like this for Race's fireworks on Saturday. I suppose we all do, don't you?'

'Are you comfortable in your room?' Millie replied coldly, ignoring the false friendliness.

'Oh, yes, very,' Celia answered readily. 'And thank you so much for putting me up. Race should have told you he was asking me back here for a few days beforehand, but it was all on the spur of the moment. I really hope you don't mind.'

'Why should I mind?' It was a challenge rather than a palliative, but Celia gave a sweetly innocent smile.

'I'm so glad,' she said easily as she came across to the door, touching Millie's arm in a friendly fashion as she passed. 'I think I will just go to my room and freshen up before lunch.'

To Millie's mind, the way she said it made it sound as if it was her own room to lay claim to, permanently.

Moments later Race followed her, passing Millie without a word to leave her standing alone in the lounge, staring at the spot where the two of them had so noticeably sprung away from each other, each hoping that she hadn't noticed.

Had they been kissing? She was sure they had, the girl's lips lifted to his, bodies close so that he would have felt the firm lift of her breasts, she aware of his hips, his groin maybe? Had he been aroused?

The thought made her feel sick. All she wanted to do was leave this house, leave him. But where would she go? Back to the East End where she had always been comfortable? It was what she would have liked to do, and she was sure one of her old neighbours would have taken her in. Except that she would have to explain herself to them and she didn't think she could bring herself to do that – airing her dirty washing!

It came to her that she had never been that happy here, not from the very start. The place was too rambling, too posh. She didn't enjoy having a cook, Mrs Dunhill, from the village coming in every day to cook for them and do a bit of housework as well. Cook-General, Race called her, him trying to be posh, stupid old twerp! But it left Millie with nothing much to do. True, she'd never been given to housework and the place in London had usually been a mess, but here she felt a need to occupy herself, if only with housework or a bit of cooking. Now that even this was denied her, she felt it. She was bored.

And all these parties – she'd been brought up to simpler things. Her idea of enjoying herself had been going to the pub with friends or to the pictures a couple of times a week. Then they'd been silent films. She'd only seen a couple of talkies before Race came into all that money and spoiled her life.

Yes, she missed going to the pictures every Tuesday and Friday night. She missed the Saturday matinees at The People's Palace or the Palladium up West. She missed sitting in the local of an evening with a few half pints of stout, with friends of her own sort who knew how to enjoy themselves, joining in a sing-song, all the old tunes. Then popping into the fried fish shop on the way home for a tuppenny bit of cod and a penn'orth of chips, eating it out of newspaper, trying to read the oil-soaked print as she did so, fingers all greasy, the acrid tang of vinegar assailing her nostrils – eating it off a plate came nowhere near the same joy – or buying a plate of cockles or whelks from the cockle stall outside the pub itself, swapping rude jokes while they sprinkled salt and pepper and vinegar over the chewy, juicy shellfish. Later, having married, she and her friends would pop into each other's houses for a cuppa and a natter and talk about their husbands.

Since moving here all that was gone. If she ever did leave Race, she would definitely go back there, pick up the old threads. She might be far happier without him. Or would she? Maybe she was jumping the gun. Maybe Celia was just a flash-in-the-pan thing. Young and vibrant, what would she want with an old fool like him? Sooner or later she'd tire of him, especially when he started to show his temper, which was never a nice experience.

Maybe it would be wise to stick it out, hope he'd see sense or Celia meet some younger man with money? Because it was Race's money she was after, Millie was certain of that.

Best then to bide her time. She didn't want any more rows with him. Let dear, darling Celia find out for herself how nasty he could be. At least there was some satisfaction to be got from that thought.

Four

She was getting fair fed up with Race tearing himself inside out making endless arrangements for this fabulous party of his.

'Honestly, yer'd think he was inviting the blessed king 'imself to come and attend,' Millie said to Mrs Dunhill, whose services would not be required on that evening, Race hiring professional catering staff and all the trimmings. Mrs Dunhill had been given to understand that her cooking would not be good enough for such a do. Feeling somewhat put out, she could only sympathise with her employer's wife.

'Just as well I'm not doing it though,' she'd said to Millie. 'All that worry would only have given me more grey hairs than I've already got.'

Millie wasn't particularly interested in Mrs Dunhill's problems – she had enough of her own.

'I sometimes wish he'd never come into all this money,' she said as she sat in the kitchen while her cook worked around her. She enjoyed sitting here. It felt homely, a little closer to what she had been used to in London, though her kitchen had been tiny compared to this one and nowhere near as tidy. But there she'd had nothing to worry herself about, not all that much money, so not many of the problems she had discovered money, or more accurately a man with too much of it for his own good, could bring. And with Mrs Dunhill there was no need to put on the posh talk. Mrs Dunhill was like herself, a plain woman with no time for airs and graces.

'I think we was 'appier before he came into all this wealth,' she went on, watching the woman rolling out pastry for the steak and kidney pie for their dinner. She was a plain cook, hence, Millie supposed, the need for fancy catering staff for Race's grand Guy Fawkes party, him showing off like bloody royalty, the soppy arse, no idea people were probably laughing at him.

Like his damned stupid ballroom. True, it did hold quite a lot of guests, but *ballroom*? Hardly, even though he fancied his luck showing it off to them.

'I really detest that room,' she mused as Mrs Dunhill carefully laid the rolled-out pastry over the meat in the pie dish. 'Ballroom he calls it, ain't nothing cosy about it, ain't nothing cosy about this whole blinkin' house. Did yer know we used to live in a two-up-two-down terrace in London?'

'Yes, I remember you saying,' Sarah Dunhill murmured as she began to brush beaten egg on top of the pastry. She felt comfortable with Millie Butterfield, who had no airs and graces and asked her to call her by her first name, and in turn called her Sarah. They were two of a kind; Millie might have been an East End person of modest means, but Sarah too was of modest means for all she lived in a village surrounded by countryside, her home a tiny three-roomed bungalow with a small kitchen, no bathroom and an outside toilet. Having lost her husband to appendicitis that turned to peritonitis, she lived with her daughter Ann who was getting married next year. Her work as a cook to a family who paid quite well helped supplement her widow's pension.

'And that damned stupid chandelier he had put up. Thinks it's the real bee's knees! I just think it's out of place. Apparently it used to hang in some great reception room in some big London flat or mansion somewhere around the Kensington area, real posh place by all accounts. Belonged to some single, really wealthy woman so the story goes. According to the antique's dealer my Race bought it from, she made all her money dabbling in investments, but then it all went wrong and she lost everything and she was so desperate that she apparently committed suicide.'

Sarah Dunhill stopped brushing her pastry with egg mixture to stare at her employer's wife. 'She what?'

'Committed suicide. So the dealer said.'

Quickly she related the tale as told to Race by the dealer, of a lover much younger than the woman who left her after she'd lost all her wealth in the Wall Street Crash in 1929, leaving her broke and devastated at his going.

'The dealer said she was in 'er thirties but very striking and beautiful and dressed like someone in 'er twenties, and she was proper deep in love with this man, much younger than she was, and who made the most of it while she 'ad money. I suppose she was what they call a cradle snatcher.'

'I know what that is,' Sarah said, all ears now, pastry brush poised idly.

'So in love, so the dealer said, that when she was left with no lover an' no money, she must have gone funny and hung herself.'

Again she related what Race had told her about the suicide, or the woman's attempt of it which ended up with her being killed. Seeing her cook listening intently, she even began to embroider it a little.

'The man told my Race that the chandelier itself could be haunted. I mean to say, something like that 'appening, it could very well be.'

'How do you mean?' asked Sarah, her eyes now wide in something near to horror, she having something of a superstitious nature.

'Well, she could of thought that by committing suicide she'd make the man what left her feel guilty. Maybe she intended only to pretend to do it, or if she did, to come back and haunt him, or anyone else she fancied, to warn off being sucked into believing people were loyal when they're not, you know...' Millie broke off, aware of the other woman's horrified expression. She gave a laugh. 'Fer goodness sake, love, it's only a tale the dealer told my husband and he'd swallow anything. But it got him to buy it, him being 'appy wiv a bit of drama to pass on to his posh friends about the thing.'

'So it's not true.'

'Oh, I'm sure it is. My husband said the dealer was really upset when he was telling him and he was sure it was genuine. He said he had tears in his eyes and the way he spoke really shook him. He said the dealer was a foreign bloke, and of course they're really religious and believe in ... what's it called? Things like purgatory, something about suicides made to go there forever and never being let into paradise and instead doomed to wander the world or something. I'm not religious but who knows, maybe it's true, who's to say. I don't know. I suppose that's why I don't like the thing much, even though I've never really been a superstitious person.'

But Sarah Dunhill was. At home that day after work she told her daughter the story and then her neighbour and some of those at the WI she attended at the village hall. Soon it began to go round the village, a juicy tale like this, that the big room where the chandelier hung was possibly haunted.

Sarah Dunhill even contemplated giving in her notice, but the money was a great boost to her pension and she couldn't afford to and the work was easy enough. Anywhere else she might be asked to slave, and so she stayed on but kept well out of the room her employer loved to call his chandelier ballroom.

The buffet looked sumptuous, though the party wasn't as large as he had hoped for. Of all those he had invited, only thirty-five or so turned up, the rest apparently feeling the need to be with family on this busy night.

It didn't seem to worry Race, despite having spent a good deal on a decent dance band and a mound of fireworks. All he seemed interested in was that blasted Celia, she flirting with him like mad, he taking it seriously, silly old fool! Millie seethed as she came downstairs to join the gathering.

She was determined not to let Celia's presence get her down. Taking special care, she wore one of the wonderful evening gowns Race had bought her on the cruise. Having had her hair and make-up and her nails done that afternoon at the local hairdressers, she felt that she looked, if not pretty, at least well turned out.

She might as well not have bothered for all the notice Race took of her. Still hardly speaking, these last few days he'd even taken himself off to sleep in another room. It hurt, but she said nothing except to tell herself good riddance. It was a change not to have him snoring beside her, hearing him humph each time he turned over in his sleep, jerking her out of hers.

The music was already in full swing as she came down, most of the guests already dancing. It made her fingers curl having to endure watching him and Celia enjoying one dance after another as if she wasn't there or was completely invisible.

During the interval she couldn't touch any of the wonderful buffet, apart from picking at it, and when the dancing resumed she again found herself totally ignored. Was he doing it just to spite her, or was there more to it than that?

There couldn't be, she told herself, quenching a desire to hurry back up to her room. Instead she made an effort to strike up a conversation with Marjory Henrey, the wife of a councillor Race

was friendly with. Trying her best to speak nicely, she was sure it jarred on the other woman's
ears. They had nothing in common and with her
mind more on Race's antics, she knew she was
talking a lot of nonsense and finally moved
away, probably to the woman's relief.

It was time for the firework display, the guests
trooping out to watch it. Millie stayed indoors,
listening to the appreciative oohs and aahs at
each series of sharp explosions, but resisted the
urge to escape upstairs and be on her own. Race
must not be left alone with that woman. She
needed to be around, needed to watch him.

With the guests returning, the dancing re-
starting, she helped herself to another glass of
champagne. She'd had quite a few already, but
holding a glass was in a way a form of support,
though by now this present one tasted of nothing.

As she sipped she heard Celia's tinkling laugh
ring out across the room at something Race had
whispered in her ear. The action was almost
intimate and the girl's light laugh seemed to go
right through her. Draining her glass in one gulp
she plonked it back on the waiter's tray, making
the rest clink alarmingly enough to turn several
heads in her direction. Again came the tempta-
tion to run. But to leave now would only make
her look an even bigger fool than she already
felt, and make guests aware of what was going
on. Her hands shook as she fumbled in her evening bag for the little silver cigarette case Race
had given her on her last birthday. Quickly she lit
the cigarette, puffing agitatedly at it.

The number finished. Race escorted his partner

towards a small group of guests near the end door, his guiding hand placed lightly on the curve of her slim back. Millie was certain he knew she was watching and was doing it deliberately to pay her out for the row they'd had over Celia.

Having reached the group, Celia said something that made them laugh over the quiet chatter in the room, and she turned briefly to glance in Millie's direction, a wide smile on her lips. They were making fun of her.

A wave of sick anger flowing through her, Millie turned and took yet another flute of champagne from the waiter's tray. Her hand shook. She felt slightly dizzy and knew she was becoming a little drunk, but she didn't care. The band had struck up with a tango, a dance she and Race had often done together in earlier days. It was the first dance she'd ever had with him. He'd asked if he could take her to see a show up West. A year later they were married. He'd been into petty crime even then but she hadn't minded; people where she'd lived were into much the same things and he'd made enough from it to give them a moderate living. But he'd always been loyal to her.

Now he was in the money he was playing a totally different game, fancying himself with a woman less than half his age, and it took all her willpower to control her rapidly mounting fury, those two in each other's arms, he having lost none of his dancing skills, his partner following him with ease, lithe and supple as Millie had once been.

Emptying her glass, she reached for another, missed, tipping it over, the waiter's instant reaction being to move swiftly back from the spillage, even apologising for the mishap. She heard herself let out a ripe epithet followed by a somewhat hysterical giggle.

People were looking at her. The giggle died as she became aware of what she was doing. The two dancers having swept towards her, Celia looked straight at her as they passed.

'Are you all right, dear?'

How dare she call her dear! It was like a sarcastic dig, and on impulse Millie grabbed another full glass off the tray and aimed its contents straight at the enemy. The girl was already clear of the erratic aim but someone else gave a short scream of shock as the liquid splashed an expensive gown. Several dancers hesitated in their stride. Someone made a grasp at Millie's arm, but she swerved and tottered across the floor, yelling abuse at Race as she went, almost falling through the door to stumble up the wide stairs to safety.

It wasn't as safe as she'd expected. Minutes later Race barged into her room. Striding to the dressing table where she'd sat in an effort to calm her jangling nerves, he pulled her to her feet.

'What the bloody hell d'you think you're playing at?' he yelled at her.

'What the 'ell d'yer think *you're* playing at?' she yelled back, yanking her arm free of his grip.

He made another grab at her but she evaded it, gracelessly tottering over to her bed, keeping it between her and him, all the time yelling at him, her speech deteriorating by the second.

'I've bin watching yer making eyes at that bitch, whispering in 'er ear and 'er giggling and stroking yer shoulder and you with yer arm around 'er waist, touchin' 'er up. I got eyes. I can see what's going on.'

'Nothing's going on! You're just being bloody silly.'

'Don't give me that, yer dirty old sod!' she raged, voice rising to a shriek. 'You ain't slept in this bed since she arrived three days ago. No, yer've bin in 'er room, 'aving it off with 'er and 'er no more than a tart, and you, you filthy old...'

In two or three leaps he was round the bed, lunging for her. She felt her head thrown sideways as a stinging swipe caught her hard across the left cheek.

She gave a yelp, her palm to the stinging flesh, and saw that his raised hand was now closed into a fist. But the blow never landed. For moments on end it hung raised, trembling in uncertainty, finally falling away. In all their married life he had never hit her, though she felt he'd come close to it many a time when riled by her plain speaking as she saw it.

Stunned, she backed away, wanting in turn to aim a blow at him for the slap but afraid. She knew that Race wasn't one to confront when his temper was up. Many had felt the pain of his not-too-light kick and feared how far he could go. Now she felt that fear, the blaze of his blue eyes of a moment ago as if he would kill her. She wasn't easily frightened and had stood up to many a woman in a brawl in her younger days, but that brief, insane glare in his eyes had terrified her.

Now the terror gave way to humiliation and cold anger. She would never forgive him for it. Sobered by shock, she drew herself up to stare him in the eyes, unflinching. It was the thin end of the wedge. Having struck her once, he could do so again and she wasn't putting up with it, or with his bloody philandering.

'Right!' she said coldly. 'If you want to mess about with some young tart, then you do it without me here to watch.'

Strange how her carefully studied speech had returned. 'I'm not staying here to see you make a fool of yourself. I'm going back to where I belong and you can do what you like.'

'Then you can bloody go!' he returned, his tone hard.

She hadn't expected that, had expected him to apologise for his loss of control, begin to vindicate himself by trying to convince her that there was nothing in his association with Celia Howard, that he'd let himself be carried away. But he meant what he'd said, she could tell, and her self-esteem wasn't going to let her belittle herself by begging to stay, nor did she want to.

'Alright, I'm doin' just that,' she said slowly, her cheek still stinging, her speech slipping back. 'I'll be off first thing in the morning and you can go back down to yer precious guests and enjoy yerself with that soppy bitch. First thing termorrer morning, I'm packing me things and going to Annie Morgan's place. She'll put me up at the drop of an 'at.'

Annie Morgan had been one of her best and oldest friends before Race had come into money. How she rued that windfall of his.

His face was like granite. 'I'll send you enough money on a regular basis so's you can rent a decent place for yourself,' he said.

'Don't bother,' she said, but she had no money of her own and she couldn't stay with Annie indefinitely.

'You'll need somewhere to live from now on.'

It sounded so definite that her heart unexpectedly sank. He was casting her off. He *wanted* to be rid of her. She hadn't even realised. It felt like a death-knell, like being committed to prison for a crime, and none of it her fault. But she wasn't going to crawl. It would make no difference anyway – he was besotted by this younger, prettier woman.

The thought came as she faced him: how long would it last before he was asking her to come back? If he did, would she eat humble pie and crawl back? No, she would not. Not now. She had her pride, would die before humiliating herself like some poor little abandoned woman accepting the grace of her master. She was made of sterner stuff. She was what she was.

'Fine,' she concluded.

She saw him give a small nod. Was it contrition, a moment of regret after all these years of marriage, or was it relief in the hope of starting a new life with someone younger and fresher? She stood very still as he turned and left the room without a single backward glance, resisting the urge to run after him, to yell abuse at him. Her heart was feeling like it was broken, as they like to say in romances, dismay flooding over her, but she fought the feeling; taking her emotions in hand she resolutely told herself that if this was what he wanted he was welcome. Their marriage was over and she was blowed if she was going to plead with him.

Straightening her back, she went over to the wardrobe and reaching up for a suitcase, lifted it down off its shelf.

Five

There was nothing to compare with this life, this one he was now living. Six months had already passed, so fast, like lightning. There were moments he found himself missing Millie, but so much was going on – parties, new friends, new things to do. And then there was Cee, always attentive, steering him through any maudlin moments.

'Darling, you've got me now. And I won't ever leave you. You love me, don't you, darling?'

Of course he did, she was his life, his very being, couldn't imagine himself without her now. When they made love, he was a young buck again, age no restriction, and anyway, fifty-five wasn't old. She knew how to please a man – sometimes pliable under his body, other times playing the vamp to his extreme pleasure, taking the initiative, he totally under her control. It was unique, new, exciting. He'd never done such things with Millie even when they were first married, certain restrictions of the times dictating decorum. Cee made him feel animal, powerful, virile, revelling in her sighs and gasps of ecstasy. They played games, he the libertine and she his concubine, utterly at his mercy.

She was fun to be with, always persuading him

into something new. These six months they'd gone abroad several times, flying off to Cannes on a whim to play the casinos, she daring him, squealing with excitement each time he won. He seemed always to win, any losses shrugged aside, luck his friend these days, and it was she who brought him that luck.

Money was coming in from several good investments. It seemed he couldn't go wrong. And Cee was marvellous, giving him every attention so that he was proud to spend out on her, give her anything and everything she wanted. It made him proud to have her on his arm, flaunting the lovely clothes he'd buy her, revelling in showing off the diamonds on her delicate fingers, the pearls at her throat and on her ears.

Slender and tall, she was the same height as him. Millie had been much smaller, petite in her young days, but flesh had made her look short and dumpy. Having Cee on his arm gave him status and poise where Millie had made him conscious of the difference between them. No one questioned the fact that Millie was no longer around. He wondered if they had even noticed. She'd never been particularly liked, her own fault, but everyone crowded around Cee, wanting to be with her and, rather than being jealous, it made him proud to see the young men trying to get near her, even more proud to see her spurn them in preference to himself. Through her he was the centre of his new world.

Millie had disappeared right out of his life. She had found herself a nice little flat in Stepney Green and had all her old friends around her. So long as he sent her enough money, she seemed content, their separation far more amicable then he had hoped. She was in her element and there was no need to worry about her coming back causing trouble.

As the months went by with Cee at his side, he could see his life continuing in an endless round of bliss. No one could be so fortunate, he thought, as he collapsed in bed beside her after a huge successful party, utterly exhausted, her ecstatic cries of being brought to a climax still in his head. 'I love you so much it hurts,' he whispered between breaths.

'Darling,' she whispered back, leaning towards him to plant a kiss on his cheek.

Life was sweet. He never wanted it to end.

'Darling, I can't come with you, not this week-end.'

They were going to some country tennis party up in Suffolk. He looked at her a little annoyed and astonished. She'd never cried out of any-thing before.

'Why not?' His question was more in the form of a demand, but she smiled sweetly at him, her pure white, even teeth piercing his very soul, but this time with a tinge of sadness to the smile.

'I've had a letter from a friend of mine, darling. She's quite seriously ill and I must go to her. She's living in South Kensington.'

She never spoke about friends and a shadow of suspicion passed over him. He was a jealous man, he knew, and more so of Cee. While he enjoyed seeing men trying to get close to her, comfortable in the knowledge that she loved him enough not to let male looks go to her head, he'd often feared the day when she would tire of him.

'What's the matter with her?' he demanded. 'What's her name?'

'Her name is Sylvia Peckham. She says she is suffering from some sort of cancer. She doesn't say what.' Her soft smile trembled to a saddened grimace at the thought. 'I don't want to talk about it.'

Instantly he was mortified by his attitude. 'Then I'll cancel the tennis party and drive you there.'

'No, darling,' she said sweetly. 'It would mean you waiting about and she would not want anyone seeing her whom she doesn't know. You do understand? You go and have a good time. I'll get a taxi to the station. I'll be there in a couple of hours but I might have to stay with her the weekend. I can hardly rush away. I'll see you on Monday, darling.'

Not much he could do. The only gratifying thing was that everyone asked after her at the party, making him so proud that she was his.

On her return, it was good to have her back. He hadn't realised how much he would miss her, even if it was only for a weekend.

'How did it go?' he asked the moment she got home. Her reply was to break into a flood of tears, very unusual for her, he having to hold her to him, feeling the heaving of her body against his chest.

'I'm so sorry, darling,' she sobbed, recovering a little. 'I didn't mean to break down but I've been so upset. She says it could be terminal, but if she can be cured it could take an awfully long time. Darling, I shall have to go and see her from time to time. I hate to leave you, but what can I do? She was my best friend before I came to you and I feel so guilty having not seen her for so long. But now I have to go and see her as often as possible to make up for it. You do understand, don't you, darling?'

What else could he say? She wasn't just beautiful, she was sweet, caring, she had cared for him and his welfare all this time, how could he deny her this duty as she saw it to be?

For the next few months she was with her friend almost every weekend, but not once would she allow him to go with her,

'She looks so pitiful. She wouldn't want a stranger seeing her like this.'

And now it was sometimes during the week, too. Each time he complained she fell into such floods of tears that his heart melted, and his was not a heart that melted easily. But every now and again she did consent to be at his side when he gave important parties.

'I have to consider your feelings,' she'd say quietly when he was troubled over her self-sacrifice. 'I should be with you as often as I can.'

This Whitsun bank holiday she'd returned home early saying her friend had gone into hospital for some check-ups.

'This is Sylvia's brother, Ronny,' she said, introducing the young man she had brought with her. 'He looks after her nearly every day. He

61

hardly gets a break so I said he should come down over the weekend for a rest from it while she is in hospital. You don't mind, do you, darling, if we put him up for the night?'

The man had smiled self-consciously at Race's narrow regard. 'I hope I'm not intruding,' he said softly. 'I must go back tomorrow to visit Sylvia.'

'Make yourself at home,' Race told him sourly. The man was young, good-looking, prompting immediate wariness. But Cee came over to hold Race's arm, cuddling against him, her eyes gazing into his with adoration glistening in them, her kiss on his cheek already promising the passion to come later.

Today had been one of his celebrated garden parties, the now setting sun having shone the whole evening, and Cee had hardly left his side. By evening, the ballroom crowded, music playing, champagne corks popping, lauger rose up to the chandelier which he hardly noticed these days, he and Cee standing arm in arm talking to this one and that, Ronny forgotten.

Exhausted by two in the morning, the last guests having left, he put his arm about her to go up to bed. Ronny Peckham had already retired to a room prepared for him. The waiters and hired staff had departed, Rosie Watts their housemaid had left for home in the village, as had Mrs Dunhill, their cook. The house lay silent. Halfway up the grand staircase, Cee sighed and moved out of his hold.

'Darling, would you mind if I stayed down here a little while longer? I've such a headache. Lying down will only aggravate it. I think I'll sit up for a little in the library, see if I can clear it. No need to stay with me.'

Grudgingly he left her making herself comfortable on a settee with a glass of hot milk and aspirin, promising to be up as soon as she felt better.

It was hard to sleep with her not there beside him. Yet he couldn't go bothering her. After a while he drifted off, waking up to find it still dark and getting up to gaze out of the window.

A dog fox was barking somewhere in the nearby woods then all was quiet. A little later there came a series of far-off screams, high-pitched and frantic, ceasing suddenly. The fox had caught himself a rabbit. Race smiled as he turned from the window. Then he frowned. Where was Cee? How long since he'd been asleep? He looked at his bedside clock. Two thirty. He had been asleep for no more than fifteen or twenty minutes. He wondered how she was feeling.

Crossing the hallway and taking the back stairs to the old corridor below, he crept into the library. The light was off but the moon casting its glow across the room showed an empty couch. Where was she?

Coming out, he crossed the passage, stealing into the ballroom. That too was in darkness, but as he entered there came a sudden frantic flurry. Snapping down the nearest wall light switch, he saw a couple who had been lying together on one of the sofas leap to a sitting position. The girl had covered her face with an arm against the sudden glare, head bent into the crook of her elbow. She was naked, as was the man, her blonde fuzz and thighs glistening wetly in the light, her breasts too.

The man was trying to cover his own lower parts with his hands. His skin too was glistening. He'd had her and she in turn had lain across him, spreading their lovemaking over both their bodies. A wave of disgust swept through Race for a second before he realised the girl was Celia. Instantly rage seemed to leap from the very core of him like a shaft of red hot metal.

Celia gave a cry but he didn't hear as in one leap he launched himself at the man, she racing past him for the still open door. Race hardly saw her go as he caught her cowering lover a single hefty blow, all the weight of fury and pain behind it. He went down like a felled animal but Race wasn't done. Hauling the half-stunned man to his feet, whom he now knew to be the one Celia had brought with her to his party, he punched that face again and again before dragging the now unresisting Ronny towards the door.

He stood no chance with Race's hands about his throat, his skull repeatedly bashed against the door jamb, powerless to retaliate or defend himself. Eventually his yells of pain subsided, but in red rage Race continued to beat the now limply jerking head against the wood until his strength finally gave out.

Letting the body fall to the floor, he stood back, breathing hard. The man lay quite still, limp and unnatural, and Race knew he had to be dead. He'd beaten up many a man but had never killed before. Yet he felt no remorse, only this continuing slow, simmering fury. Cee – where was she?

Turning, he walked at a steady pace to the main staircase, along the upstairs passage to their bedroom, his face set cold. She'd said she loved him. Liar! He'd been used, played for a fool, wanted only for his money and what he could give her. How long had she been deceiving him? His mind whirling, he burst into the bedroom, looking about for her. She had locked herself in the adjoining bathroom. He could hear her sobbing. How dare she sob? The sight of those two springing apart still raged in his head.

Without calling her name, a name he could no longer say, he began to wrench at the bathroom door, and when it did not yield, to throw himself at it, feeling it give a little under his weight. Again and again he lunged, hearing her shriek at each blow, but the effort was making his rage mount more and more until it was consuming him, adding to his weight against the wood.

Finally it burst inward and there she was, crouched on the tiled floor, still naked but for a thin towel across her body as a flimsy protection.

'Don't hurt me!' she was begging, but he hardly heard her as he stood over her, she cringing from the blind rage on his face. 'He made me ... don't hurt me, please. I...'

Her plea broke off to a sharp shriek of terror, like that of a rabbit he'd heard caught by a fox as he whipped the towel from her grasp, taking one end in each hand to encircle her half-raised head with it, the ends wrapping around her neck to drag them together and pull with all his might.

How long he pulled he had no idea, but coming finally to his senses he saw that her body had gone limp. Her beautiful grey eyes were bulging. The delicate skin of her face was suffused and swollen – her beautiful face. Slowly he let go the towel as if fearing to hurt her more, saw the head flop lifeless.

He heard his own cry of agony as he fell to his knees to shake her awake. 'Cee! Oh God! Cee, wake up! Cee, please, please wake up!'

How long he called for her to wake up he didn't know, kneeling beside the limp body, clasping it to his chest, rocking it back and forth. It was like holding a piece of foam.

How long he remained there he had no idea, but slowly came the realisation that he had lost her, and then that he could not leave her there. It took a long time for any real thought to come into his head as to what to do next.

Crying, choking, he began dragging her from the bathroom into the bedroom. There he lifted her up and laid her on the bed. Her limbs flopped as he laid her down. Not knowing what to do next, her lifted her into his arms again and went out into the hallway, going down the main stairs as if in a dream, a nightmare of a dream that seemed to move so slowly, like someone sleep-walking. Soon he would wake up. Somehow he found himself in that place he had once so happily called the ballroom, the light still on and there the body of the man he had pummelled, as still as death.

Kneeling by the sofa he lay Cee on the floor,

all the while blubbering, 'Forgive me, I didn't mean to do it. Please forgive me, my beautiful darling, I didn't mean this to happen,' over and over.

Slowly insanity began to wane, a seed of reality returning and with it renewed hurt. And anger. Played for a fool, the woman he'd stupidly thought had given her whole heart to him had proved herself to be no more than a damned cheap gold digger and he, fucking idiot, had fallen for it, had had the piss taken out of him. It was that more than finding her with some other man that now got him; robbed of his self-esteem, knowing himself to have been made a fool of, damn them to bloody hell, the pair of them!

His tears evaporating, he felt her wrist. Nothing. She was dead, the only one he'd ever really loved in his life. He truly believed that. Pushing away a new wave of remorse, he rose to his feet to check the man's pulse. He half expected him to groan, but there wasn't a flicker. He felt a satisfaction in this death, wishing he'd taken it slower, killing the bastard, seeing him suffer, begging pathetically for mercy...

The grandfather clock in the passage struck, making him start.

Three o'clock! Was that all it was? Something had to be done about these two, and quick. His mind raced now with the thought of where to dispose of the bodies. In the grounds somewhere ... but they could be found there.

This Ronny Peckham, what if he would be missed, traced here? It came to him that there'd been no friend called Sylvia. They'd made it all up and he'd let himself believe it. To trump up the tale of a friend with cancer – it was despicable.

And Cee, she had no family, but any curious acquaintance might look for her, enquiries made, police suspecting foul play, digging up the grounds, questioning. He could already see his world falling apart.

The frantic debate ceased abruptly when he remembered that hidden door behind the back stairs of the older part of the house with steps down to the tiny, windowless cellar, undiscovered by all except him. It had probably been used by the butler for keeping wine cool. But that was way back. No butlers these days. He could bury the bodies there, and as people began to wonder about Cee, he would put on a show of hurt and dejection, saying she'd left him for this Ronny chap with no idea where they were, had maybe even gone abroad.

People would be sorry for him, but after a while he would have to pull himself together, maybe even ask Millie back. But first there was a job to be done.

Six

A rose-pink sunrise that had not yet penetrated the low-lit passage saw Race emerging from the tiny cellar. It had been a night he wanted to forget.

Working solidly with a pickaxe and shovel he'd brought from one of the outbuildings to help penetrate the thin cement floor, each dull stroke was a blow to his own heart, each impact wrenching a sob from him. Not for the man – he couldn't have cared less for the man whose name he refused to let enter his head – but for what he himself had done to the girl he'd loved with such trust and devotion.

He hadn't meant to harm her. Dear God, he'd never have done such a thing had he not been so incensed by events. He hadn't been himself, out of his mind with grief and that blinding over-whelming knowledge of having been so grossly wronged by the woman he had allowed to become his life. Yet try as he might to heap recriminations solely on the man, he could only blame himself as he toiled in the faint light from the passage above to dig Celia's grave respectfully deep enough to cradle her lovely body, now wrapped in a large, soft, pure white tablecloth he'd found in the kitchen.

He'd not realised how hard it would be digging her pitiful grave, the ground beneath the thin cement floor hard, dry clay, needing the pickaxe and all his strength to penetrate. It seemed to take hours until, his arms aching, he was forced to give up, bury her as best he could, all the time spluttering a frantic prayer over and over between choking paroxysms of tears: 'Please, my darling, my only love, forgive me. Please, dear God, forgive me. Punish me if you must, but I did love her, dear God forgive me, I truly loved her,' as he replaced the bone dry soil with as much reverence as it allowed.

With hardly enough strength left to dig little more than a shallow hole for the man, the un-wrapped corpse kicked in without ceremony and with just enough earth to hide it, he concluded the burial with a hefty aim of spittle, an earlier aim having already defiled the now covered body.

Paying the untidy mound no more attention, he moved back to kneel beside the grave of his darling, and between each grieving convulsion he forgave her, now convinced that she had been led astray against her will.

All the time he'd been digging that grave, visions had crowded his shattered mind: the great following of mourners there would have been had this been a natural death of his beloved, all sadly paying homage to a lovely, tragic girl, taken in the prime of her life; the horse-drawn hearse, black plumes nodding on the heads of two jet black horses, coffin and hearse smother-ed with flowers; the church crowded, the music subdued; at the graveside the stifled sobs as her body in its casket was lowered gently into its resting place. Such were the scrambled abstractions of his grieving mind.

By the time he climbed back up the few stairs, both bodies safely hidden, he felt all in, yet still his mind whirled, trying to block out what he'd done to her. Before lowering her into her poor grave he'd kissed her tenderly. He would never kiss her again.

Tomorrow he would have liked to go down there just once more to put lilies on the place where she lay. But that would have afforded no purpose. What he needed to do now was to securely nail up the door, never again to open it, leave her to sleep. First thing tomorrow he would hire workmen to entirely redecorate the passage with pine cladding, he would say to brighten it up a bit. Once that was done, no one would ever guess a small door lay behind it. The men would not care; unsuspecting, they'd do what they were ordered to do, happy to take the money he would pay them.

A moment of cold rationality was stealing over him. He needed to hide all trace of what had happened. Returning to the ballroom, he was surprised to find less blood than expected. Very few spots on the floor and though the flat paintwork of the doorjamb had extensive smears, it took only moments to clean off with wet cloths from the kitchen. That done, he gathered up the scattered clothing, taking it all upstairs to cram into the overnight bag Cee's lover had brought with him, together with everything he'd been using – soap, shaving gear, comb and hairbrush, down to the very last collar stud.

He did the same with Celia's stuff, packing every last thing away in two large suitcases, then surveying both rooms for anything that could have been overlooked, but wardrobes were bare and looking somewhat forlorn, their doors left open, bedclothes tidy. Lugging it all down the back stairs, dry eyed and calculating, he unceremoniously flung everything into the tiny wine cellar, the act instantly flooding his eyes anew, constricting his throat.

Nailing up the door was like nailing up his past, that love he had so fondly cherished, lost forever. Convulsive spasms of anguish almost choking him, he gathered up his tools and let himself out of the back door to stand there watching the sky growing lighter. It promised to be a fine day but one she would never see. Drawing in a deep breath to gulp back a renewed onslaught of tears, he returned the tools to the shed where he'd got them from.

The job was finished but she would always be here, walking through the house, through the ballroom, the faint sound of dance music following her. He wanted that. But the place itself would no longer hold any joy for him. He'd be better getting rid of it, yet he knew he'd never bring himself to do so, so long as she lay here. He *wanted* her to walk these rooms, *wanted* her to haunt him, forever. Memories of *Wuthering Heights*, of Cathy and Heathcliff, prompted more tears and a need to hurry back indoors away from this bright, cheerful sunrise. In there he would be nearer to her.

With that poor comfort he strove to get through the next few days. To help, he was drinking, yet each day saw his heart grow heavier, his world emptier. He had told Mrs Dunhill that Celia had left him, had run off with a young man she had brought to his party, that he had no idea where they'd gone, maybe even abroad. Trying to commiserate, she said as to how she'd always thought the girl very nice on the face of it, but now having heard the truth, felt she wasn't worth grieving over. Assuming she had helped settle her employer's mind to some extent, she cheerfully busied herself getting his breakfast, a little hurt that nothing got touched.

In utter despair, knowing he'd lost his only love forever, he watched the innocent workmen finish the job they'd been paid to do. Lost and bewildered, the emptiness inside him growing, he would find himself weeping in the empty silence of his echoing house, bursting into tears in the loneliness of his bedroom.

Sleepless, he was getting through half a bottle of whisky a night to try and help him sleep, but by the early hours, still awake, he'd take himself out of the house to blearily stare at the tennis court he'd built some time ago for him and Cee to enjoy and for his hordes of guests to use, or gaze down at the swimming pool seeing again her lithe body cutting the blue water.

Sometimes he'd walk unsteadily among the trees to hover by the small lake he'd had made, where they would feed the fish he'd stocked it with. Staring down into the nine-foot depths of water, he would conjure up the reflection of her beautiful face on the still surface.

It was on such a night, some five or six nights later, that he could stand it no longer. Having finished the last half of yet another bottle of whisky, he staggered outside in the early hours to find himself again by the lake. With a three-quarter moon lighting up the quiet night of his estate, he gazed down into its depths for a moment then, with no other thoughts entering his mind, let himself fall effortlessly forward with such longing in his heart to join his beloved Celia that he hardly heard or felt the splash as the water closed over his head.

He was found next morning by his hired gardener. The police were sent for, their findings that he must have slipped while under the influence of alcohol, had probably sunk like a stone, feet probably caught for a time by weeds on the lake bottom, the body later rising to the surface where it was discovered.

Millie Butterfield didn't cry when she was told the news. She was sad, of course, recalling the good days, blaming herself a little for not standing by him as people who have lost someone often find themselves beset by whatever guilt their heart can conjure up – for not doing what they think they should have done, or doing something they shouldn't have done while the bereaved was alive.

She was, however, consoled by the fact that her husband's money was now hers. She was a rich woman and she planned to take full advantage of it, and in time maybe settle down and start again with someone else – who knows. But her first thought was to get rid of that blasted hateful house. Her solicitor was surprised to hear that she didn't want to keep it.

'Think, my dear, what you could do with it. Turn it into a small hotel, or more modestly a bed and breakfast establishment, or even hire it out for parties.'

Parties! She'd had enough of parties. How could he know the heartbreak that bloody awful place had brought her? She wasn't going to tell him. Let him carry on thinking her odd. She was quite content. She had friends, lots of places to go with them, pubs, cinemas, the odd theatre, holidays of course, even abroad maybe, spend whatever she liked so long as she was discreet about it so as not to isolate herself from friends with less cash in their pockets. In the same manner she would find herself a better house, but not too grand and still in the area she loved.

She wasn't like Race had been, with his expensive tastes and his flamboyant need to show off. She'd never been one to show off and she wasn't prepared to let people know just how much she was worth. Let them believe her husband had gambled away most of his money, leaving her just enough to live on comfortably and maybe a little besides, in case they got too suspicious and took her as seeing herself better than them, though she knew they wouldn't, not her sort of friends, good friends, the absolute salt of the earth.

Within a couple of months she'd put the place

he had striven to make so impressive on the market, to be sold with all its contents, lock, stock and barrel. Being so large it had taken almost a year to sell, but by the spring she had a bite – an offer from a pair of young newly-weds, admittedly for a little less than she'd hoped, but she was only too glad to accept it, happy to see the bleeding place go.

Within another six weeks the contracts had been signed, leaving her pleased and relieved to see the keys handed over, her only thought, good riddance to bad rubbish. They were bleeding welcome to it. She wouldn't be surprised if the damned place was haunted. It had never bought no bugger any luck and that was the truth!

Seven

In awed silence the young couple stared around the immense room they'd entered from a door off a narrow passage. The man consulted the brochure he held. 'It says this is the chandelier ballroom.'

The girl gave an explosive laugh. 'What on earth does that mean?'

He didn't look up from the page as he pointed to the ceiling above them. 'I suppose it means that.'

Together they glanced upwards to study the hugely elaborate object, he with awe, she grimacing. 'What a stupid thing to have in any house.'

'I suppose it had its uses,' he said, looking down at the brochure again. 'It says here that the room was used as a ballroom.'

'How silly! It's nowhere near large enough for a ballroom.'

'That's what the people selling this house called it. They probably held big parties here.' He gazed about him then up at the chandelier again with its two-tiered branches of gleaming brass arms and its beautiful crystal shades. 'Actually, I think the thing finishes this room off perfectly. It must be worth quite a bit. I wonder what possessed the woman who's selling the place to leave it here?'

The girl shrugged. 'The agent said she was leaving everything here, just as it is. So she must know what she's doing. Odd though. Anyway, we don't want her old rubbish. We want our own decent stuff.'

'Everything she has left here is decent – expensive. I don't think we could match it, not for some time yet. So while it's here we might as well make use of it – if we buy the place that is. Do you like it?'

She ignored the question. 'Another thing, we'd have to replace the wall to the hallway. I don't like stairs in a room, there's no privacy.'

'There are the back stairs.'

'And you saw the state of them,' she countered, grimacing. 'A lot of the house at the rear would need modernising if we do buy it.'

He had to agree, though it was only certain areas. The kitchen and utility room had been modernised, as had the five bedrooms, the walk-in bathroom/toilet off the master bedroom and the second bathroom and toilet along the hall, but he knew what she meant. He had to admit that parts of it *were* a bit old-fashioned, though for him that was the charm of it.

Entering by the rear door, having for the moment mislaid the key to the front door, they had gone straight up the old stairs to look at the views, Joyce more interested in them than the layout of the house.

Living with her parents in Surrey, leaving a beautiful home with extensive views across the Surrey Weald to be his wife, the last thing she wanted was to live somewhere crowded on either side by houses. His home on the other hand had been in South Kensington, cheek-by-jowl with other buildings, albeit of the finer sort. He just hoped he would soon get used to living in the country.

They had looked at places around where she had lived but most were too expensive. Both their parents had money, but hers having forked out a huge sum for the upcoming wedding of their only daughter, in fact their only child, as well as paying for the honeymoon in the south of France, felt they had given enough.

His father, on the other hand, although a stock-broker in the City, as he himself was, was a tight-fisted old devil and would have thought it out-rageous to be asked to put down a mortgage for his son, one of three, who if he didn't keep an eye on them would have drained him dry given half a chance, according to him.

So, even with both sets of parents pretty com-fortably off, finding the down payment for this place had been a bit of a struggle. Arnold felt they had come across a snip with this house, despite it being in Essex, if a better part of Essex. And if Joyce liked it, then this was what he would settle on.

Every one of the five bedrooms was large, the windows imposing, the décor needing nothing done to it. And there was the furniture. What had possessed the widow whose home it had been to sell it down to the last stick of furniture, even to the last knife and fork, he'd never know, but the woman's eccentricity, if that's what it was, was to his advantage.

'It's such a good price she's asking. It would be silly to turn it down,' he'd said as they came back down the main stairs leading straight into this huge room, with its elaborate chandelier which he now switched on just to see how it looked, the room immediately flooded with light despite the bright sunshine flowing in through each of the five tall, beautifully curtained windows.

'I suppose,' Joyce replied a little begrudgingly, still staring about her. 'I must say I do like the house. But we'll definitely have to wall off these stairs. And,' she added as he switched off the chandelier, 'we'll have to get rid of that ridiculous thing – it's far too garish for my liking.'

He made no comment but secretly knew he was going to leave that lovely thing exactly where it was no matter what she said, as they went on through what would become a hallway again if they bought the house, to look at the lounge, then into the narrow wood-clad passage with its doors to the sitting room, the library, the dining room with the kitchen and utility room at the far end.

'We'll have to do something about this passage too,' she remarked as they entered it. 'Not much natural light at all.'

It was the only drawback, but impossible to alter. 'We'll put doors between the lounge and the three other rooms, make them interconnected,' he offered, 'so you won't have to use the passage except to go to the kitchen, the downstairs cloakroom and the main hall when we rebuild that wall.'

For the first time since coming in, Joyce smiled. He was encouraged.

'Shall we put a deposit on it then?' he asked as they came out to the trim Morris he had left standing in the wide drive, gratified to see her nod in agreement.

The house was theirs. It hadn't been easy reaching a mutually agreeable price. Loathing any kind of haggling, Joyce had left it to Arnold to do the talking, the vendor, Mrs Butterfield, a forbidding adversary, small in stature though she was.

In her mid-fifties, tight-faced, tight-lipped, as if having gone through a hard time of some sort, she had probably once been quite plump, the sagging flesh of her forearms conveying that fact. Now she was thin rather than slim. Her blue eyes brittle, she had glared up at Arnold as if bearing him an intense grudge. It almost turned Joyce off, she only wanting for the negotiation to end and for them to walk away, except that she had fallen in love with the place, other than the need for a few alterations.

She was glad Arnold had taken charge of haggling and hadn't once included her in the negotiations, assuming her to be in full agreement with everything he'd said. Indeed she had been. There'd been more on her mind at the time with her wedding drawing ever nearer, all the arrangements still only half complete. Nor was she one to enjoy standing out, which as the bride she would have to, and the nearer the day approached, the more her nerves had mounted.

Now the wedding was behind her, her nerves

had fallen back into their rightful place. Yesterday the keys had been handed over and today they'd finally moved into their new home.

Some of the furniture belonging to Mrs Butterfield having been taken out and their own installed this very morning, everything placed exactly where it should go, the van men having left, it felt that the house was theirs at last. And at a far lower price, Arnold said, than he had expected.

To celebrate he suggested taking a stroll around the area, maybe ending up in one of the two local pubs in the village for a quick drink, and later that evening they'd go out for a celebratory meal somewhere nice.

In the Baker's Arms, the middle-aged couple at the next table, each with a half pint of light ale in front of them, kept glancing their way until finally the man whose complexion was almost nut brown, addressed them directly, a broad, cheerful smile lighting up his large face.

'Forgive me for asking, you must be our new neighbours,' his tone was jovial. 'We have the house on the corner to Rye Lane, you know. We wondered who'd be buying Crossways Lodge, didn't we, Pat?'

Pat nodded, smiling across at Joyce, who immediately inclined her head then looked away, saying, 'I need to just go and tidy my face,' before getting up and walking off.

Arnold wanted to apologise for her. She could be a little offhand at times. People were apt to take it as unsociable but it was only that she was of a rather retiring nature, unable to make friends as easily as some might.

They had met by sheer chance, in a library, he asking if she knew where the history section was, she saying she had no idea but returning his smile, an unusual response for her, he was to discover much later. They'd bumped into each other again after he'd found the section he'd been looking for, waving his book at her, saying brightly that he had found what he wanted. To his delight she held up her own book saying that she too had found what she'd been looking for. He'd asked what it was and she said it was on gardening, prompting him to say that living in Chelsea his family had no garden but that one day he hoped to have a place of his own with one. They'd got talking and it had developed from there. That had been two years ago.

He'd found that Joyce wasn't an easy person to get on with – full of self-doubt and discomforting indecision – but by then he was in love. When he finally proposed she'd almost recoiled, but eventually she accepted his proposal. The families met and hers harried her to set the date. At first she had agreed but then had a fit of uncertainty, saying he wasn't the steady partner she'd have preferred. True he liked to have fun, tried coaxing her into having fun too, aware that she didn't enjoy the sort of pleasures he did, going to parties, meeting new friends, having lots of holidays. It had been a blow until she confessed that she suffered such collywobbles about the whole business of weddings, finding herself forced into the limelight perhaps for the first time in her twenty-one years.

Her whole life had been a sheltered one –

coddled, protected, educated at a college for young ladies, her friends vetted, her movements watched by doting parents who feared her getting into mischief or hurting herself. They had even vetted him, checking his background, his upbringing, before ever allowing things to get serious.

With arrangements for the wedding fixed a second time, her excuse to back out had been that she felt she wasn't ready to fly the nest and settle down to married life. The third time, she again wanted to back out, this two days before the wedding, with everything in place. Her parents finally informed her that she couldn't let guests down, everyone having bought expensive wedding presents, and she had a duty to go through with it. This time she had capitulated without a murmur.

Only on their honeymoon did he discover how frigid she could be, but slowly she had melted to him, and now, having moved into her own home, she seemed ready to unwind and behave like a true wife, maybe not as much as he would have liked but at least to some extent.

'Is your wife all right?' the man was saying. 'She seems to be a little on edge.'

It was a rather forward question and Arnold replied hastily, jerked back to the present. 'No, she's fine. It's all the business of buying the house, getting settled in, that sort of thing.'

The man promptly reached over, hand extended. 'Albert Hessington, by the way.'

'Arnold Johns-Pitman,' Arnold supplied as he took the offered hand.

'This is my wife, Patricia,' Hessington went on, she in turn reaching out her hand, her somewhat plump form half rising to do so.

'So,' said Hessington as his wife sat back in her chair, 'settling in, are we?'

'Very much so,' said Arnold, half glancing towards where Joyce had disappeared through a rather ramshackle doorway.

'Of course I suppose you know the history,' Hessington was saying, leaning forward again in a confidential sort of way.

'Just what we read in the agent's leaflets,' Arnold said.

There came a nodding and gnawing of lips from the other man, his voice dropping to a whisper. 'You know the owner, Mr Butterfield, odd sort of fellow, from the East End of London as far as could be told, terribly eager to make friends in the community, anyone of any importance, liked to throw huge parties nearly every other week or so – he was drowned in his own pond, you know. His wife left him when he took up with some young woman, flighty sort. When she walked off with a younger man, so it's said, Butterfield was found days later face down in that pond, drowned. Police said it was an accident, but some around here believe it was suicide. But there, all in the past,' he concluded as Joyce reappeared from the toilets, negotiating her way between the few rather well-used empty tables.

Nothing more was said as the others moved back in their seats with a nod to Joyce, who again inclined her head without smiling and took a sip of her whisky and ginger.

There was a round of goodbyes and good-lucks-in-the-new-home as the other two eventually got up and left. Joyce's grey eyes followed their departure. 'What did they want?' she asked coldly.

'Nothing much,' he said, 'just welcoming us into the neighbourhood, that's all.'

He wasn't prepared to tell her what they'd said about a suspected suicide. The estate agent, crafty so-and-so, had vaguely pointed to a matter of the previous owner having died some time back in an unfortunate accident. 'Which is why,' he had added jovially, 'the widow has put the house up for sale.'

Obviously eager to sell the property, what the agent hadn't mentioned was that the accident had been by drowning in the property's very own pond. As Arnold saw it, the man's object had been 'the least said the better'. After all, his job was to sell houses, not put people off.

He'd had no cause to question the man about it at the time. The death of the previous owner was one of the many reasons for the wife to sell their home and he had thought little about it. Now it seemed that what had been supposed an accident had been seen by the locals as suicide, with a plausible cause for it, and even he felt a little disconcerted. He didn't feel happy keeping these suspicions from Joyce, flimsy though they were, just village gossip no doubt. But she being of a nervous, somewhat superstitious nature, it was best not to mention any of it to her.

What was done was done and having already

developed a keen love for the place, he wasn't prepared to have her worrying herself, peeking into nooks and crannies of which there were many, jumping at each crack of the furniture when the sun was on it or night cooled the wood, she interpreting every unnamed sound as sinister. It was best for both of them that she remained ignorant for the time being. Let her get used to the sounds that older houses were apt to make, at least that older part of theirs.

'You must have talked about something!' Joyce said as she sat back to sip at her drink.

'Not really,' he lied. 'They merely wished us both every happiness in our new home, then got on with their drinks and left.'

That seemed to content her, except to remark, 'I hope we don't get too many locals knocking on our door, wishing us every happiness, hoping that we'll invite them in so they can have a look round. People can be so nosey!'

'Perhaps they were among those who used to be invited to all the parties that were held here, according to the estate agent. He said the place was perfect for parties.'

'Well, I don't care much for holding parties merely for other people's benefit,' Joyce remarked huffily. 'If they are contemplating that, they are going to be very disappointed. This is our home and I do not intend to hold open house for any Tom, Dick and Harry. I hope you agree, darling.'

Even as he nodded, he hoped that didn't include their own friends. Joyce could border on the unsociable at times, a private person, but he had no wish for the house to be turned into a prison. But her parents tended to be people unto themselves and he guessed it was only natural for her to be of the same ilk. Married for such a short while, he was finding out that he still had a lot to learn about her.

Summer had gone by like a dream. They were well into autumn and it had taken all that time to have the wall to the hallway rebuilt, parts of the house redecorated and others modernised to their own taste. He'd also enlarged the conservatory leading off the room that held the chandelier and extended the patio where they would be able to sit next summer, looking for a nice tan. If the days weren't quite so warm of course they'd benefit from the comfort of the conservatory.

The new area had also given them the advantage of broad, open views over the countryside right to the horizon which the gentle elevation of the village enjoyed. As an access to both conservatory and patio he had had the large window on that side of the ballroom – the name stuck despite Joyce insisting on calling it the big room – formed into a French window. It still hadn't made her like the room and in fact she only ever entered to go through to the patio on fine days.

'I do wish you would get rid of that chandelier,' she suggested when the hall wall was eventually rebuilt, making the room less vast. 'It does look quite ridiculous now the room is that much smaller. It's so out of place now and, as I see it, only adds to the cold feeling I keep getting in here. I can never feel comfortable in here, no matter how I try.'

She was probably right about the room. He had to admit it never quite seemed an easy place to relax in. It held a vaguely lonely feeling, no warmth to it, as if it lamented the days of music and dancing and scores of guests. No matter how hard he tried, it seemed to retain an air of forlorn remoteness, as if bemoaning some sort of fall from grace.

Imagination, he told himself, and dismissed it from his mind. Yet he was loath to do anything about it – why, he didn't know – even more loath to get rid of the imposing chandelier. Even his parents seemed to have fallen in love with it and when he spoke of having it taken down they had been appalled. Joyce's father didn't seem to care if it came down or not, but her mother had shuddered and said it should be got rid of, though she wouldn't say why. *Women*! he thought as he dismissed his mother-in-law's reaction. *He* liked it and this was his home – he would decide what to keep and what to get rid of. It was a beautiful thing and maybe it was a strange sensation for a level-headed stockbroker to feel, but every time he looked at it his skin would tingle pleasantly

No, he wasn't prepared to take it down, no matter what Joyce and her mother said.

Eight

Florence Evans, whom the newly-weds had engaged as a cook/housekeeper as soon as they'd moved in, had found them to be a decent couple. The man was indeed very nice, though she'd not been quite sure about the young lady.

A year later she'd become used to Joyce's somewhat aloof nature. Though she took it that she couldn't help being the way she was, Florrie sometimes wished she'd unbend a little, be more at ease with her, a bit more friendly and natural. But that was her nature and nothing one could do about it.

She'd expected to be called Florrie as time went on, but it remained Mrs Evans still, though Mr Johns, as he liked to be called – 'bit of a mouthful every time you address me,' he'd said – did use her first name. It seemed silly not to, she living in, but Mrs Johns-Pitman couldn't help being what she was. She'd still not made any friends around here and it must have felt very lonely at times. But as they say: each to his own or her own.

Even so, it was a good salary. She got one day off a week as well as Saturday afternoons when she went visiting. A widow with no children, there was only her sister's family, but she had plenty of friends. If only Mrs Johns-Pitman could relax a little, she too would find friends. But that was her affair of course.

After almost a year Joyce was finally acclimatising to her new home, certainly these last three months now that the weather had improved and daylight was began to linger a little later each evening.

She still had some serious doubts about the move. It hadn't occurred to her that she might feel lonely. All her life had been spent with her parents, her schools and at her college for young ladies. In the company of others if not all that close to them, they'd been there all around her, the buzz of conversation, the sudden peals of laughter, the constant movement of people, something going on every day, occupying every hour, the passing of time unheeded. Living here had come as rather a shock.

Their first summer had been nice, she and Arnold going here and there, exploring the surrounding areas and showing their parents around. But winter had proved a trial, she finding herself completely alone for the first time in her life, he going off to the city each morning, parking his car at Shenfield to take the train the rest of the way and not coming home until seven in the evening. The days had dragged.

'You ought to find something to occupy yourself,' was his response to any complaint she made. He loved it here, but he wasn't here all day.

'You've got Mrs Evans and Doris for company,' he said. Doris, their general help, came from the village each day except for Saturday afternoons, her half day off, and Sundays. But as an employer there was only so much one could talk to them about.

'Find yourself a few hobbies,' Arnold had said brightly, confident that his advice would solve her problems.

But there hadn't been that many things to do, particularly in winter. Reading, of course. Writing letters, but the few young women she'd once made friends with in her teens had moved on. The same went for telephoning them. She'd tell them they were free to visit any time they fancied, though not with the house still to be finished. It was finished now but she hadn't pushed her invitations. If any had come she wouldn't have known what to say to them.

With the finer weather, there had been more to do. The swimming pool cleaned and refilled, she'd taken advantage of it on one or two warmer afternoons. At weekends she and Arnold had spend time clearing the tennis court, which during the winter had accumulated a green hue of moss, and they could now use it, she as good a player as he was. They seldom had occasion to go out other than visiting either parents and sometimes his two brothers and their wives. Other times they'd go to see a film at nearby Brentwood or Romford, occasionally to one of the big London cinemas – Fred Astaire and Ginger Rogers were her favourite stars with their dancing and his singing, especially in the film, *The Gay Divorcee*.

It was now May and Sunday would be their first wedding anniversary.

'I thought I'd take you up to London for the whole weekend,' Arnold told her. 'I have it all planned, darling. I thought I'd surprise you. We'll take in a London show, have a wonderful dinner at the Ritz hotel and stay overnight, then on Sunday I'll take you sightseeing.'

Joyce frowned. She didn't want to sound churlish, especially as he looked so eager, but over the year she had become a little cloistered. It was all right for him, he was at home there, living all his life in London and working there with his stockbroker father. She'd spent hers in the countryside. Even when at finishing school she had been well away from any large town. They made her nervous. It wasn't too bad just for the one afternoon, shopping maybe or even seeing a show and then home, but to stay overnight, all that bustle and hubbub for a whole weekend...

'I'd rather not,' she said more bluntly than she'd intended, quickly altering her tone. How could she upset him after such a generous idea? 'I was thinking more of throwing a dinner party on the Sunday and inviting just the family, our parents, maybe your brothers and their wives. It's our first wedding anniversary and I don't really want to spend it going out and sleeping in a strange bed and having to eat with lots of strangers around. It would be so much nicer here in our own home.'

It sounded selfish and for a while he looked disappointed, but then he brightened. 'Just as well I've not booked anything up. But if that's what you want, darling, that's what we'll do. Though it could mean a lot of hard work for you.'

'Why?' She had begun to feel excited, her first dinner party. 'Mrs Evans is here. And I'm sure Doris will be happy to wait at table over the weekend for a little extra money.

'It will be nice having our families here together,' she went on. Her parents often visited them and had been to stay at Christmas, most likely would spend Christmas here for many years to come. His parents had been only the once, as had his brothers, Howard twenty-six and Douglas twenty-eight, both a little older than he – nice people but she didn't really know them that well, even though his brothers were very sociable, as were their wives, Evelyn and Barbara.

Howard had a son, and Douglas a son and daughter, all under twelve, consequently having proved a bit of a trial during their visit, scampering around, getting in the way, filling the air with piercing, animated voices, fingering her precious ornaments that could get broken. She'd been glad to see them go. But now, having disappointed Arnold's plans to take her up to London, it was only fair to have his family here for their anniversary, though she would request that all three children be left at home, perhaps in the care of a relative, this being a celebration for adults only.

She had yet to become a mother, though there was little sign so far of that happening. Every now and again she did feel vaguely broody, but with quite a tidy mortgage sitting on his shoulders, the house far larger than two people should need, Arnold had insisted they wait at least another year or two. It wasn't really a bother but it didn't sit well with her mother.

Daphne and Edward Everington were the first to arrive about eleven thirty on the Saturday. Daphne instantly glanced at her daughter's midriff, having given her a peck on the cheek.

'No sign of any family yet, dear?' she asked as she handed her lightweight, three-quarter-length swagger coat, together with her pill-box hat, to young Doris, already holding Mr Everington's trilby.

Doris eyed the suitcase standing in the hall. Did that mean a longer stay than just these two days? Being asked to work this Sunday would give her a little more money to spend on evenings out with her friends, but serving extra meals and being at their every beck and call, which she looked likely to be and for Lord knows how long, wasn't her idea of work,

'No, Mummy, nothing yet,' Joyce answered her mother's question a little off-handedly as she led her parents into the front lounge. 'Arnold and I feel it far too soon to begin thinking of starting a family.'

'Of course, darling, plenty of time, I expect,' murmured her mother, ignoring the rebuff, as they entered the comfortable room with its two soft brown leather sofas, matching deep armchairs and quiet décor. Arnold was already pouring welcome drinks for everyone from the cabinet in the corner by the large bay window.

Taking the sherry he handed her, Daphne settled herself in an armchair, Joyce in the other, while the two men stood by the cabinet with a brandy each. She looked across at her daughter.

'We rather thought we might stay over until Monday afternoon, if that's all right with you, dear,' she said, sipping her sherry. 'Quite handy, Arnold and your father not having to be at the office that day, public holiday you know, with the Royal Silver Jubilee.' A far away look came into her blue eyes. 'Our dear King George and Queen Mary, twenty-five years on the throne, incredible how time flies. I can remember the Coronation as if it were yesterday. 1911. I was there to see them pass in their state coach, you know. She looked so beautiful, so young. I was fifteen, hadn't yet met your father of course.' She took another sip of sherry then glanced up at Joyce. 'I hope you don't mind us staying one extra day?'

'Why should I mind?' Joyce replied, resigning herself to one more day of questioning as to exactly when she did intend to start a family, querying if she had any health problems that might prevent her from bearing a child, the woman still clinging to a need to protect her daughter. 'It would be nice having you,' she ended lamely.

Having finished their brandy, Arnold and her father had gone out onto the patio for a cigarette, leaving Joyce to endure her mother's account of life at home now she was no longer there. She was telling her how much she still missed her, when Arnold's parents arrived, bringing the men back into the lounge. Hardly ten minutes after having been welcomed with a glass of wine or brandy, Daphne accepting a second sherry just to be sociable, in came Arnold's two brothers and their wives, calling for yet another round and a topping up of any half-empty glass.

Gertrude Johns-Pitman, a short, broad-bodied woman, so different from her tall, lean husband, waved her hand to a second glass with an almost apologetic expression on her blunt features as she whispered, 'I really seldom if ever drink more than one, thank you.'

'I am much the same,' Daphne put in as she accepted her third.

Her mother's cheeks had begun to glow and Joyce suggested they retreat out to the patio where the men could smoke and the women enjoy the fresh air, to which they agreed.

It was good to sit here in the partial shade from the house, the sun not coming round until early afternoon, its summer rays already proving hotter than usual, and it was a relief to see her mother's cheeks slowly regain their usual pale colour.

The men moving off to inspect the three acres of grounds so grandly termed an estate by the previous owner, though the small clumps of trees made it seem larger, the women sat on in the sublime comfort of reclining patio chairs.

Content not to be drawn into any conversation, Joyce cast her gaze over the wide views of rolling countryside seen through scattered woods with hardly any house to spoil it. Often looking out on it, it would feel as if it was all hers to the distant horizon, so long as she didn't look the other way and see the village with its few shops, church, village hall and two pubs bordering the road that ran through it.

Her mother had fallen silent while Gertrude and her daughters-in-law went on chatting. She'd begun to look pensive. After a while Joyce felt bound to ask her if anything was wrong. She turned to her, her voice a whisper.

'That big room of yours with the chandelier, I've never felt comfortable there.' She paused as if embarrassed then went on, 'Do you know what I mean? Have you ever felt anything strange about it?'

'Not that I know of,' Joyce answered, keeping her own voice low, but it was a lie in a way.

'Arnold calls it the chandelier room, but I don't like the term,' her mother went on.

Indeed he did, though she preferred to call it merely the big room – why she couldn't say, except that it didn't seem right to mention the chandelier, again she couldn't have explained why. Nor why she seldom lingered in the room for any length of time. Despite it having been reduced to a somewhat more acceptable size by rebuilding the wall between it and the hall, there was a disquieting, empty feel to it.

Now her mother had felt it too. It may have been the three glasses of sherry she'd had, but halfway across the room she'd given a huge shudder.

'I really do not like this room!' she'd burst out loudly and vehemently, causing the others to glance at her in surprise.

'It's a lovely room,' Mrs Johns-Pitman had re-marked. 'So bright, and that beautiful chandelier sets it off perfectly – just the right size for such a big room.'

Daphne had come to a halt, gazing almost furtively about her. 'Can't you sense it, a strange chill? I feel it whenever I come in here.'

Joyce said nothing. She too had often experienced a similar feeling, but she didn't want her mother pointing it out to others.

'I can't feel anything,' Howard's wife remark-ed, faintly condescending amusement in her tone.

The men had merely exchanged grins as they'd continued through to the conservatory and out to the patio, more interested in having a smoke, Joyce not happy to have cigarette or cigar smoke tainting her home.

'It's definitely here in this room,' Daphne kept saying, the other three women moving a little closer to her as if to console. Joyce guessed they had probably all seen her high colour and assum-ed her to be ever so slightly tipsy. She could even imagine them smiling to themselves as they coaxed her outside into the garden.

Once seated at ease on the patio, shielded by the house from the morning sun which would soon make its way round, necessitating the use of sun shades, she seemed to forget her fear, lying back in her chair to enjoy the morning warmth, until the whispered exchange with her daughter.

Joyce continued to feel unsettled over what her

mother had said. She too disliked the odd feeling that room sometime gave her, though there seemed no explanation for it. At first she'd attributed it to the size of the room, and for a while the rebuilding of the wall had made a difference. But around the end of October the disconcerting sensation had begun to creep back. Then she'd shrugged it off as an attack of autumn doldrums that can take a hold of some people lamenting the end of summer, dreading the start of winter with its creeping cold, sunshine, long dark nights and short overcast days.

Now her mother who, she had to admit, was a little sensitive to atmospheres, had also taken a dislike to that room. Yet why, when no one else seemed to?

On Sunday evening Arnold's family went home, allowing the four of them to settle down to a quiet evening together, Arnold and her father engrossed in conversation, the radio playing, she and her mother nibbling sandwiches Mrs Evans had made before retiring.

'I must just trot off to the bathroom, dear,' her mother whispered discreetly with a smile. When she came back the smile had disappeared, replaced by an expression of bewilderment.

'Who is that woman?' she asked Joyce quietly, as though fearing to alert the men's attention

Joyce looked at her in surprise. 'What woman?'

'In your big room.'

As Joyce stared at her she went on, 'She was by the French windows. The door was open and you usually keep it shut, don't you, and I looked in and there she was, at the far end of the room with her back to me.' Her mother was talking fast, whispering. 'She must have heard me. She turned and looked at me, then up at the chandelier. I looked at it too. I looked back to ask who she was but she'd gone. I thought she'd slipped into the conservatory but I couldn't see her. She simply disappeared. Who is she?'

Joyce felt a shudder run through her but thought quickly. 'I don't know, unless it was Doris, our housemaid. She lives in the village. She must have popped back for something she'd forgotten.'

But Doris would never have popped back for anything at this hour. A respectful young girl, she'd have waited for Monday morning. Who then was the person her mother had seen, if it had been a person in the sense of flesh and blood? The thought brought the skin on her arms up in goose pimples and tingled the back of her neck. Yet she had no reason to feel like that.

At least her reply seemed to have settled her mother somewhat as she said, 'Well, it would have been more polite for the girl to have come to the front door to speak to you first instead of creeping around the place like that! Heaven knows who could have been lurking there with us here unaware.'

Again Joyce felt her flesh grow chill. Who exactly had her mother seen and why should it have made her flesh creep? What was the answer, if an answer there was?

Nine

It was the following February that she found the answer. These past months she'd slowly got to know a few people in Wadely, though none that well: a passing smile in the local hairdressers, a nod or two in the post office or one or two of the four shops, hardly enough to spark off a conversation.

It being fine last summer there'd been no need for friends, her parents making regular trips out to see her, she and Arnold visiting both them and his parents as well as one or other of his brothers a couple of times. There had been that fortnight holiday in Switzerland in late summer, a couple of weekend jaunts to the south coast. And there was the garden. They had a gardener but she enjoyed pottering round. Time had just flown by, giving her little time to feel lonely.

Autumn had changed that. The days growing shorter, nights drawing in, Arnold's long hours away from home working with his stockbroker father in the City left her again feeling uneasy on her own, though never sure why. Thoughts of what her mother had said she'd seen by the French windows that day last May had plagued her constantly, and though she herself hadn't seen anything odd, the episode returned again and again to disturb her thoughts, making her yearn for Arnold to come home.

In desperation she'd forced herself to join the WI, rather nervously at first, anything to help fill at least some of those empty hours. Not that good at mixing and getting acquainted with new people, instead she'd sought the back row of those who came to listen to whatever speaker was there and had shunned volunteering for any of those little WI tasks others enjoyed.

No one appeared particular drawn to her, but that was how she preferred it. She was a private person and had made no close friends even at school or at that college for young ladies. It hadn't worried her and it didn't now, though soon she would have to socialise or be seen as odd.

It was only after several meetings that she found courage enough to speak to anyone, that because one of them, a woman in her late twenties with a naturally outgoing chatty nature, spoke to her first, seeming to want to take her under her wing somewhat.

Introducing herself as Jennifer Wainwright, she came and sat next to Joyce as they drank coffee, proceeding to tell her all about herself: that she ran the post office; that her husband had gone off with another woman three years ago. 'We'd been married for nearly ten years but we were married very young. I don't think we were suited anyway. I don't miss him, far too busy to want him back and there were no children. In time I might meet someone else, I'm still young enough and you meet all sorts in my job.

But no hurry.'

She gave an easy laugh, talking so rapidly there was little need for Joyce to say much, which was a blessing. She didn't care for people knowing too much of her private life. But Jennifer was open, easy to get along with, so much so that by February she had practically invited herself to Joyce's home for morning coffee, or rather Joyce found herself pushed into inviting her. Anyway, she rather liked Jennifer, maybe because she was that bit older and a less overbearing mother-figure than her own mother.

'It's such a nice house you have,' she remarked now, gazing around the cosy sitting room over their coffee and biscuits. Joyce had offered cake but Jennifer had patted her rather noticeable tummy. 'Too much sweet stuff, need to watch the waist,' she had said brightly.

She was still gazing about the room, nibbling a chocolate digestive instead. 'This place is quite old, you know. At least the rear part is. Built around the beginning of last century I believe, 1820s or thereabouts, a sort of manor house, wealthy family, quite large I was told – the house, not the family.' She laughed then grew serious. 'This part was built by new people about the beginning of this century who had bits of the older one pulled down, so all this is quite new. But this has its own history.'

She leaned forward, replacing her cup on the little round occasional table to peer into Joyce's eyes. 'But then I suppose you know about that.'

'About what?' Joyce asked innocently.

'About the suicide.'

A knot formed itself deep inside Joyce's stomach, though why she wasn't certain. 'What suicide?'

'The last chap who had this place, surely you know – your pond, the one in the wood on your property – he drowned in it. The police said it was an accident but people here think it was suicide. Surely you know?'

No, she hadn't known. No one had told her. Instantly the thought came of what her mother said she'd seen. But she'd described a woman. Even so, it brought a shudder, and as Jennifer left she rang Arnold. His secretary said he was out of his office for the rest of the day at a meeting.

On tenterhooks and unable to settle, she counted the hours until he'd arrive home, and the moment he walked in the door, weary but as cheerful as a cricket, before he could even kiss her cheek hello, she tackled him on what Jennifer Wainwright had told her.

'Did you know?' she burst out, gabbling in her pent-up anxiety. 'I rang you but you were out. Your secretary said you'd be out of the office with clients all day. She put the phone down before I could tell her to let you know I'd rung. Obviously she didn't or you'd have rung back.'

She didn't much care for Gillian, his secretary. She had met her last Christmas at his office party and hadn't liked the way she had hung around him the whole time. But at this moment her mind was not on his secretary.

'I needed to talk to you so urgently,' she complained now. 'Did you know that the man who

105

had this house before us was drowned in our very own pond?'

She hadn't realised she'd not given him his usual homecoming kiss, having worked herself up into a stew for half a day, and instantly interpreted his surprise for one of concealment.

'You already knew, didn't you?' she challenged as she saw him nibble uncertainly at his lower lip.

'I should have told you, love. But you'd have got yourself into a state, just as you have now. How much did she tell you?'

Tears filled her eyes. 'Everything! She told me everything! What everyone here believes. That it was suicide. She was surprised I didn't know. But you knew. And you never told me. When were you told? Who told you?'

'Hold on, love!' He was attempting to soothe, moving to the cloak cupboard to hang up his coat. 'It was that couple we met when we went across to the pub for a celebration drink when we first moved in, you remember.'

He was making a meal of his explanation, speaking far too casually.

'All that time ago! And you never said a word. Why didn't you tell me then?' She was trembling, shaken by what she now realised were the true facts. Her voice fell to a whisper. 'Why didn't you tell me then?'

He was trying to calm her, his tone even, his hand held out towards her.

'Darling, you're letting your imagination run away with you,' he began as she shrugged away from the outstretched arm. 'People here just assumed it to have been suicide. Just talk, speculation. It's what those in villages tend to do and you shouldn't take any notice. The police concluded it was an accident and they should know. Anyway, it was a few years ago, all over and done with.'

But it wasn't over and done with. How could she explain the strange feeling she got from that room, her eyes ever searching for what her mother had seen? He said she was letting her imagination run away with her after what she'd heard from that scaremongering Wainwright woman. But she wasn't. Her mother had seen something, had sensed the same eeriness she felt about that room. They couldn't both be wrong.

Maybe it was best to keep her views to herself, let him think she had taken his advice and put it behind her. She tried to tell herself she *was* imagining things, her fear based on pure rumour. But the room with its great chandelier remained disquieting. In fact, even to go through it to the conservatory would put her on edge. Not that she ever saw anything herself.

Was she just being foolish, yielding to a vivid imagination as Arnold had said? The rest of the house was charming and she loved it. It was just that room. She tried hard to tell herself that there was no logical reason for it, except for the seed Jennifer had sewn in her mind, and perhaps she *was* being over-imaginative, but then there was her mother. Could two people get the same strange sensation from the same part of the house? Maybe she was being silly, for it was only her mother who had seen something strange, no one else. Yet that was no consolation, it was still there with her.

Their second anniversary saw their families down once more to celebrate, Arnold and his father taking time off from their office, Joyce's father with his own business also able to get away.

This time her mother seemed not to notice anything odd about the room whose chandelier still took centre stage, even passing a remark that Arnold was right not to get rid of it.

'It makes the room,' she observed lightly as they went through to the conservatory for lunch rather than out to the patio, it being a cloudy day. Joyce felt nothing either. The big room was just fine and she vowed not to allow Jennifer Wainwright to scare her ever again.

Summer melted into autumn. Still with no recurrence of that odd sensation in the room, slowly Joyce forgot about the episodes. Jennifer had never again made any mention of the suicide business. Anyway, so much was going on. They were entertaining much more these days, friends Arnold knew mostly, and family of course. Having holidayed in Italy for two weeks in September, she felt rejuvenated. She and Jennifer had become firm friends, there were WI outings to go on, but often just the two of them would drive off somewhere for the day in Jennifer's car. The shortening autumn days and the fact that it was dark before Arnold came home from the office no longer bothered her. She had Jennifer now.

Autumn drifted into winter. A week before

Christmas, Joyce was expected to attend Arnold's father's usual office party, as she had since becoming Arnold's fiancée. She'd found it hard work then and it was still not her cup of tea, still uncomfortable talking with people she hardly knew, and as always she had dreaded this one.

Now she stood awkwardly to one side, the dregs of the same glass of champagne she had started with warming in her hand, aware that she would have to take another ready for the usual toasts. Those about her gathered in conversational groups, the talk seeming to be mostly of recent dire events – King Edward giving up the throne for that dreadful Mrs Simpson, the fascist Hitler threat in Germany and the Mosleyites in the East End, the great Crystal Palace fire, such a pity after all its prestigious years. They hardly noticed her, though Arnold's father Howard and his wife did come over to talk to her for a while until called away. She felt isolated.

Arnold had once or twice come to see if she was all right. She had told him each time that she was fine and he had walked away after telling her she should mix a little, seeming to feel that his advice would do the trick. At the moment he seemed well occupied with his immediate staff, two young men and three young women, one of them apparently the copy typist, one very young girl who was probably a filing clerk, and the third one Arnold's secretary Gillian. It was she to whom Arnold seemed to chat mostly, and from her corner Joyce eyed her cautiously.

Gillian Daniels was slender, in her twenties, maybe a year or two older than herself. In fact

Joyce thought she had a rather mature look, fair hair permanently waved, the curls framing the heart-shaped face. She was extremely pretty, Joyce noted with a stab of jealousy, and very confident. The more she watched the way Arnold was talking to her, far nearer to her than he should be, laughing with her, touching her arm every now and again to convey some point or other, looking into her eyes or so it seemed, the more that jealousy mounted and with it a vague anger which she told herself was sheer annoyance at the immature way he was behaving. But deep inside, she knew it was anger. All the way home in their car, it simmered inside her until as they approached their own home Arnold made the mistake of glancing at her, frowning.

'Are you all right, darling? You're being very quiet.'

He'd been talking incessantly about how well the party had gone, how much it has cost and how successful it had been compared to other years, to which she had hardly responded until finally he too had gone quiet, concentrating on his driving.

Now he apparently needed to tackle her on her persistent silence. 'Is something wrong, my sweet? Are you not feeling well? You've been very withdrawn all evening.'

'There's nothing wrong with me,' she remarked in the classic statement used by all women when hurt.

'I'm sure there is,' he insisted, turning his eyes to the road. 'I can feel it. I tried to bring you out, tried to get you talking to others. My parents

110

even came over to talk to you, but you persisted in standing to one side on your own the whole evening. I don't know what others must have thought.'

'You know I'm not good at parties,' she said simply.

It was cold. The smell of snow was in the air and all she wanted was to get home, enjoy a warming cup of Horlicks, go to bed and forget the evening.

'I can't pretend to be sociable when I'm not at ease. And I wasn't.'

'Why not?'

Joyce hesitated. How could she tell him why? What she had said was partly the truth, but seeing him nodding sagely at his secretary's every word, laughing uproariously whenever the need called for it as though it had come from the lips of some great wit, had spoiled any interest she might have had in taking part in the small talk around her. She thought quickly. 'I didn't know anyone well enough to barge into their private conversations.'

'Even so,' he persisted, making her fingers screw up, 'you could have made an effort, or ... well ... anything...'

He let his voice trail off as he swung the car into the drive and she was glad he said no more about it as they got ready for bed, though he too had become unusually quiet. Hardly saying goodnight as they slipped beneath the warm covers, he didn't even kiss her before turning over, his back to her.

The moment his head touched the pillows, his

breathing grew regular and deep. She continued to lie awake watching the shadows of trees being cast upon the cream-coloured walls by a frosty moon that every now and again escaped the fast-moving, snow-laden clouds.

Like some bad dream her mind churned over what had seemed to her his excessive friendliness towards his pretty secretary. Finally she did drop off, sleep proving a healer so that by morning she was already scolding herself for her foolishness. Arnold was true as any husband could be, kind and generous and he loved her. She had been the one at fault.

By Christmas Day, their third in this house, she had put it out of her mind completely, her thoughts taken up by both their parents spending Christmas Day with them, Arnold's parents going on to their son Howard and his family for Boxing Day, taking Douglas and his wife and children with them, which was a relief to her.

She had dreaded the children coming but could not really object without appearing petty. Fortunately they were put to bed early, to her intense relief, wearied by their energetic excitement over their toys, she having to move all breakables discreetly out of reach.

The evening saw her mother-in-law, quite a decent pianist though her touch was a little on the heavy side, entertaining them with a few nocturnes and etudes, a good deal slower than Chopin had ever intended. Arnold's father recited an endless string of Kipling poems in his rich baritone. Worn out trying to be sociable, she was glad to finally go to bed, the women going up earlier than the men, leaving them downstairs to talk into the small hours, smoking and discussing business and the world situation.

Friday saw her own parents depart, giving her and Arnold the weekend to themselves to quietly unwind, the radiogram playing, her own worries and suspicions fading like summer-warmed clouds. They were spending the New Year alone too, she having insisted and Arnold apparently only too happy to go along with her, making her feel that 1937 would find them at one with each other even if the rest of the world seemed in turmoil.

The disconcerting feelings she'd had about parts of her house during the year seemed to have faded too. If her mother still had such feelings she had not once mentioned them at Christmas, so probably it had all been imagined, her mother putting ideas into her head by reading something into it that wasn't there.

She looked forward to spring and all the things they would do together, swimming again once the pool was cleared of winter's ravages, the tennis court rid of moss that had grown during the cold weather. She would spend time overseeing the pruning of the trees that obscured the lovely long views of countryside and having the drooping stems of climbing roses retrained. She would replant the kitchen garden and tend the shrubs lining the driveway. Yes, she couldn't wait for spring.

At that moment she could never have foreseen that this coming year would change her life forever.

Ten

It was wonderful to feel the spring air again, balmy and full of life, all the bad news that was in the world going over her head with the arrival of bright long days. In January Arnold took her to Sadler's Wells to see *Giselle* danced by Margot Fonteyn, her debut replacing the famous Alicia Markova. Joyce found herself virtually in tears at Fonteyn's heartbreaking depiction of a girl going slowly mad, to die for love of her prince, young Robert Helpmann, rising from her grave an ethereal spirit, so much so that it tore a wavering sob from Joyce's lips. If I lost Arnold's love, came the overwhelming thought, I'd go mad. I think I would die too.

So enthralled was she with the rendering by the graceful new prima ballerina, who seemed to float rather than dance as if not made of flesh and blood at all, that the very thought of losing Arnold became only too real. Though the magic lingered long after they'd left the theatre, the dismal feeling that had gripped her during the performance did eventually fade.

She told Jennifer Wainwright all about it when they met over coffee, going into such detail that Jennifer finally had to disguise a yawn.

'I'm afraid I'm not that interested in ballet and

opera,' she said, apologetically patting her lips. 'Now a comedy film or a good thriller ... I'm more James Cagney, Gary Cooper or Bob Hope.'

Fancy not liking ballet! Jennifer was a philistine! But Joyce forgave her. One thing she was grateful for was that she had never again mentioned that suicide, though from time to time it still haunted Joyce, just a little.

They would go to the pictures sometimes, and it was there they watched the newsreel of the Coronation of King George VI and Queen Elizabeth. It had taken place on the twelfth of May.

'Fancy it being on the exact same date as our wedding day, even if that was three years ago,' she said excitedly to Arnold, making him smile.

He was more attentive these days, almost as he'd been during their first year of marriage, taking her to so many more places than last year. They were going to far more London theatres, having meals out, going off on little jaunts to the coast. Now a partner in his father's firm, they had no money worries these days. He'd bought a new car, a sleek 1937 BMW, now able to afford such luxuries, and would proudly drive them to wherever she fancied. He'd also promised a holiday in Venice around September during his two weeks off. The only regrettable thing was that lately he was being compelled to work longer hours, as a partner having an interest in seeing the firm prosper.

'There's such pressure at work,' he explained. 'All this trouble in the world, stocks and shares going wild, we've our work cut out just to keep up.'

They'd not celebrated their third wedding anniversary the way they had those first two years. 'We don't want to keep inviting people down to celebrate it,' he'd said. 'I'd rather we take ourselves off somewhere instead, just the two of us.'

She was inclined to agree and that weekend, with their anniversary falling on the Wednesday, they had driven to Norfolk on the Saturday to a good hotel, returning home on the Sunday night.

There was one fly in the ointment which, despite it happening more often than it should, he never made a lot of, but at which she could feel his frustration – their sexual relationship.

They'd enjoyed a lovely Saturday, a splendid lunch, then wandering along the shore under a hot, bright sun, leaving only as the low cliffs cast an afternoon shadow across the sand with the sun moving round to the west.

Returning to the hotel they'd sat on the covered veranda for the rest of the afternoon with long, cool drinks before changing for dinner; afterwards had gone to a show, returning for a nightcap and bed.

Under the covers he held her close as they spoke of the wonderful day they'd had. He was telling her how much he loved her and she felt his hand slide up under her nightdress. Instantly her body tensed. Why it should feel this way, she had no idea. She loved him with all her heart, would weep in self-indulgent fear that one day something dreadful could happen to him, an accident or some unexpected illness, to take him from her. To be left in the world alone, without

116

him, would be unbearable. Yet the moment he touched her, her muscles would go rigid. She wanted him to make love to her, she really did, but her reaction had always been the same from the very first day of their marriage.

Those early days she had put it down to a virginal fear, as perhaps many a young bride might go through. Now she knew it for what it was – she did not like the sexual side of marriage. She did not like it with a paranoid fear she could not explain, not to her mother who might chide her, have tried to advise her, even scold her for what she would see as her foolishness, and certainly not to him who might think her a little mad.

He *had* been patient, perhaps hoping she might eventually adjust to what was after all a natural side to marriage. Indeed she had often gone as far as clinging to him, even allowing him to explore her. But something deep inside would crawl up – the only name she could find for it – the moment he grew ready, her legs refusing to yield to him, and though he tried to talk her into allowing them to part to receive him, she just couldn't. There had been entry once or twice, but so tense had she been that it had hurt, so terribly that she had cried out, causing him to withdraw in fear of hurting her further.

At first he hadn't been angry, merely attentive, but slowly his patience had ebbed and he would show his frustration with her, not violently – Arnold could never be of a violent nature – but by his very disappointment with her. Aware of it she would cry and he'd hold her to him and soothe her, saying it didn't matter, though as time went by he had bothered her less and less.

This time in that Norfolk hotel he had pulled away from her without saying a word, had not attempted to cuddle her to him but had merely turned over on his side with his back to her, almost like one relieved that nothing had happened.

'I'm so sorry, darling,' she had murmured as she lay full of remorse, but he hadn't replied. Whether he slept she didn't know. There had been no regular breathing of someone asleep. She had tried to speak to him but again had received no reply and finally she too had turned over to nurse her guilt. By Sunday it was as if it hadn't happened, he his old self again. They'd spent the day relaxing in the sun, enjoying their meals, and in the afternoon had left for home. But the episode was still there in her mind, lingering as it always did, and she wondered if it was in his too. If it was he hadn't shown it, making her feel worse, thinking, would it or could it ever change, could she make it change if only for his sake. He was such a good man, he deserved better from her.

Late this Monday afternoon, knowing she should have phoned much earlier but unable to wait until he came home, she rang him at work still full of remorse at her conduct to say how sorry she was for her unreasonable reluctance of sex, fearing he might have been brooding over it all day.

His secretary answered as always, telling her to hold while she put her through. The girl was usually in the outer office, but Joyce realised she was in Arnold's, she hearing his voice instantly enquire, 'Who is it, my dearest?'

Dearest! *My* dearest! Joyce's heart froze, seeming to drop as though made of some huge piece of ice.

Through a fog she heard the girl whisper, 'It's your wife, darling,' followed by Arnold's frustrated hiss, 'Damn!'

Seconds later came his voice, loud and clear and cheerful, 'Hello, love. Anything wrong?'

Unable to speak, she let the phone drop back onto its cradle, her thoughts in turmoil as she stood there staring down at the thing. Had she heard correctly? But there was no mistaking that easy tone of endearment and that whispered epithet, 'Damn!'

It felt as if her world had collapsed. No wonder he found no anger at her refusal of his love.

Devastated, she dreaded him coming home. And when he did, coming in all bright and easy of mind, asking how she was, how her day had gone, she was barely able to face him, much less smile at him. Yet smile she did, saying her day had gone well. He mustn't know what she'd overheard. Or was it just a mistake – had she misheard?

Already doubting her thoughts, that night she slept beside him as a wife should, bore his goodnight kiss on her cheek, then turned over pretending sleep. He had immediately drifted off, his breathing soon regulating to gentle slumber. Yet as she lay awake she knew she hadn't misheard.

Each day she thought of him and that secretary, visualising them together. Had they made love? If so, where? The way he'd called her 'my dearest' – yes of course they'd made love. She felt sick each time she imagined them together, she the fool who'd been kept in the dark. Yet she loved him still. Hurt and grieving as she was, she loved him still. The weeks went by and she could find no will to confront him with what she'd overheard, but her heart grieved. Slowly, she found it even harder to bear. With him still pretending to be the loving husband, all the time playing her false, grief was turning to bitterness, yet still she loved him.

Finally unable to stand the mounting pressure any longer, she sought her mother's arms like a child who has been tormented by others, and to her she poured out her anguish. But instead of taking her in her arms so as to console her, Daphne regarded her daughter from the armchair in her lounge with something close to tolerant scepticism.

'I do know how you feel about your marital duties, Joyce, being a little like that way myself with your father. And I think that you are probably blaming yourself and have therefore read something into Arnold's words that may not have been intended in the way you interpreted them. It is easily done.'

'But I know what I heard, Mummy!'

'You could have made a mistake, my dear. People often call others darling...'

'It was *my* darling, as plain as I hear you, and

when he was told it was me on the phone, I distinctly heard him say, "damn!"'

'You could have been interrupting some important matter—'

'Oh yes, important is right!' she broke in, pressing the backs of her fingers to her lips in anguish. 'I can't bear to think what they were doing before I phoned.'

Her mother rose and went over to her still-seated daughter to bend and take her lightly in her arms. 'And you've been brooding over this all this time. You should have come to me before now. I'd have advised you that it is all in your imagination, that they'd been doing nothing at all underhand.'

Joyce hardly heard her. 'What have I done for him to need to turn to someone else? Where have I failed him?'

'You have not failed him,' her mother said patiently. 'It's all in your mind.'

Joyce wasn't listening, her mind running ahead, tears streaming down her cheeks. 'I really thought he loved me! But he's having an affair.'

'Of course he isn't. And he does love you, my dear.'

She paused in thought, then still bending over her daughter, her arms about her, said, 'What I think you need is to be away from him for a while.'

'And leave him in that woman's clutches?'

'My dear, he's in no one's clutches,' Daphne rebuked. 'What I am saying is that perhaps being apart from each other for a while might be a good thing. Absence makes the heart grow fonder. If you were to have, let us say, a few weeks away from him, he will soon begin to miss you and come running back...'

'So you *do* think he's having an affair?'

'No, I do not!'

Her mother released her almost in exasperation, returning to her armchair. From there she leaned towards her daughter, speaking to her slowly and purposefully.

'Now listen to me, Joyce. Whatever you may think or have read into what you thought you heard, he is still true to you. He may appear to have cooled a little. It does happen. It may be he has merely begun to take you for granted. Men are not as deeply involved as women. You must prove to him that you don't need him as much as he imagines you do.' She leaned back in her chair as one coming to a decision. 'Now what I suggest is you and I taking a little holiday, maybe on the Continent, say for a month or two. I shall make the arrangements. Your father will not think it odd the two of us going off somewhere together, mother and daughter with a little wish to be together. Without you, Arnold will soon realise how much he needs you.'

She waited while Joyce took it all in, then assuming it to have been concluded, said quietly, 'Now dry your eyes and think sensibly. It will do him good having to do without you. You'll see. It might be good for both of you.'

She smiled as Joyce nodded slowly, more resigned than eager to agree with whatever she suggested.

'Then it's settled,' she concluded firmly, sure

that this was the right thing for her daughter. 'You may leave everything to me, my dear. I will speak to Arnold and tell him what we have planned. I will choose my words to make it sound quite innocuous so you will have nothing to worry about.'

Within a week she was explaining to Arnold that she had persuaded Joyce that it would be nice for them to spend a little time together, despite the fact that he had spoken of taking Joyce away himself in September.

'I feel we both need a break,' she said briskly. 'And September is still quite a way off. We'll be home a good two months before then. It will be nice for her and for me, a mother and her daughter – a little trip to Florence, I think.'

She was surprised by his ready agreement. 'Joyce always wanted to go there and you both have a great interest in art. I think she would enjoy wandering around Italian art galleries, and I hear the city is beautiful.'

Daphne said nothing, but to her mind his agreeing seemed almost too eager, in fact it set her thinking. What if her daughter was right to suspect something going on between him and his secretary? But that was nonsense. Arnold was a sober-minded young man, dedicated to his work, who'd never dream of deceiving the wife he loved. It was all in Joyce's imagination.

At least a holiday together, away from him for a while, would give her something else to think about, help cure her of these fanciful ideas.

All Arnold felt was a surge of relief. For weeks

Joyce had been growing ever more distant, turning her cheek away from his kiss when he arrived home from working in the City. She was hardly talking to him, and when compelled to was abrupt and unsmiling, her eyes avoiding direct contact with his.

When he'd asked if she was feeling out of sorts, her only replies had been things like, 'Nothing wrong with me!' or 'Why should I be?', not going into any further detail as to why she was behaving so strangely, the counter enquiry off-putting, affording no hope of any normal conversation. For him there was nothing to account for her behaviour, and he was almost glad when she and her mother boarded the train to the coast and the channel ferry, the two of them taking the train to Italy.

Eleven

Free of anxiety for the first time since he and Gillian began their relationship, Arnold didn't have to rush home and account for his lateness with carefully structured lies. His constant fear was that sooner or later he'd be found out. He loved Joyce, though not in the way he felt about Gillian. She was exciting, could rouse him with a single look from those blue-green eyes.

She'd become his secretary around eighteen months ago. Then he'd merely thought what a lovely girl she was. It was later, when her hand, happening to brush his in the course of working together, sent a massive tingle through his body. His expression must have given him away for she seemed to know immediately what it was he'd felt. From there they'd drawn closer, until that evening in his office a few months ago, he compelled to stay late with some work, it finally resulted in what they'd both known would happen one day.

Everyone else had gone but she'd volunteered to stay on to help him. When he'd thanked her for her dedication as she stood beside him helping to sort the sheaf of documents on his desk, she'd murmured in a low seductive tone, 'I wouldn't call it dedication. I'd say it's something quite different.'

He'd looked up at her, for the first time in his life realised what it was like to feel an over-whelming desire for someone other than his wife. Sensing the change in his manner, she'd moved even closer to him, hand on his arm, slim fingers caressing it. Seconds later he was clasping her to him, his lips hungrily seeking hers with a need to take possession of her. The rest had been frantic, exquisite, she lying across his desk, face down, thighs exposed, gasping with pleasure as she received him. So natural, so wonderful. He had never done this with Joyce. She would never have allowed it.

Since then they'd begun taking advantage of hotel rooms. It was like a drug to him, he wanting more and more, and he found himself dreading his wife's return. It was she, he told himself, who had driven him into Gillian's arms with her frigidity. She only had herself to blame. Surely it wasn't natural for a woman not to enjoy sex? A man can stand only so much abstinence. Yet he did love her. So long as she never found out about him and Gillian they'd get along just fine, and surely it would be a relief to her that he would never trouble her again in that direction.

Three weeks since she had left and still three more weeks to go before she would return. Strangely he was beginning to feel a little put out by the enjoyable time her postcards said she was having in Italy with her mother. She should never have gone, leaving him open to tempta-tion. Had she been here he might have overcome that, he told himself, believing every word of it.

He needed her back just to have her waiting when he returned home. Coming home to that large house all alone was beginning to be unbearable. Yet it was unthinkable, bringing Gillian here to fill those empty hours. The time they spent together was another world, and she played no part in the one that was his and Joyce's. By the third week, not having her here was beginning to play on his mind. Gillian was all very well but he needed stability, needed someone to welcome him when he walked in through his door.

He hadn't intended to, but these last few days he had become terse with Gillian and last night they'd had a row in the hotel room, she saying that he was becoming a bore, she didn't want to hear about the length of time his wife had been away, didn't want his divided time; that she was no whore to be used as and when he wanted, and when his wife returned would he assume they should rush their lovemaking so he could get back to that silly woman?

'And how long do we carry on like that?' she blazed at him when he confessed to being content with the way things were. 'How long am I to be considered your bit of pleasure on the side?'

'It's not like that,' he said in confusion at her sudden outburst.

'So what *is* it like then?' she demanded, growing more aggressive. 'I tell you this, Arnold, I'm not prepared to sit around forever waiting for you to make up your mind which of us you want. Either you love me or you don't. And if you do, how long do we wait before you ask your wife for a divorce?'

The word had shocked him. Until then such a move hadn't occurred to him and suddenly he knew how much he wanted Joyce back with all her faults. Yet these evenings making love, wild and passionate, had become his life, his salvation.

'I'll put her in the picture the moment she comes home, I promise,' he lied. It seemed to content Gillian and they'd made love, harsh words forgotten, he almost throwing himself on her and she reciprocating with frantic enjoyment.

But this evening an innocent remark that this time next week his wife would be home, she immediately interpreting the tone as bordering on the wistful, had started another row in which she screamed abuse at him, so much so that he lost his temper, blaring out that if she thought so little of him it might be best for both of them to call it a day and she was free to leave any time she wanted. He hadn't meant it, but Gillian was furious.

'What d'you mean, leave?' she demanded, jumping to the completely wrong conclusion. 'Do I take it you're trying to say I'm being sacked?'

He hadn't meant it that way of course, but beside himself with hurt pride, having been called a weak and pathetic wimp, he burst out before he could stop himself: 'If you like!'

'Oh no you don't!' she yelled back at him. Joyce had never yelled at him in three years of marriage. 'No one sacks me! And on what grounds – that you've been shagging me and you've now got the wind up? But you can have my resignation with pleasure! I don't need a stupid twit under his wife's thumb for a lover. I want a man, one who knows what he wants. So go back to the dear little wife and play the humble little hubby and damned good riddance!'

That was it – four weeks of mad, wonderful, anxiety-free passion, over. He wanted to say he didn't mean what he'd said, but he knew he couldn't. It was then he realised he had merely been carried away by the excitement of sex. It would have had to come to an end eventually because he could never have divorced Joyce. He'd never tell her what he'd been up to. Better she remained oblivious. Had it gone on she would undoubtedly have found out and then were would he have been? Just as well things had come to a head. It was beginning to worry him. So long as she didn't seek retribution, try to blackmail him. But he didn't think she would stoop that low.

To his intense relief, Gillian handed in her notice the next day. He knew he must have really upset her but was too relieved to worry, which in itself proved that he couldn't have been that much in love with her, just in love with the thrill of it. She handed her notice to his father, saying she'd been offered a better job starting immediately, not needing to work out her notice.

His father hadn't queried it except to remark, 'Seems you must have seriously offended her over a few things to say the least, the way she stormed into my office. She was fuming and I was not going have my junior partner being asked to match his word against hers. No doubt something you said or did. You'll need to be a bit careful how you handle your secretary, Arnold. Touchy people, secretaries. Especially the young, clever, good-looking ones.'

To Arnold's ears the remark seemed to hold a double meaning and he swallowed hard even as he smiled and said he would remember that.

All he wanted now was for Joyce to come home, for everything to get back to normal. She had sent a hasty postcard saying she'd be home on Saturday, seventeenth July, a week earlier than expected, leaving him to thank his lucky stars that he and Gillian had parted company just in time.

He was actually looking forward to seeing her, to carrying on his life where it had left off all those months back. But he was a little mystified by her having cut short her holiday. Her postcard had been almost terse, giving no reason, and for an insane moment he'd wondered if Gillian had got in touch with her and told all. As his secretary she could have got hold of any one of those postcards he'd kept in his desk drawer, each with an address of the hotel Joyce was staying in. Could she have been that underhand? What was it – a woman scorned? He remained on edge as he waited for Saturday to arrive, his heart beating sickeningly every time he thought of it.

She was happy to be back in England. It had been a good holiday and she was feeling so much calmer than when she left, though something

130

about Italy had felt rather strained. The people had been friendly and easy-going, but there'd been a lot of military presence that had rather unnerved her.

Waiting for her as she and her mother got off the train from Dover was Arnold and her father. Arnold held a huge bouquet of red roses that almost hid the upper part of him, and a satisfying thought flooded into her head as he thrust the bouquet at her – yes, he did love her and had really missed her these past weeks. It was written all over his face as he caught her to him, almost crushing the blooms, to plant a kiss on her lips which immediately embarrassed her with people still alighting from the train. She was sure some of them had grinned secretly, seeing it.

Her father had simply pecked his wife's cheek, presented to him as though she too felt uncomfortable with even this small demonstration of affection with people around. The modest bunch of summer blooms was, however, accepted with a little more grace, a small thank you and a smile while a porter gathered up the mound of luggage onto a station trolley.

Saying goodbye to her parents who'd be travelling home, Joyce settled herself gratefully in the passenger seat of their own car, her own luggage piled in the boot and on the back seat.

'It's so nice to be going home,' she whispered as they drove out of London.

'It's nice to have you home,' he answered, his sentiments sounding oddly mechanical, his eyes concentrating on the road ahead. 'You had a nice time though?'

'Oh, marvellous!' she gushed, instantly embarking on nearly every detail of her holiday, it all coming alive again for her as she spoke. 'I think it was just what I needed.'

She half closed her eyes, the lids feeling heavy after a long homeward journey. 'Mother was so good, she took me everywhere. I almost felt I didn't want to come home, but now I'm so glad I am. Oh, and by the way, I've got you a few really nice presents from Italy. I hope you like them. They're...'

She let her words trail off, realising that he hadn't been responding to her account of her holiday for some time. She was about to jerk him into paying a little more attention to what she'd been saying, but weariness was overcoming her, her eyelids drooping lower and lower and, hardly aware of it, she drifted off into a doze.

She awoke with a start and sat up as the car swung into the long gravel drive with its flower borders and well-trimmed shrubs. The house looked unexpectedly different, like seeing a long-forgotten acquaintance again, unable to readjust to the once so familiar. She'd only been away a couple of months yet everything struck her as being larger than she remembered, the tall windows even taller, the wide bay window even wider, the upper windows too strangely different, all of it momentarily unreal. Seconds later all had fallen into place, everything back to normal, familiar again, a phenomena anyone coming home from a long holiday might experience and find amusing. Yet she felt suddenly disconcerted, a tiny shiver rippling through her.

It wasn't the end of it. Stepping inside the door while Arnold unloaded the suitcases, she felt a cold draught moving along the hallway to meet her. It seemed to be coming from what Arnold loved to call the chandelier room, and she noticed that its door was open. She gave a shudder and hurried into the sitting room to escape.

Having deposited the suitcases in the hall, Arnold followed her into the room, immediately noticing her drawn expression.

'Are you feeling all right?' he queried.

'Just tired,' she answered, sitting down in the armchair by the bay window.

'I expect you are. You slept most of the way home,' he added. 'I reckon you could do with a nice cup of tea.' He turned as their cook-cum-housekeeper came bustling in.

'Oh, Mrs Evans, I know we'll be having dinner soon and I hope you don't mind, but we could do wonders at the moment to a cup of tea.'

Her chubby face beamed. 'Funny you should say that, Mr Johns. I was coming in to ask that very thing. I expect you could both do with a little bit of cake too. I made a nice Dundee this morning. I don't think it'll spoil your dinner.'

'Thank you,' Joyce said feebly, and as the woman made to go out, she called after her, 'And Mrs Evans, could you close the door to the big room as you pass? There's quite a draught coming from there.'

'Yes, of course. I didn't realise it was open.'

'It's probably the French windows,' Arnold said as she went out. 'It's been such a warm day and as Mrs Evans was here I left them open. I'll go after her and close them now.'

Left alone, the late afternoon sun pouring warmth on her back, Joyce sat staring at the sitting room door as if should her gaze wander something strange might manifest itself. Such an irrational fear that she became angry with herself and deliberately turned away to stare out of the window at the lovely slanting sunshine. Moments later Arnold returned to drop onto the sofa and begin asking more about the holiday and if she was still happy for them to go on the one he'd planned in September, being as she already seemed to have had such a good time with this one.

'Of course,' she told him without hesitation. 'I'm looking forward to it very much.'

It seemed a relief to him to hear her say so and he immediately embarked on what he had planned for it. Slowly she relaxed, feeling better with herself.

Later, going upstairs with a lighter heart to freshen up and dress for dinner, she noticed the door of the chandelier room open again and a faint draught touching her arms. Rooted to the spot she called to Arnold who came hurrying out into the hall at her frantic cry.

'You said you'd closed those French windows!' she accused.

'I did. They might have blown open again.'

'There's no wind.'

'Then I couldn't have shut them properly, could I?' He sounded off-hand, moving off to check, leaving her standing halfway up the stairs.

'No, they are closed,' he said, coming back into the hall now, firmly shutting the door behind him, but before he could look up at her she had run off up the stairs, disappearing along the passage to their bedroom. Collapsing onto the bed she was aware that she was trembling, fighting to calm herself. Slowly the trembling ceased and by the time he'd followed her up to get ready for dinner, she was herself again, annoyed at her silly behaviour.

Twelve

Sunday, a day to linger under the covers a little longer, to rise to a leisurely breakfast, take things slowly and do very little, maybe read, have a little swim, or perhaps wander about the garden, though today it was too hot for that.

This morning Arnold had gone off to play golf. He'd asked her to go too, had tried teaching her some time ago, but she wasn't keen on it and today it was too hot to be traipsing across the greens in the full sunshine and she was still weary from yesterday, all that travelling home from Italy.

When he returned from golf they'd had lunch and settled back for a peaceful couple of hours. Mrs Evans had gone out for an hour or two to see a friend but would be back in time to prepare dinner for them. Around three, Arnold began to get restless and said he was going for a walk, asking if she wanted to go along but she'd declined saying it was far too hot.

Rather she sought the cool library away from the strong sunlight that streamed into the lounge. Passing the door to the big room, she felt stupidly relieved to see it closed.

It was pleasant in the library, reading, but for some reason she couldn't relax. Deciding to take a walk in the garden, she went down the hall to the front door, passing the closed door to the big room.

It would have been quicker going through there to the garden, but she preferred not to go that way. Instead she used the front door, taking the path leading around to the rear of the house. Somehow, glimpsing the road at the end of the drive made her feel part of the outside world. It was very quiet. A solitary car passed but most people were hiding from the July heat.

For a while it was fine, but soon the heat drove her back indoors by the same route, but halfway down the hall she stopped short. The door to the big room now stood open, a faint draught touching her cheek.

Joyce's heart missed a beat then began thumping wildly – there was only her in the house.

She stood, petrified, trying to fight the panic that threatened to take control, trying to tell herself she was a grown woman and this was her house, that the French windows must have been left open. A hot day, reason enough to leave them ajar, and forgetting to shut this door properly, a draught had caused it to open on its own.

Drawing a deep breath, she forced herself to peep into the room. They were indeed wide open, but she wasn't going over to close them. She would shut this door firmly and go back to the safety of the library until Arnold returned home.

As she made to back out of the room, a movement caught her eye. There, lounging in one of the wickerwork easy chairs in the conservatory was the figure of a youngish woman. Joyce gasped.

'Excuse me!' she challenged sharply, raising her voice with some authority, no longer in fear but shocked that some stranger, probably off the road, had had the audacity to enter her home uninvited to plonk herself in her conservatory. 'Who are you? What do you want?'

The woman turned towards her, one slim arm draped over the arm-rest. She was extremely pretty from what Joyce could see of her, and she didn't know why but for a second her mind went to that secretary of Arnold's. The blonde hair like Gillian Daniels' but shorter, maybe recently cut, slim like her, the same heart-shaped face, though from a distance and through panes of glass it was difficult to be sure. If it was her, what was she doing here? Before she could challenge her again, the woman rose and in one swift movement slipped out through the conservatory door into the garden.

Forgetting the odd feeling the room always gave her, Joyce bounded across it, into the conservatory and out through its now open door to the garden. On the patio she stopped, looked about. No sign of the person, whoever she was. But it could only have been Gillian Daniels. Who else? What about Arnold's excuse of going for a walk – had it been arranged for her to meet him? Had golf this morning also been just an excuse?

Even as she chided herself for such silly ideas, her mind went back to that Christmas party, they standing far too close for mere work colleagues.

Was that why he'd been so pleased at her taking a holiday abroad, so they could have things all to themselves? Her stomach crawled at the thought, her heart thumping like a piston. Despite the hot sun, her skin was cold.

To her confused mind, the sheer risk of those two actually thinking they could meet here in her own home and expect to get away with it didn't occur to her. Nor did the fact that the person she'd seen in the conservatory wore a dress that hardly reached down to the knees where it should have been calf-length. And the hair – the last time she'd seen Gillian Daniels, it had been longer, a chin-length page-boy bob. So short a time to have taken it all in, maybe she only thought she saw what she did, but she *had* seen, and now her sole aim was to find Arnold and confront him with her suspicions.

Where was he now? Was he waiting for Gillian somewhere just beyond that small group of trees where the pond was, out of sight of the house? What would she do if she caught them together? She couldn't face that prospect, losing her temper and making a fool of herself, an equal fool if she merely walked off in indignant silence. In the end, choked by tears, she went back into the house, furious with herself for the coward she knew she was.

He came back indoors half an hour later, smiling and at ease. She had to force herself to ask if he'd had a nice walk, where he had gone.

His reply was casual. 'I went to the end of our land and hopped over the fence on to that little lane that runs along the back. It was so quiet and peaceful I just kept on walking. Had to turn back eventually, couldn't be late for dinner. But it was really enjoyable. You ought to have come.'

He was lying, rambling aimlessly. Liars ramble and that was what he was doing. They flush, and she was sure he looked flushed, though it could have been the heat. She merely nodded and went off upstairs, needing to get away from him and his lies. Whether he noticed her coolness she couldn't say, though she was sure he would eventually begin to wonder at her distant attitude.

Over their evening meal she could hardly look at him as they ate in relative silence. At one time he looked up from his dinner to regard her and ask if she was not feeling well.

'I'm ... fine,' she managed, hardy able to keep her voice steady. 'It's this heat.'

'It'll be a pretty hot night,' he said, but she couldn't trust herself to answer. The food was like sawdust in her mouth, almost refusing to be swallowed. Near to tears, she dared not let them show and have to explain herself. What if she was wrong? But she had seen that woman as plain as could be. Who else would it have been but that secretary of his?

In retrospect she was growing surer than ever that the woman she'd seen had been her. If Arnold noticed the trouble she was having in eating he gave no sign, continuing to eat steadily himself, enjoying the stewed pears and cream that followed, though Joyce refused hers, aware of the surprised frown on Mrs Evans' brow.

As soon as dinner was over, she pleaded a

headache from the warmth of the day, saying she needed to lie down. She did not stir when, as daylight faded, Arnold came up to bed, asking if she was feeling better, she pretending to be asleep.

A few days later it seemed her suspicions had been realised when he took her by surprise by voicing concern about the holiday they were to have in September, saying he was wondering if they should really think about cancelling. The arrangements had been to drive through Germany, on to Switzerland and back home through France. The hotels already booked, it was a strange move. He'd also intended they go on to Italy, but as she had already gone there with her mother, there was no point to it. Now he was looking to cancel it altogether.

'I'm worried about the way things are going in Germany just now,' he told her as she raised a querying eyebrow at him. 'The papers are reporting enormous Nazi rallies and demonstrations against Jewish citizens. It seems Hitler and his Nazis are beginning to throw their weight around a little too much. And the way Mussolini's fascists are behaving ... Well, you said yourself that you saw some of it while you were in Italy, didn't you?'

He was talking too much, as if trying to fill a void of which he was now becoming aware. He paused for her response, forcing her to answer.

She had to say something. 'I saw quite a few soldiers about, that's all,' she said tersely, unable to look at him without her fingers curling into small, tight balls.

141

'You said they were rather off-putting and it worried you.'

'They might have put me on edge a little, yes.'

'Well, I don't want to have you put on edge again if we go. In fact I'm not happy taking you to anywhere near any countries like Germany with the present state of things. I think it might be best to cancel.'

Under normal circumstances she'd have been deeply disappointed, would have pointed out all that money lost through cancellation. As it was she hadn't been looking forward to sharing any holiday with him, with what she now suspected, and anyway she'd had a lovely holiday in Italy with her mother. When asked if she'd be too disappointed if he was to cancel, all she said was that it was up to him.

If he detected hostility he gave no indication, which to her mind only accentuated his guilt. Sooner or later she was going to have to tackle him on that person she'd seen in their conservatory. She was now sure it had been Gillian Daniels. The way she had fled had been proof of something going on between him and his secretary – his ex-secretary. He'd told her a couple of weeks ago that she'd left her job, was now working for a firm of solicitors, still in the City. It all sounded innocent, but of course he could now see her without others knowing. The fact that he intended to get out of taking his own wife on holiday was, if anything, even more proof.

She couldn't help herself. 'Do you still sometimes see Gillian?' she asked, trying to make it sound casual. She was sure he'd coloured a little even as he shook his head, but there was little more she could ask on that score without looking as if she were prying, or worse, portraying mistrust.

She felt all alone in her suspicions, needing someone to talk to and be reassured that Arnold was trustworthy, and her thoughts turned to Jennifer Wainwright. They'd become good enough friends for Joyce to confide in her, and so long as she swore Jennifer to secrecy she knew she could rely on her to observe it, and maybe give good advice too.

'You do tend to live on your nerves,' was her advice, which she wasn't exactly expecting. 'Are you sure it wasn't someone off the road with cheek enough to look for a cool place to sit down for ten minutes?'

It was so ridiculous a suggestion that Joyce broke into unintended laughter until her friend was obliged to join in with her.

'No, I am sorry,' she said, recovering her composure. 'But seriously, did you really think your Arnold would be having an affair with someone? He loves you. He wouldn't dream of two-timing you. But I don't know what to say about who you saw. It was all I could think of. I'm sorry.'

Sitting over coffee in Joyce's library, Jennifer thought awhile then said carefully with a small self-evasive smile, 'I don't want to sound as if I think you're being stupid, Joyce, but I wonder if you might have seen your own reflection in the conservatory glass. It could happen,' she ended hastily, seeing Joyce's lips tighten. 'I mean it could happen to anyone.'

'And see my reflection get up from that wicker chair and walk out?' she queried. Jennifer thought a moment then shook her head, smiling at the foolishness of the suggestion.

'Well, I don't know, but maybe...' She fell silent, the silence going on for so long that Joyce found herself forced to prompt her.

'Maybe, what?'

'Well...' she hesitated, then, 'What if it was ... well, a ghost?'

'Oh, come now!' Joyce smothered a false laugh to cover the shudder that ran through her knowing how often she felt some strangeness about the big room. 'Why should the place be haunted?'

'Well...' Again Jennifer hesitated then ploughed on. 'Those people who owned your place previously. I've told you about the man who drowned in your pond and...'

'It was a woman I saw,' Joyce broke in almost savagely. 'Not a man.'

Jennifer sighed. 'Well, I really don't know what to say. But I don't think your Arnold would be unfaithful to you. He's not the type.'

Joyce relented, wanting to believe her. 'Maybe you're right. It could have been someone who shouldn't have been there, taking advantage of a cool place to sit. Maybe I am being a bit silly, imagining Arnold going off with someone else.'

'Of course you are. He's a lovely man, your Arnold. And he loves you, I know he does. I mean, there he is taking you away on a lovely holiday on the Continent in September. You don't know how lucky you are to have a husband like him.'

She sounded so wistful, obviously reminded of the husband she had lost to some scheming woman, that Joyce hastily changed the subject. Even with no real advice forthcoming, she did feel a little better for having talked it over with her friend.

Yet despite Jennifer's reassurances, as the days went by, what she now swore she had seen that afternoon was beginning to build up again in her mind. All the little things put together slowly multiplied into a renewed gnawing suspicion; one she felt she could not prove, in fact one she found herself fearing to prove, all imaginings of ghostly presences swept away.

Thirteen

With the autumn nights drawing in, Arnold was coming home later and later from the City – for reasons other than work, she painfully suspected now.

It hadn't upset her that he'd cancelled their September holiday for the reasons he had explained at the time, and with which she had agreed, not caring for the uncomfortable feeling Italy had given her when she and her mother had been there. Nor was she sorry. The thought of having to endure his pretence at faithfulness would have been intolerable, even though there was still no proof of any infidelity, nothing to go on except what she suspected, he certainly not about to confess all.

The woman she'd seen that day in summer had not been here again, maybe having realised the danger of discovery. For the time being it was well to let them both believe she was still in the dark. But it constantly disturbed her peace of mind. While not having courage enough to face Arnold with what she was convinced was going on, in a way so long as she remained unsure there was the hope that it was all in her imagination, although that was not exactly any consolation.

October gave way to November and rain. To-night she could hear it drumming on the conservatory roof, so loudly it was even audible in the hall. Coming from the lounge where she had been trying to read to take her mind off the fact that Arnold was again late coming home, having rung to say he'd been delayed at work, she became aware of a draught from the now half open door of the big room. She could have sworn it had been shut earlier, and surely the French windows must be closed. Who'd need to open them this time of year? She couldn't exactly remember when she had last closed them, days ago perhaps. Back in the summer the catch had proved to be faulty. Arnold had said he would have it fixed and she assumed he had. Even so, it still refused to respond to anything but a firm slam. At the time she thought he should have had a proper lock made with a key, but he'd said there was no need. 'The door to the garden already has a lock and a key, so there's no point.'

She had yielded as she always did to his superior knowledge, but if that blessed catch was still faulty she was going to talk to him about it when he finally got home.

Irritated, she marched across the room to the conservatory door, in her annoyance for once feeling none of the strange sensations that usually bothered her. She hadn't even stopped to switch on the light, saying to herself that he should have dealt with this ages ago. At least she would be able to give vent to some of that pent up anger and indecision she had been harbouring for so long.

This time the door was firmly shut. So what had caused the draught floating into the hall? For a moment she stood wondering, then becoming suddenly aware of the chill the room seemed to hold for her, she quickly retraced her steps to the door to the hall.

Reaching it, something made her pause, turn and glance back. Dim and indistinct, with no moon on such a wet night, she fancied she saw a figure standing at the far end, hardly discernible, its back to her. Her breath almost stopped in her throat, then exploded from her as she burst out in a trembling voice:

'What are you? What are you doing here?'

The figure turned slowly to face her, sending a cold shiver coursing through her veins, Jennifer Wainwright's words coming back to her: 'You know people do still believe your house has a ghost?'

At the time she had scoffed, but now, rooted to the spot like one totally paralysed, all she could manage in a tiny wavering voice was, 'Please ... go away ... leave us alone.'

Gripped by growing terror, she almost wanted it to be Gillian Daniels, someone solid and real on whom to vent her anger. But this wasn't Gillian Daniels. A figure, still indistinct yet just clear enough to be seen clothed in the same shapeless, short, low-waisted summer dress she now remembered noticing before, the fair hair in the style of a decade ago. Now, as if from a distance, quiet words came from the figure: 'Your husband is playing you false...'

It was those words that made her come to her

senses. The paralysing fear left her in a rush. 'What do you mean?' she burst out. 'What do you think you are playing at? Who are you?' Words flew from her lips in a rush of sheer anger. 'You've no right to be here.'

This woman was no ghost. She was as real as she herself. 'Did that Gillian Daniels send you?' she demanded. 'If so then you'd best go, as soon as you like, before I call the police!'

'Look to your man – he plays you false.' The words were repeated, cutting through her angry torrent. 'All men are liars.'

The voice trailed away and for a moment Joyce stared on from her end of the room, convinced now. No ghost; this was someone connected with the girl Arnold was messing around with. Why? Was it to rile her so much that she'd row with him, throw him out, leaving the way clear for them with no need to meet in secrecy? She wouldn't put it past the wicked bitch.

'Look, I'm going to phone the police!' All fear dissipated, she made to leave, but for some reason, she didn't know why, turned back to further her warning, only to find the person no longer there.

Where had she gone? The French windows were still closed yet she was no longer here. Unable to bring herself to go and investigate, instead backing out of the room, the only logical answer was that it had to have been an interloper. The woman had to still be in the room, hiding behind a sofa or an armchair – anything to give her substance. It was the only answer. She needed to phone the police straight away.

But lifting the receiver she stood gazing at it. What if the trespasser had been Gillian? It hadn't looked like Gillian. It had all happened so fast she wasn't sure now what she'd seen, though it could only have been her. But why come here in weather like this and Arnold not yet home?

Thinking back on it, it now occurred to her that the person had been bone dry, not a spot of rain in her hair, not a drop of damp on her clothes, as though she'd been in the house for some time, waiting for him to get home.

That had to be it. It all seemed logical – any straw to cling on to rather than those first eerie thoughts that had all but overwhelmed her until she'd felt she couldn't breathe. Any stranger could have broken in, could have been lurking for God knows how long, hiding. But wasn't that thought just as bad? Anything could have happened. Mrs Evans, busy in the kitchen with the evening meal, would have been too engrossed to hear anything until too late.

A key turning in the lock of the front door made her almost leap out of her skin. Moments later a half-drenched Arnold stepped into the hall.

'My God, it's teeming out there!' he burst out, seeing her. He was already struggling out of his wet greatcoat, vigorously shaking his hat ready to hang it up on the hallstand. 'I got soaked just getting here from the car. I've just left it in the drive. I'm not messing about out there in this weather putting it in the garage. It can stay where it is till the morning.' His voice trailed off as he noticed the look on her face. 'What's wrong? Is something the matter?'

'No, nothing,' she said sharply, recovering enough to turn away from him to go and tell Mrs Evans he was home and she could serve dinner now. But her mind was racing. Who and what had she seen in that room? And why warn her about Arnold? Gillian Daniels wouldn't have done that. Even so, she was sure it had something to do with her.

Arnold was in the sitting room standing by the window staring out at the rain when she returned. He turned and looked at her as she came in and, seeing the strained expression on her face, asked again, 'Is there something the matter, darling?'

Unable to contain her feelings any longer, she burst out, 'Liar!' her voice shrill. 'You know very well what the matter is. That ... that woman!'

He had stepped back from her onslaught. 'What woman?'

'That secretary of yours!'

'You mean Helen Ainsworth?'

'I mean that Gillian Daniels.'

His voice remained calm. 'She left. I told you. She left the firm to go somewhere else.'

'And you're still seeing her!'

He was frowning, but his voice had adopted a cautious tone, or so it sounded. 'Why should I still be seeing her? She no longer works for me.'

'You're seeing each other, I know. I've seen her here – twice. That day in the summer, you said you were taking a walk but I know it was to meet her. She was waiting in the conservatory.

She saw me and rushed out. You came back and said you'd been for a long walk, alone, even said I should have gone with you, but that was all lies. You were with her.'

He made to interrupt, but she waved away his effort, words tumbling out of her mouth. 'She was here again this evening, just a few minutes ago. She spoke to me. I turned away but when I turned back she'd disappeared. It's raining but her clothes were dry as a bone. And you came in moments later so she had to have come here with you in your car.'

Her wild words fell away as she caught her breath in an anguished sob. 'I know what you two are up to, Arnold. Don't try pulling the wool over my eyes. You and her are having an affair, aren't you?'

'How can you ever think such a thing?' he burst out, but he was looking decidedly uneasy. He moved forward to take hold of her but she sprang away, screaming at him not to touch her, so much so that he stepped away again, stood looking at her as if at a loss as to what to do.

A light tap on the door seemed to break his confusion, Mrs Evans coming into the room to tell them dinner was ready to be put on the dining room table. Now she asked cautiously if everything was all right.

'Everything's fine, Mrs Evans,' he said a little too abruptly. 'My wife is just a wee bit upset, that's all. Everything's all right.'

'If you say so,' came the reply. 'I'll take the dinner into the dining room then, shall I?'

Not waiting for an answer she closed the door

very gently, her heavy footsteps retreating while Arnold turned his attention back to his weeping wife, his tone sounding as if it was fighting to be firm. 'I suggest we go and have dinner and you can tell me what all this is about.'

As if he didn't know. She looked at him narrowly through a mist of tears. 'Do I really need to?' she said with a wavering sarcasm. 'I'll not eat with you until you tell me the truth.'

'Darling, you're letting your imagination run away with you.'

How dare he call her darling! The very set of his face betrayed his every word. Whoever that woman was whom she'd seen was making him squirm, pointing to a guilty conscience. How dare he treat her as though she were a child needing to be soothed!

'You've got yourself all upset about nothing, my love. Maybe what you thought you saw was just a trick of the light. Now come and have something to eat.'

She watched him walk past her. Her tongue seemed to cleave to the roof of her mouth in disbelief that he was treating her as if she was an idiot. He was in the rear passage making for the dining room before she galvanised into life, bounding after him to catch him up as he got to the dining room.

'You grubby pig!' she raged as she followed him into the room. 'That's why you were so happy for me to go on holiday, so you two could have a free hand. You said she enjoyed her job so why did she leave? So no one would discover what you were both up to. She said you were a liar!'

'Who said I was a liar? What're you talking about?' he demanded, turning on her fiercely.

'Your bloody ex-secretary.' She seldom swore. Her voice coarsening, she hardly recognised herself.

Arnold continued to hold himself in check. By the table, he gazed calmly at her. 'Get a grip on yourself, Joyce, you're overwrought thinking you saw someone who wasn't there at all.'

'I know who I saw!' She railed at him. 'You brought her here in your car, made her wait in the big room. You know I hate going in there and so you'd both be safe there, wait for me to go to bed, then you could enjoy each other. How many times – in my house – how many times?'

Her voice had risen to a screech yet his had hardly altered from its smooth attempt to assuage. 'Stop this nonsense, darling. Sit down and let's enjoy our dinner.'

'I'm not your darling!'

'You are. Now come and sit down.'

So bloody calm. She could see guilt in his eyes even as he demanded she sit down and enjoy her dinner. Enjoy dinner, when he was aware of what she knew, that him and that bitch had been sleeping together all the time she'd been away, were still thinking they could deceive her.

Something seemed to snap, loathing enveloping her whole body, blood pulsing through her temples like searing flames. She began to scream. It was as if someone else was screaming, hysterically, on and on, powerless to stop.

She felt him take her by the shoulders, tried to

154

free herself, but his grip was relentless. He was shaking her. She didn't want him to shake her. On the table beside the joint of lamb waiting to be carved and served up lay the carving knife.

Someone was still screaming as she reached out in a need to be free of that grip, in panic raised her arm, thrust downward, found herself instantly released, almost falling backwards.

The screaming had ceased. Now she lay on the floor sobbing. Beside her lay the knife, he kneeling beside it. He was looking at her in an odd sort of way, staring at her, eyes wide with disbelief, one hand clutching his neck. From it blood was flowing slowly, over his hand, his shirt, his tie, running down his arm. Then slowly he toppled sideways. Someone was in the room, was crying out in alarm, but she had no idea who it was.

Mrs Evans had heard the commotion but at first thought it best not to interfere. She had done that a little while ago, going into the sitting room to enquire if everything was all right and almost told to mind her own business. She hadn't wanted to interfere again, but to her ears that scream-ing hadn't been right. It had become hysterical, like someone having a brainstorm. That second time she had just known that she had to interrupt.

The funeral of Mr Arnold Johns-Pitman was car-ried out after the inquest, but it seemed to those attending that his widow wasn't quite right, standing dry-eyed at the graveside between her parents, her face blank, her lips slack.

On the other side of the grave, as if to be as far

155

from the widow as possible, the deceased's parents, his brothers and their wives stood stiff with grief, but also hostility. A little way off a police van stood ready to take the widow back to await her trial.

Some weeks later, on the reluctant evidence of her cook, found guilty of homicide while mentally disturbed, she was committed to a mental institution for treatment. Those watching the wreck of a woman being led gently away agreed that the findings had been just, that she had completely lost her wits and was still out of her mind by the way she'd been unable to follow what was being said; unable even to remember how it had all happened. Constantly becoming hysterical, she had rambled on about a woman whom she had said had been her husband's lover Gillian Daniels, or someone like her, who had come to haunt her and warn her not to trust him, then disappearing in front of her.

Gillian Daniels was proved to have been somewhere else entirely at those times, and locals who'd come to listen to the trial were convinced that Joyce Johns-Pitman had indeed seen *the* ghost. They remembered again the previous owner of Crossways Lodge drowning himself in his own pond, even though this ghost had been female according to the accused.

Some weeks after Joyce Johns-Pitman had been committed, Florrie Evans, now without a job, went into the post office to post a few letters and naturally brought up the subject of her own ordeal at the trial, how she'd hated having to stand witness against her employer.

'She was usually such a quiet soul,' she said to the post mistress. 'I felt so guilty having to talk against her on that witness stand, her someone I worked for ever since she came to live there. I don't think she was ever happy living there, and I felt so sorry for her despite what she did.'

Passing her money over to Jennifer Wainwright, she went on, 'But I was the chief witness apparently, me coming into the room just as she ... well, you know. You were at the trial too. You were friends with her.'

'I always found her to be a nice person,' Jennifer Wainwright put in as she eased a couple of tupenny stamps from the perforated main leaf. With no one else waiting to be served there was time to talk. 'A bit on the quiet side. I never would have dreamed her capable of doing what she did. I think I feel more sorry for her than her poor husband.'

'You knew he was carrying on with some other woman?' whispered Florrie.

Jennifer managed to look surprised. Joyce had confided her suspicions to her some time back but she was not going to divulge that to anyone, priding herself on not being one for tittle-tattle.

'She did go strange though,' Florrie went on. 'I found her kneeling beside him ranting on about that room with the chandelier and a strange woman warning her not to trust him. But there was no one else in that house at the time but me and her. Young Doris had gone home and, well, you heard it all at the trial, her talking about some woman appearing from nowhere, a ghost she said, though who I've no idea.'

Jennifer kept her opinions to herself, remembering how Joyce had shuddered as she spoke of the first time she'd seen that apparition, as she had called it later. The only person Jennifer could think of as being an apparition would have been that poor man Horace Butterfield who drowned in the lake.

Some said it had been suicide, the man besotted with that gold digger he'd thought was as much in love with him as he was with her. Everyone but him could see what she was. The wife had walked off and left him over it. But that Celia running off with another man must have got to him so badly.

Jennifer believed it had been suicide. But Joyce had spoken of seeing a woman dressed in clothes ten years out of date. It did get a person thinking. Even if that Celia had died since, she'd been extremely fashionable, skirts reaching well below the knees, so whoever Joyce saw couldn't have been her, no more than it could have been the girl Joyce's husband had been seeing.

True, Joyce had always insisted she felt something odd about that room with its chandelier, that it gave her the shudders whenever she entered it; had said her mother too had felt it on occasions. Whatever it was, it had led to her finding her husband carrying on with that secretary of his and, like the worm that turns, so had she.

Jennifer couldn't blame her entirely. Any woman in her state of mind might have done the same. Maybe not to the extreme that Joyce had, but that opinion was best kept to herself, she thought, as two people came up to stand behind Florrie at the postal counter, terminating the conversation.

What continually plagued Jennifer's mind was Joyce's description of the dress worn by whoever she'd imagined she'd seen in that room, seeming more the style of the late twenties than the mid-thirties. Wondering if it had anything to do with the chandelier Joyce hated so much, she had delved deeper, finally remembering what Butterfield's cook had once said when describing the lovely ballroom her employer had constructed, the glittering parties he'd thrown and how much his guests had admired that splendid chandelier of his. He'd always been ready to tell them the story attached to it of a woman jilted by her lover after losing all her money in the Wall Street Crash of 1929 and her attempted suicide by hanging herself from it, laughingly adding that it had given way and fallen on her instead, killing her instantly.

Was that the answer to Joyce's dislike of the thing, of the out-of-date dress of the apparition she said she'd seen? That solution had come as such a revelation that she couldn't wait to confide it to Florrie Evans. But she had reckoned without Florrie's love of gossip. The woman saw no point in keeping such a wonderful tale to herself and before long it had spread like wildfire around the whole village, to the macabre delight of everyone who heard it – real proof of that house being haunted!

Fourteen

Six months since the tragedy and the house was still empty.

Locals had assumed that the murdered man's parents would have placed it on the market immediately, glad to be rid of the bad memories the loss of their son had left them with. But if they had done so they'd certainly not bothered with its upkeep. It lay behind a now overgrown hedge, hardly visible from the road, and if one ventured beyond the low, wrought-iron gates – not that anyone was brave enough to do so – it would have been to a weed-grown drive, bordered by ragged, untrimmed shrubbery, grass lawns uncut, while the windows of the house gaped at the intruder like empty eye sockets, despite the curtains still being in place.

Whether the furniture had been removed was anyone's guess, for not even the family of the woman who'd murdered her husband had come nigh or by. No one knew what was going on. Rumours abounded. At the murder trial it was said that the wife of the dead man had ranted on about having been spoken to by, as she put it, the ghost of some strange woman in what she termed the chandelier room. It was all that was needed to set people talking about Crossways

Lodge being haunted.

'They say she'd always been susceptible to odd goings-on,' someone said in the post office after the trial. 'It seems she said the woman she saw actually warned her that her husband was being unfaithful. And I think it came out in court that he had been.'

For all her resolve to keep her one-time friend's confidences to herself, the post mistress Jennifer Wainwright talking to Florrie Evans one day when the post office was quiet couldn't help making a comment of her own on how Joyce Johns-Pitman had told her on one occasion all about what she'd seen.

Florrie nodded sagely. 'Her mother said that even she felt very queer about that room, even wondered if it had anything to do with that chandelier itself, the one that hung in that room, though goodness knows what.'

Jennifer Wainwright made a personal note to delve into the tale a little deeper if she could, loving a mystery. Now she said, 'I don't know how true it is but when those other people, the Butterfields, had the place, the chap Horace who used to hold all those grand parties, who was drowned in that lake of his, once told someone I knew that that chandelier had a bit of a history to it. He apparently boasted about it. Said the people he bought it from when he first came to live here told him that some wealthy woman in London had tried to hang herself from it but it fell on her and killed her.' She gave a small titter. 'Maybe it was her Joyce Johns-Pitman saw before she killed her husband?'

'I didn't know that,' said Florrie Evans. 'But I quite believe you. She said at her trial that it was a woman, definitely a woman, not a man.'

'But it makes you think,' said Jennifer Wainwright as the bell on the post office door tinkled and two people came in, necessitating her to let the matter drop. It was better not to spread too much gossip around the place.

She had, however, reckoned without Florrie Evans' loose tongue, with no need for her to keep quiet over what she had seen going on from day to day in the Johns-Pitman household, and it didn't take long for speculation to become truth in the minds of local people.

It now became clear why the place was still empty after six months. After all, who would want to lay out good money for a house that was possibly haunted?

The six months became a year and still Crossways Lodge remained on the market, no one apparently interested. There had been several look at it but none had expressed a desire to buy, despite the price having been lowered several times. The only reason Johns-Pitman could think was that word had gone around of the heart-stopping tragedy that had happened there. Nor did it take long for local tittle-tattle to reach the ears of any potential buyer of it being haunted and the tale attached to it.

'All I want is to be rid of the bloody place!' Johns-Pitman said vehemently to his wife. 'I'd give it away if that was possible.' But of course it wasn't, nor could it be demolished, a protection order attached to part of it.

'I really should go over there to check on it,' he said reluctantly. The mere thought of venturing anywhere near the place where his son had been murdered made him quail, hard-headed professional person though he was.

Gertrude Johns-Pitman shuddered, imagining he might expect her to accompany him. 'I'm afraid I couldn't go within miles of the place.'

'Nevertheless, we can't go on leaving it to itself. I'm going to have to go sometime to see what condition it's in.'

'But the agent does that, surely? You pay him to have it inspected regularly and kept tidy.'

'So he says, but if I don't go over there, he could say anything.'

'I'm sure he cannot be such a rogue as that,' she scoffed. 'He has his reputation to think about, surely.'

But Howard senior frowned. 'Maybe I should tell him my plan to go there at some time.' Though when that would be, he didn't even want to think. 'It'll make him check that his own people are doing what I pay him to do. He does not seem to be putting much energy into trying to sell it.'

Came the thought that maybe he should procure another real estate agent, but all he did in the end with no heart for anything was to write and enquire how the upkeep of the place was going. It wasn't like him at all, but the loss of his youngest son in such circumstances had knocked all the stuffing out of him.

Bad enough his son's face coming back to him

whenever he closed his eyes, his dreams filled with muddled scenes – Arnold a young lad swimming in the sea, playing football for his school, graduating, clasping his bride to him at his wedding, laughing, strong, intelligent – leaving an unbearable weight in his heart as well as a deep hatred for the woman who'd robbed him of that promising future he would have had, her only punishment to be committed to a mental institution.

Once the house was sold and off his hands he'd be able to rest more easily. In the meantime he wrote to the agent in the strongest terms. Maybe the man did need a squib up his arse!

It wasn't that he needed the money from the sale of the house. His investments were sound, his company thriving, more now as repercussions of the past recession faded, replaced by sighs of relief at Prime Minister Neville Chamberlain bravely averting the threat of war. That September had brought joy, seeing their Prime Minister brandishing a paper the German Chancellor had signed proclaiming 'Peace in Our Time', happy in the belief that everyone could now get on with their lives.

Surely the house would sell now, thought Johns-Pitman. At last he'd be rid of that, if not the heartbreaking loss of his youngest son to that mad woman who had ranted and raved in court of a ghost telling her that her husband was being unfaithful, causing her to lose control enough to stab a carving knife into his neck.

It was summer again. Still the house hadn't sold.

'I cannot understand it,' said the agent, Mr Morris. 'I do assure you your property is being kept in excellent order. I have people there constantly overseeing its upkeep so I really cannot understand it.'

After another stern reprimand from Johns-Pitman on the apparent lack of attention being given to the property, with a word of warning of it being put into the hands of a more competent firm of estate agents, he had pulled out all the stops to make certain that the place was now bright as a new pin.

'It's an attractive enough property. All I can say is it has to do with the times. War hanging over our heads again isn't making it easy, but I do assure you I am doing all I can. I cannot say better than that and I am sure we will see a realistic buyer before long.'

But he too had heard the rumours that still abounded around the area of the place being haunted, rumours that had grown in strength and inventiveness. There was now not one ghost but two. How the story of the chandelier had got about, no one was certain, but got about it had.

Mr Morris secretly felt that most potential buyers had got to hear of it and had backed off for that very reason. He still lived in hope that some hardy soul would shrug off the stories as pure piffle and put a substantial down payment on it. The place was becoming a drain on his own resources, despite reaping a steady income for all his services.

To the people of Wadely village, the brightening up of the haunted house, as it had come to be called, could only mean that it would soon be occupied by new people. But what if the ghost or ghosts refused to be laid to rest? For months every local waited in suspense, their attention finally averted by the sad and regrettable voice of Neville Chamberlain announcing that the country was at war.

'We won't sell that blasted place now,' Johns-Pitman complained bitterly, even as he thought of his two remaining sons who, if war continued for too long, could be conscripted despite being married men. 'The only thing, being empty, is that we might end up with a lot of young evacuees.'

A second wave of children were pouring out of London to the country and safety, away from possible bombing. The first wave had arrived before war had been declared. This time it was even more serious. 'God knows what state it'll end up in by the time it's all over.'

But it wasn't to be. Within weeks an elderly couple with no family had snapped the house up, the price having been lowered considerably owing to the times. They were laying out their entire savings with the idea that if bombs did begin dropping on the part of London where they had been living, the country would be the best place for them. The place had gone for a song in the end, such was Johns-Pitman's despair that he had become willing to be rid of it at any price. He didn't need the money, but he did need peace of mind, able to wash his hands of the place entirely.

The elderly couple living safe from the air raids that began in May 1940 felt fortunate to be out of it. Unfortunately, at the end of May they visited a couple of old friends living in the East End, deciding to go home the following morning, the air raid sirens already having gone off. Seeing no point in the four of them huddling together in one tiny, cold air raid shelter for hours, especially as all was quiet with a temporary lull in the raid, the occupants and their guests were still indoors when the house received a direct hit.

At the start of the war the couple had made wills, leaving everything to each other, but stating that if both passed away at the same time, everything was to go to their only surviving relative, the woman's elderly brother Benjamin Lacey who lived in Vancouver in Canada. He was entirely alone, having lost his wife a few years back; their son, an only child, had been killed thirty years ago in an accident at the age of twelve.

Benjamin was sorry to hear of his sister's death, his memory momentarily winging back to when they'd been children. But that was over sixty years ago and he hadn't seen his sister for nigh on forty years. He wouldn't even know what she'd looked like, being that they hadn't written to each other for years. He had no interest in going back to England, and even if he had, was too old now to travel all that way, even without the risk of enemy submarines lurking in the Atlantic.

Among the old couple's possessions was a sizeable house in some village called Wadely or

Great Wadely in Essex, Benjamin learnt. Bit of an ancient place by the sound of it and he guessed pretty run down too. He was comfortably off enough not to bother with all that legal messing about trying to sell it, and he had no wish to be worried to death at his age having to sort out a place probably on the verge of falling down anyway.

Let it stay, he told himself. He didn't have many more years on this earth and he wanted to enjoy what was left. He had a nice apartment on the first floor of a block of flats near to a pretty good shopping area. He could take a stroll down to the picturesque harbour where the big liners would berth end on end. Vancouver was ice-free, had a temperate climate, was surrounded by green forest and purple mountains; it had nice beaches and he still swam occasionally, though much less these past few months. He had friends, was a member of a couple of social clubs for the elderly – plenty to occupy his time and a decent pension to go with it. His sister and brother-in-law's tumble-down house would be more of a nuisance than an asset, probably more trouble than it was worth going through all that paperwork trying to sell it.

Washing his hands of it, old Ben Lacey proceeded to get on with his own life, the house in Wadely again left to sit empty and forsaken over the next three years as the war dragged on. Few had any interest in buying houses, even to get out of London and away from what people were calling the Little Blitz being waged on specific places of importance, South Wales, Hull, Bristol,

168

and of course London, and that only lasting a couple of months.

In Wadeley, the house, still furnished with its chandelier hanging in place now covered in dust, settled into slow, elegant deterioration, the old tales of ghostly goings on there gaining vigour until no one cared to venture anywhere near it, while little boys would dare each other to creep up its once again weed-covered drive and bang on the door.

Towards the end of those three years, Ben Lacey, now in a home for the elderly, received an official letter from the powers that be in England requesting he might care to give his consent for his empty property to be used as a billet for military personnel, assuring him that at the end of the war it would be returned to him in good order. Not caring one way or the other, he was content to allow it.

Once again Crossways Lodge found its rooms cleaned up, its grounds tidied, hedges bordering the road trimmed though remaining purposely tall so as to screen the place from interested eyes. Army huts were erected in the grounds with washrooms, latrines, mess hall and other various amenities the military allowed its men.

Soldiers would frequent the village, shopkeepers' takings looking up, the two local pubs doing a roaring trade, the post office too, selling as it did lots of goods other than stamps. Even the local tea shop saw a good trade. The old empty house, brought back to life, suddenly became a hive of activity, locals and little boys robbed of tales of funny goings on there.

The house itself was for the staff, undergoing a complete change with the absent owner's furniture carefully removed and stored in the several outbuildings, the large room to be the officers' mess with more conventional furniture, the conservatory installed with a bar for drinks, stools and tables, its missing or cracked panes of glass having been replaced. Some of the other ground floor rooms became offices and storage rooms for files and such, the kitchen remaining as it was, while the upper rooms were used as living quarters for the staff.

Few used the back door other than the kitchen staff, and the far end of the narrow rear passage would often become cluttered with bits of rubbish and a deal of kitchen waste waiting to be stacked outside the back door for taking away. Few also used the old back stairs to gain the upper floors, officers preferring to use the main front door to the large hall to reach their rooms, or to go into the big room that was now the officers' mess and the bar, or else to their place of work in the several downstairs offices.

The chandelier in the large room had been removed and carefully packed away to reside in one of the outbuildings for the duration of the war, however long that would be, although the powers at the top already felt they had the end to it in their sights at last.

Nothing had been said of course, but around autumn a vast movement of troops all across southern England had the population wondering, raising hopes that the end could indeed be in sight, as empty shops, business premises, houses, schools and social halls were used as billets for troops and skilled men. Crossways Lodge in the village of Wadely near Brentwood was one of many chosen, being handy to a major arterial road and Tilbury, in readiness for when the call came for what many people were praying would be the long-hoped-for invasion of enemy occupied territory, the so-called but so far undisclosed second front.

Thus twenty-one-year-old Corporal Norman Bowers from a village in Derbyshire was one of those who found himself billeted at Crossways Lodge in Wadeley in the autumn of 1943.

Fifteen

At the end of a wet and dreary October day, Corporal Bowers straightened his shoulders with relief that he'd soon be able to rest, get cleaned up and have something decent to eat after hours of gruelling travel with full pack on, a few sandwiches and the odd cup of lukewarm tea.

Following Sergeant Price across the well-trodden grass, he could see lines of huts spread across what had probably once been a fine estate. The house was big – for officers of course, lucky buggers! To one side was a NAAFI canteen, instantly reminding him how hungry he was, near the house a small swimming pool with no water in it, further on a tennis court, locked, though any keen officers would probably be able to procure a key for its use.

Sergeant Price finally halted them outside one of the Nissen huts. 'Right, Corporal, see 'em settled in ... Quietly! See they unpack and clean up before eating. You *are* up to doing that, I take it, Corporal?' he added with a touch of sarcasm that made Norman Bowers' skin crawl. 'Grub in the mess hall, you've got half an hour. After that, too late, you go without!'

Turning smartly, he marched off as if he'd just risen from a good night's sleep instead of having spent a whole day on a train and then in the back of a rattling army truck the rest of the way to this place.

Left to themselves, each man proceeded to claim his bed by throwing his equipment on it. Some flopped full length on theirs or sat on the edge, hands clasped loosely between the knees, heads lowered in weariness. Travelling for eight or nine hours was no joke on a packed, dawdling train that seemed to stop nearly every quarter of an hour or so for no known reason – the joys of wartime travel for everyone, not just the military – all the way from Conwy in North Wales to some out-of-the-way railway station in south Essex.

Since the end of summer they had been detailed to load endless planks of wood, iron rails, iron poles and anything else needed onto trucks destined for the docks. There was a rumour that it had something to do with a planned second front, but no one had any details. Nor had anyone been told why they'd suddenly been uprooted and sent off to Essex on the other side of the country. But then theirs wasn't to reason why, theirs was but to go where they were sent, no matter how daft the reason; all they knew was that they'd be on continuous training and man-oeuvres in readiness for something big, whatever and whenever that would be.

His stuff stashed away, Norman Bowers picked up his washing kit. Some of the men had already sloped off to the ablutions situated just behind the big house, others still too weary to bother as yet. But soon they'd have to follow their mates if they didn't want to miss getting something to eat.

Norman thought of Sergeant Nigel Price, who'd gone off to make sure the rest of his men had settled in. He grinned as he thought about the man who rather saw himself something, God's gift to women – tall and well-built, a good-looking man around twenty-eight, probably married, but if he was it didn't seem to curb his pleasure for girls and before long he would most likely find himself a few of them in this village. Sporting a small moustache, he held himself very upright, his bright blue eyes ever on the prowl, not only for some likely tart but for any man who might appear to cross him.

Some sergeants were tolerably fair-minded. Price was not. A sarcastic bugger, no one ever knew how to take him. What seemed a genuine friendly remark usually turned out to be pure sarcasm, and hard luck on the poor unsuspecting soldier taking it to be a cordial gesture. Most maintained he did it on purpose just to see a man get himself into hot water.

Along with others, Norman couldn't stand him, nor, it seemed, could Price stand his corporal. Being a corporal it was impossible to avoid him, the man taking a particular delight in putting him down at every turn, calling him a twit in front of everyone, a nincompoop, a jumped-up petty snob who thought himself an intellectual, preferring studying books to getting stuck in, a cut above everyone else and him not even with a high school education to back it up.

As he never ceased to do, Norman thought of it

as he made his way towards the ablutions. The trouble was, Price was right on some things. Yes, he read widely, his parents had made sure of that, and yes he *was* secondary school material, but he was proud of what he'd achieved on just that, proud too of his upbringing. His parents were self-respecting, he their only child. They lived in the small village of Swinage in Derbyshire, went regularly to church, having made sure he went along with them from an early age. They played a large part in many functions in the area. His mother was an infant teacher in the local school, a Brown Owl and the chairwoman of the local WI. She was also on the church hall committee. His father had the village store and post office above which they lived, ran the boys club, the youth football team and was a member of the village cricket team, excelling himself as a strong leader.

Norman had therefore been brought up to regard himself as they themselves did, a little above the ordinary locals, and to excel in all he did. He could have gone to high school and maybe on to university, but his father had viewed it unnecessary to prove himself, instead deemed himself well enough equipped to teach his son a deal more on a one-to-one basis than any college or university might have done, and in fact he was right, procuring books for him he might never have read. He felt he had a lot to thank his parents for

As to Sergeant Price, according to someone of the sort that seemed to know everything about everyone, he'd been to college but failed to get any high grades. How that person knew was a mystery, but it had got around and could account for Price's choleric attitude towards others, especially towards himself thought Norman bitterly as he stood stripped under the trickling shower.

He knew Price was deeply envious of his being more widely read and therefore a deal more intelligent than he. He'd heard that at one time Price had possessed aspirations of being smiled upon by the Commissions Board for officer material, and maybe bitter disappointment at being passed over was one reason for his trying to belittle Norman at every turn.

Norman felt he himself might have been selected had it not been for having gone no further than secondary school, and there had been no point in trying. Having been taught at home no matter how intensively by a father whose intellect might have been superior to some officers he could name, was still no recommendation for selection. But he didn't need recognition from any Commissions Board to know that he was far superior to Price in intelligence and intellect.

'Did you 'ear that?' Private Dick Hobbs asked Lance Corporal Bob Macatty as they left the showers, their corporal still showering himself.

Bob, known as Mac, shouldered his damp towel, his washing kit tucked under his arm. 'Hear what?'

'That what Sarn't Price said ter Corp'ral Bowers when he asked if Bowers was up to carrying out an order. Sarky bugger! If I'd been Bowers, I'd of felt like biffin' 'im! Mind you, them two

176

are a pair well matched. They both fink somefink of themselfs. Me, I don't fink much of eiver of 'em. I mean, that Bowers do fink 'imself a cut above the rest of us, don' you fink?'

Bob Macatty didn't reply. He got on okay with Bowers. So he could be a bit superior at times and maybe he wasn't all that good a mixer, thought of as being a bit on the snooty side. Probably the way he'd been brought up, from what he'd heard. But Mac could forgive him. He was an only child and maybe that was the reason he was a bit withdrawn. Mac, on the other hand, was one of six and knew his way around the world.

Dick Hobbs was nattering on, seeming not to notice that his previous question had not been responded to.

'Yer can't deny though, got a good 'ead on 'is shoulders. Would've made a proper officer. Real clever bugger – too clever fer words, that's 'is trouble. Makes yer feel real small sometimes. Me, I steer clear of 'im when I can – like yer do. Beats me 'ow you tolerate 'im.'

Still not responding, Mac felt a wave of pity for Bowers. The man needed a friend. And he was tolerable enough so long as you overlooked his failings. Everyone had failings. Mac supposed he himself did.

'You and 'im often used ter go down the local tergever when we was stationed in Wales,' Hobbs stated. 'How did yer find him?'

'I found him okay,' Mac finally answered, giving nothing away. They'd reached their hut, each making for his own bed space, Hobbs to do

177

whatever he intended to do before going off to eat, Mac to think about Bowers.

They were just casual friends, only the stripes on their arms keeping them as such. He doubted it would be a lasting friendship. Once they were separated as happened to army chums in wartime, he'd forget him, but for now they'd probably carry on going down to the local together whenever they obtained a pass, like when they'd been in North Wales, swapping snippets about their lives before being called up, maybe talking about girls, but with Norman not very often, finding it a bit of a one-sided subject.

Mac had no trouble finding girls but Norm was far too reserved to even approach one, let alone ask for a date. He was a good-looking blighter too. Such a waste! It was a shame. Maybe when they went down to the local pub, hopefully to see what there was on offer – not that he held out much hope for Norm – if he found a decent bit of skirt he might ask if she had a friend she could introduce to Norman. Perhaps it would even get him off to a head start for once.

A couple of months had gone by and still no luck with Norman Bowers. The moment Mac began to approach any group of girls, the man would instantly make an excuse to get back to camp or go to the gents', moments later to emerge and skedaddle off before the girls could be introduced to him.

This evening, standing at the bar of the Baker's Arms surrounded by a continuous boom of men's voices and raucous guffaws, occasionally pierced by high female laughter, Norm was airing his most recent brush with Sergeant Price.

'Being a corporal doesn't make it easy trying to keep out of his way,' he mumbled into the pint of black and tan he was drinking.

This morning he'd come under fire during training, Price ridiculing him in front of the men for the dim-witted know-all he really was, all over one of them having reported a minute or two late for duty. Price had slagged him down in front of everyone and nothing Bowers could say or do. An unwitting snort of amusement from one of those present had merely brought a glower from Price, before he used it to upbraid his corporal further for failing to keep the men in order. 'Can't even do that, can you?' he'd bellowed. 'Think you can command this lot? You couldn't command a turd!'

Hours later, Norman was still smarting from the humiliation.

'You should try not to take it so much to heart, Norm,' Mac told him. 'It's not just you. He's like that with everyone.'

Norman disliked his name being shortened, but with an effort curbed the impulse to correct him. The last thing he wanted was to lose the man's friendship. Mac saw no evil in anyone, but from time to time could betray a faintly thin skin and without Mac he'd have no one. He knew what the men thought of him, maybe not as badly as they thought of their sergeant, but sergeants were a breed apart whereas corporals were more like one of them, and ostracism was the last thing he wanted.

The Baker's Arms this Saturday night was full of locals as well as men from the camp, the noise louder than usual, the atmosphere jolly and thick with tobacco smoke. It often happened that some of the locals would play darts against some of the soldiers and tonight was no exception.

Standing at the bar with Mac, Norman watched them for a while as he sipped his black and tan, finally letting his gaze wander on around the room. By the door four young women were seated around a small table, and for a moment or two his heart pumped a little quicker before he let his eyes move away.

He realised that Mac had also spotted them and knew with a sinking heart that he would soon be making his way towards them, expecting Norman to follow. In his mind's eye he saw himself being introduced, smiled at briefly as every gaze became riveted upon Mac, the tall, good-looking one, he ignored from then on, leaving him to move away with an excuse of needing to be somewhere else. Better to make that excuse now than be humiliated later.

Mac had already come upright in preparation for going across to them. Norman took another quick peek in their direction, already concocting his excuse to leave Mac to himself. That thought was suddenly arrested by the sight of Sergeant Nigel Price entering the pub by the door where the girls were sitting. They'd looked up at his entry, continuing to stare appreciatively at him, but he already had a girl on his arm.

Quickly Norman turned back to the bar but Price had spotted him, was already making his way towards him.

'Good God, if it isn't our shrinking violet, Corp'ral Bowers. And all on his own as usual, not a woman in sight. Does his mother know he's out?'

His sergeant's powerful voice ringing across the smoky room brought all nearby eyes to look straight at his quarry, and Norman felt himself cringe inside, but it was Mac who stepped forward.

'What you on about?' he demanded.

Price fixed him with a blue-eyed glare. 'I was talking to him, not you.'

'No, you talk to me!'

'Watch yourself, Lance Corp,' came the low warning, but Mac wasn't to be deterred.

'We're not on the parade ground now. We're in a pub, off duty.'

'But still in uniform,' came the low, menacing reply.

Seeing trouble, Norman stepped forward, easing Price to one side. 'I'm sorry, Sarge, have you got something to say to me?'

His eyes for once were glaring, maybe more than he guessed, for Price stared at him for a moment, then laughed. 'Trouble with you, Bowers, you can't take a joke.'

'I see,' Norman said slowly. 'I didn't realise. I haven't seen my mother lately, so I will speak for her. If she and my father were here they would no doubt be wondering if your parents in turn know you're out. I'm only asking, of course.'

It was a pitiful excuse for a retort, but as the fluffy-haired bottle-blonde on Price's arm gave a giggle, he went red, tugging her into line and snarling at Norman, 'I'll catch you later, Bowers.'

It was a threat and Norman didn't reply, except to acknowledge the dread that made itself felt within the pit of his stomach as Price moved away, dragging the girl with him.

'Come on, love,' he said as he began shouldering a path through the throng towards the door through which he'd come. 'We've better things to do than stand yapping to some brainless twit. Might even give you a nice present for the one I'll be giving you a few minutes from now if you're good.' To which she laughed and cuddled closer to him as they made for the exit.

'What was all that about?' Mac asked mildly, while Norman continued to stare towards the door through which Price and the girl had disappeared. Norman's thoughts leapt back to the present.

'Are you really that dim?' was all he could find to say, quite savagely in his seething anger at being made to look such a fool, with no idea how rude and unsociable he sounded until he became aware of Mac gazing at him, slowly shaking his head.

'It's no wonder you put blokes' backs up, Norm,' he said quietly. 'One can see why you ain't got any friends. I'm your friend, but talk to me like that and I won't be for much longer. It's not the first time you've spoke to me like I was nothing. I've done you no harm. If you want to take your spleen out on someone, take it out on Price, not me.' With that, he drained his still half full glass of beer in one long swig, putting it back down on the bar with some force. 'Think I'll toddle off back to barracks. I've had enough for tonight. You coming or staying?'

Far from being an invitation to leave with him, it was an open desire to go back alone. Norman took the hint.

'I think I'll finish this up, maybe get another,' he said quietly, not sure why Mac should have become so upset, as the man departed having first laid a hand lightly on his shoulder without looking at him.

Left alone, Norman ordered another beer which he now didn't feel like drinking. He let his gaze wander about the room. The fug and the country pub lighting made it difficult to pick out with any clarity those sitting around the few tables on the far side, mostly family groups, neighbours and friends, while laughter continued to bounce off the ceiling to beat against his ears.

He wished he had gone with Mac out into the quiet night with its silent sky like dark velvet, stars bright as diamonds, the Milky Way a solid path above an enforced total blackout. In the quiet he could have apologised for whatever remark had been enough to put Mac's nose out of joint and maybe would have felt better than he did at this moment.

He'd like to have thumped Lieutenant Nigel Price, but he would have belittled himself, and anyway they were in uniform. It would also have demonstrated an admission of failure. Yet his insides were raging with an unaccustomed, primitive emotion he fought to stem. His parents would have had a fit had they known how angry he felt. His two years in the army hadn't yet conditioned him to give way to natural anger, and just as he'd been taught from a child he still spurned that emotion as indecent and undignified, something to be battled until it was thoroughly conquered. He even felt some pride in doing so, just as they had taught him.

Mac had said he put people's backs up. That wasn't fair. He never had the intention of upsetting others. If he did it was they who were at fault not him. Mac himself had been wrong to even say that he was the one at fault.

Norman stood, trying to pierce the fug of smoke and fumes, seeing the door at the far corner through which he yearned to escape. At the table just to one side of it sat the group of four girls laughing together. They were about his age, probably had boyfriends. Maybe they were discussing them now, swapping tales. He felt suddenly very lonely.

He'd had enough of drinking alone. He might still catch up with Mac and apologise if he'd upset him. Finishing his drink he made for the door with that goal in mind. Reaching the table where the girls were still laughing, necessitating him to edge past with little space left to manoeuvre between the table and the exit, one of them pushed back her chair to get up, tripping him so that he half fell against the door jamb. She leapt up like a bolt released by a spring, making a grab for him to help steady him, almost toppling over herself, ending up with him grabbing her instead.

'Oh, God, I'm sorry!' Her voice was high with embarrassment while at the table the other three had broken into peals of laughter.

Norman felt his face grow hot. He wanted to round on her, ask what she thought she was doing, but she was still clinging to him and he was obliged to take both her arms to steady her instead. So they stood clutching each other until he in turn was forced to apologise.

'It's all right,' she said quickly, looking up at him. 'My fault entirely. I wasn't looking what I was doing. I honestly didn't see you there.'

Her face was inches from his as she gazed up at him – a pretty face, wide blue eyes, sweet mouth with just a touch of lipstick, the lips now parted in her words of apology. Fair wavy hair framed oval features, a strand having escaped the hair clip that held it off her forehead. Norman felt his heart leap.

Sixteen

For a moment they stood together just staring at each other. Her friends had gone silent, all three now keen to see what developments might arise. 'What's your name?' she asked at last.

'Norman,' he said, wondering why on earth he had responded so easily. 'Norman Bowers.'

'I'm Valerie Prentice, usually known as Val.'

There came a giggle from the three still-seated girls. 'Well, kiss him then,' one of them hissed.

She turned on them without disengaging herself from him. 'Shut up! All of you!' But then she did step back from him. 'I'm sorry, I didn't mean to embarrass you.'

Oddly enough, for once in his life he didn't feel embarrassed by what could have been an awkward situation for him. All he felt was a strange wish to have her not go and sit down, leaving him standing there like a fool.

'It's a very nice name,' he said quickly. It was all he could find to say, but she smiled.

'Do you think so?'

'Yes, I do.' He thought desperately of something else to say, but his mind was now totally blank and it was she who spoke again.

'D'you come in here often?' It was so trite, the sort of words used by new partners on every

186

dance floor in the country.

He didn't enjoy dancing, usually going only when a couple of blokes, feeling sorry for him and assuming they were doing him a favour, practically compelled him to go along with them. Even then the only dance he could do was the waltz and that badly, preferring to sit out and watch others rather than asking a girl to dance and possibly being refused. But he had heard the words spoken, the reply usually being some flippant come-back. Hearing her say it, he wanted to laugh, but managed to control himself from giving tongue to a reply he knew would sound utterly stupid.

Instead he said simply, 'Sometimes, when we are given a pass for the evening.' It needed to be enlarged upon. 'But I enjoy coming to this pub as often as I—'

'I don't come in here much myself,' she interrupted. 'We usually go off into Brentwood or somewhere like that, but we missed the bus tonight so we decided we'd come in here instead.'

'I thought I hadn't seen you before.' Words were suddenly coming to him easily, his head filling with things he wanted to say to her about himself, everything about himself. But again she interrupted.

'How long have you been stationed here?'

'Just a couple of months.'

A voice broke in from one of the three girls sitting watching. 'Be careful, soldier, she might eat you!'

Val glanced back at them a little irritably then

back at him. 'Let's go outside, out of the way of this lot.'

He nodded, not knowing quite what to say, but found himself meekly following her as she pulled aside the blackout curtain of the first door to the tiny lobby, swishing it back into place as he stepped out with her, she going through the same procedure with the one across the outer door before opening it to emerge into the stygian darkness of the chill December air, he close behind. The night was silent but for the muffled voices within the pub.

He was feeling awkward. She had leaned her back against the side wall of the pub. What was she expecting of him? He could hardly see her face but thought she was smiling. Was it one of enticement? A girl alone in the dark with a soldier, there was only one reason for that, only one ending. This was how lots of girls in wartime got their fun – certain girls.

'Tell me all about yourself, about your life, and I'll tell you all about mine,' she began.

She hadn't reached out to him, hadn't even moved away from the wall, empty space still between them, but he was on his guard.

'Why?' he asked.

Instantly he wished he could have bitten off his tongue, expecting her to give an annoyed puff and walk back into the pub, but she didn't seem at all offended. 'So we might get to know each other,' she said innocently.

'I'm sorry,' he said for the second time that night. 'I thought ... Well, it doesn't matter.'

He wasn't being propositioned at all. The girl

was genuine, wanted to get to know him better. Did she really fancy him? But why him? He almost made to continue his apology for having made such a horrid mistake in his first assumption of her, but that might have frightened her off and he wanted her to stay, desperately wanted her to stay.

'I suppose you've guessed I live in Wadely – just down the road, the second lane on the left from here.' His eyes now growing accustomed to the darkness, he noticed that she'd eased her shoulders off the pub wall, her left hand across her body to point behind her away from the camp. 'I live with my family and we've a bunga-low. It has a big garden and we can see right across almost to the Arterial Road. We grow all our own vegetables and we've a few chickens for eggs so we don't have an egg ration. Instead we're allowed mash to feed the chickens with and get our eggs off them. At least we know they're fresh,' she finished with a laugh. 'How about you?'

Never had he felt so at ease with someone. The girl was interested, wanted to know all about him. He'd never spoken to anyone for so long, as he told her where he came from, about his home, his parents, their lives, his life before he was called up.

'I go to church too,' she said. 'Maybe not every Sunday but quite often. Lot of people here do. I don't think they go so much in big towns like Brentwood and Chelmsford and London. Maybe some do, but village people go a lot, don't they? You're from a village like me. That's nice.'

How long they talked he wasn't sure, but the time went on as they left the pub and strolled along the village street to the end then turned back to retrace their steps, he realising that he'd have to be back in camp soon or be in trouble, maybe refused a pass next time.

When he told her she said, 'That's so unfair.'

Reaching the gates across the entrance of the driveway to the big house, Norman took a deep breath, asking hurriedly while he still had the courage, 'Can I see you again?' and felt her touch his arm. She'd not even been holding it as they'd walked, more like two friends really.

Now she said, 'I'd like that. When?'

'I'll probably get a pass on Thursday, if that's all right for you?' It sounded a silly question but she gently squeezed his arm.

'I look forward to it, very much,' she said, and reaching up with her lips brushed his cheek before quickly standing back as if embarrassed.

'Thursday then,' he said, moving away towards the gate with its two men on guard duty either side. In the darkness he couldn't see her now, but he knew she was standing watching as he showed his pass and went on through. Tonight he felt as if he'd stepped into a world he'd never previously known, his heart beating with happiness as he made off towards his hut.

Over the next few days he could think of nothing but Valerie Prentice. He'd never felt like this before. She sat in his head through everything he did, her slim, petite figure, the light tone of her voice, that fair, wavy hair, those china-blue eyes. He found himself wondering what she was doing at any time of the day, imagined her at work – she'd said that she worked in the typing pool of a stationery manufacturers in nearby Brentwood and was learning shorthand at night school, hoping in time to become a secretary.

He had begun to let his imagination run riot, visualising her at home, sitting by the fire listening to the wireless with her parents and her younger brother Sidney, some evenings going off to Brentwood with her friends. What did they do there? Who did she see? Was there another boyfriend in her life and would he find himself put aside in preference to that faceless other, he already forgotten the moment she met whoever he was?

He found himself constantly on edge, longing to find out if there was anyone else, and the next few days seemed to drag, he going through each hour as best he could. Not even training and various duties dulled thoughts of her. Sergeant Price's scathing remarks no longer seemed so daunting or bit as deeply as they had once done. He now had something to look forward to.

Even sentry duty wasn't the interminable drag it normally was. When he sat on his bed polishing his brass he could conjure up her face. Eating his meals he'd wonder what she was eating. Lying in his bed at night he'd picture her lying in hers. He'd dress in the morning ready for parade and wonder what she would be wearing. In short, he knew he'd fallen in love.

Then came anxiety, fear, self-censure: anxiety that one stupid little remark would lose her; fear of what life would be like if she were to decide not to see him any more; self-censure that he was already tormenting himself after only one meeting, not him at all, yet he couldn't stop.

Daily duties helped to some extent to make the days pass quicker, and he found himself looking forward to being constantly occupied no matter how tedious and exacting the task. This Wednesday afternoon, despite spattering rain driven on a cold, stiff breeze, he and his lot had been detailed to cut and clear grass and weeds that had run riot around the two outbuildings since summer and were now dying off in unsightly masses. They worked fast, each man eager to get back inside out of the miserable, cold, rain-bearing wind.

While overseeing the work he noticed one of the outbuildings hadn't been locked. It vaguely occurred to him to report it, but most likely would mean him having to chase around for the key if it was lost, when all he wanted was to get out of the weather and into the warmth of the NAAFI with a cup of tea. Let someone else deal with it, he thought, a little vindictively.

That evening, the weather having cleared and him unable to rest for longing for tomorrow night to come, he decided a short stroll might settle him down. The noise from the NAAFI pierced the chill air, but he just wanted to be on his own for a while, wrapped up warm, to think about Valerie.

His route took him past the outbuildings, one of them still unlocked. In fact the door now lay slightly open. Surprised that no one else had noticed it, unless of course a careless officer had lost the key around here and decided against reporting it and getting into hot water, curiosity swept away his thoughts of Valerie for a moment. Moving nearer, he peered inside, almost as if he was being gently persuaded to, though it didn't really occur to him that this was so.

A full wintry moon, risen above the horizon and now very bright, slanted uninterrupted into the interior as he eased the door wider. Wondering at himself for being so curious, he stepped inside leaving the door open so as better to see. Garden tools leaned against the wooden walls. A variety of farming implements occupied most of the floor space along with cardboard boxes, some with the damp having got to them, the cardboard coming away in places to reveal glimpses of porcelain ornaments, from the house no doubt, kept safely stowed away lest they got damaged if left in the house.

Dust sheets covered various pieces of furniture. He lifted one of the sheets by the corner for a peek, to find it to be covering a grand piano. It came to him that the house must have once looked absolutely lovely. There were large mirrors propped up, their gilt frames and the mirrors themselves reflecting the rays of the moon back into the area so that whole portions of it were lit up.

Next to the grand piano was another dust sheet of an unusual shape. Curious, he lifted one edge. Instantly the moonlight reflecting off one of the mirrors pierced the object underneath, which glittered back straight into his face, taking his breath away, a huge, golden-coloured chandelier, its crystal drops shining like diamonds into his eyes.

Startled, he dropped the corner of the dust cover. Then, recovering, he lifted the sheet again. Squinting against the brightness, it went through his mind that Valerie would have cried out in delight to have seen all this, though why he should think of such a thing he had no idea. But then she was in his thoughts all the time.

But he'd stayed in here too long. Someone could easily come along and discover him here and he'd be in for a fizzer. Retracing his steps, he closed the wooden door behind him, but as he made to walk away, his foot touched something metallic. Half hidden between a tuft of grass that had been missed and the edge of the building lay an open padlock almost buried in the soft ground, but no key.

Scanning the area briefly, wondering why he felt a need to waste time on it, moments later his eyes alighted on it laying about a foot away, almost hidden in the trodden mud of a well-cleared patch. It was a wonder no one else had noticed. It had probably been pressed into the earth by the careless foot of the one who'd dropped or mislaid both objects during his hasty search. Maybe the man had had to leave with his search half done, having made up his mind to lie, say that the building was safely locked. Otherwise why had both objects remained unfound until he saw them?

A wild thought stole into Norman's head as he glanced furtively about in case anyone had seen him and wondered what he was up to. Snapping the padlock into place, he slipped the key into a pocket of his battle dress and hurried off.

In his mind a mad idea had begun to form – he who'd never had a mad idea in his life – one that was now setting his mind on the go, not even pausing to wonder why. It was almost as though someone else was putting the idea into his head and he felt excited.

Valerie would love to see the stuff in that outbuilding. What if he were to suggest he smuggle her over the perimeter fence one night? She'd see him as a bit of a dare-devil, something most girls wanted their men to be, and she would be so proud of him. She might even be proud enough of him to find him irresistible, the two of them together on one of the dust sheets. The first girl he'd ever kissed, he felt he could go further, who knows, maybe all the way. Thinking about it he felt like a lion.

In a mad moment he'd confided his feelings about her to Bob Macatty, swearing him to keep it to himself. And of course Mac would, he was that kind of person. If it did get around, it would not take Price long to make some snide remark and Norman would know the information could only have emanated from Mac, and Mac knew it too. He could trust his friend and he knew Mac was pleased for him. But the man's advice had been sober.

'Don't get too carried away, Norm. You've only known her a few hours. If you let it get to you, she could break your heart, especially the type of bloke you are.'

'What's that supposed to mean?' snapped Norman, feeling his back go up. Who did Mac think he was, deeming to judge him? What gave him the right to imagine what sort of person he was? But Mac hurriedly changed the subject, realising himself in the wrong.

'That girl I met when I left you last week. She was with some others but I chatted her up and we went off together. I even got a kiss and cuddle in the bushes on the way back here. I'm seeing her again too, on Thursday, but I'm not making too much of it like you seem to be doing. Don't forget, Norm, ship's that pass in the night – that sort of thing. We could get posted or she could get fed up. Girls can. We all can. Just take it easy, that's all...'

Seeing Norman's lips tighten once more, he added hurriedly, 'I'm only warning, that's all. No one wants to see a mate get hurt.'

Despite Mac's wisdom ringing in his ears, he still felt elated if a little anxious, so that it was an intense relief to see her standing just outside the pub waiting for him. In the moonless blackout, the sky overcast, she was almost invisible before he realised she was there, recognising her only by the cream-coloured coat she'd worn the week before. But her voice came leaping back into his memory.

'Norman! I was frightened you wouldn't come.'

She must have been feeling the same emotions that had plagued him all this week. Delight leapt in his breast as he took her hand.

'Do you fancy a drink?' he asked, not really looking forward to going into a noisy, smoke-filled bar, seething with humanity.

She looked at the darkened place that to him had now taken on the discomforting appearance of a vast black box vibrating with noise.

'I don't think so,' she said, making him feel she had the same impression of the place. 'It's so nice and quiet out here and the weather's not too bad, cold but dry. Let's just go for a stroll.'

He felt on top of the world as they walked slowly, his arm about her waist, she allowing it. She took him past her house and they stood looking at it for some time while she told him a little more of her life. They had gone on to where the lane ended in fields and by the gate had kissed and held each other. No more than that but it spoke of much more to come as time went by.

He'd wanted to conduct her safely back home, saying goodbye to her there, but she insisted on accompanying him to the camp gates.

'I'm quite safe going back home on my own. This is my village and me and my family know everyone and everyone knows me and my family. And I don't want to say goodbye to you until the very last minute.'

Filled with secret delight at her words, he let it go at that. When he finally left her at the camp gates, she let him kiss her again – a long lingering kiss, he hearing her whisper that she could hardly wait to see him again.

He knew now that this was the girl for him, visualising their lives stretching on to a distant and wonderful future together. Mac had been so wrong when told him not to let himself be carried away.

Seventeen

Norman could hardly believe they'd been going out for nigh on three months. Just before Christmas, Valerie had asked him home to meet her family, that in itself proving it to have become serious in her eyes as well as his.

It had been a traumatic evening, meeting her parents, even though they'd welcomed him. He'd been on his best behaviour, trying not to say or do anything out of place, seeing their eyes going from him to their daughter and back to him. To his mind, tension had existed all round, and he'd been glad when the evening was over.

He'd never been at ease with strangers and this had proved the most difficult situation he'd ever experienced, knowing how much rested on it. Even Valerie had looked on edge, constantly singing his praises while they regarded him narrowly, openly weighing him up. After all it was their daughter's well-being they had in mind and she still only twenty. They were trusting her future to a man they'd only just met, although she'd most likely spoken enough about him to fill a bible if he knew anything about her.

She'd sat beside him the whole time, her hand in his, singing his praises, talking for him when he became lost for words or abrupt, as people like Mac had often told him he could be. But for her he would have appeared as he'd heard people say of him, at least since he'd been called up, soldiers not so fussy about airing their views – that he wasn't easy to get along with and in fact could be downright bloody off-hand. Val had obviously never found him so and he was sure he wasn't as bad as some made him out to be. But her parents, like her, were nice people, nice to him even though he felt the tension could have been cut with a butter knife at odd moments as conversation became worryingly stilted every so often.

Her younger brother Sidney was more honest, hardly bothering to talk to him, Norman catching him eyeing him up and down when he thought he wasn't looking. The thought kept repeating itself – if only families didn't have to get in the way, life would be so much less complicated. He was glad when the evening was over and he and Valerie left to take a walk on their own.

'I hope you liked them, my parents,' she'd said, cuddling close to him as they strolled in the somewhat blustery night air. 'I'm sure they liked you.' He'd had no wish to contradict her and had merely said that he liked them as well.

Since then he'd gone regularly to the house, had begun to feel more at ease, if only a little more for he still sensed if not disapproval then a wish for her to have maybe found herself someone other than him, though nothing of this was ever intimated.

He was beginning to feel that before long he must declare his intentions towards Valerie more strongly. He wanted desperately to propose. That he was deeply in love with her was beyond any question and he knew she was deeply in love with him. But it needed more, a serious commitment.

On his mind were the peculiar times they were living in. Normally a man could bide his time, waiting at least a few more months before a proposal of marriage, maybe getting around to it gradually, the two of them thinking along the same lines. Under normal circumstances a young couple would have been able to take their time making any such move towards long-term decisions. But they no longer lived under normal circumstances. This was wartime. With the ever-mounting expectancy of an allied invasion looming, a government announcement bursting on them at any time, a man could be snatched from his girl at a moment's notice. He needed to do something about the two of them well before anything like that happened. He needed to propose to her. Would she accept? Would she understand the need for haste?

He was sure she had the same thoughts in her mind, though she said nothing and he felt with a sinking heart that she was rather shy on the subject, maybe wary of letting herself be carried away and he respected and loved her for it. It was how a girl should be, not looking to slip straight into the bushes with a man as some did.

He thought of Mac, the first evening he'd met Valerie, Mac telling him later that he too had found a girl. For Mac it had been merely a short-lived thing and he'd gone through quite a few others since, enjoying it with whoever was willing, which seemed to be all he was after. That had been Mac's way, not his.

'You mean you haven't had it off with her yet?' Mac had asked incredulously after a few weeks of Norman seeing Valerie. The query had riled him to such an extent that he had rounded on the man in no uncertain terms and had nearly lost himself a friend.

But he too was beginning to ache for something more with Val than the usual kisses and cuddles, though winter had helped to curb the need to some extent with either blowing snow, ice pavements, biting winds, frosty air or chill fog. They'd cuddle close on the bus coming back from seeing a film in nearby Brentwood or having had a meal in a café or little restaurant, all he could afford on a corporal's pay. If he was short of cash she often paid and he loved her for it. She was generous, sweet-natured, even-tempered; he couldn't fault her in anything and he was proud of her. If only she'd unbend a little to his longing, but the moment he attempted anything she'd lean away ever so slightly and he'd get the message. One day, maybe.

He'd have liked to have taken her home to meet his parents when a thirty-six-hour Christmas leave had enabled him to go and see them, the holiday being a short one, falling on a Saturday as it had. But she had declined, nicely and with some regret.

'It's only right we should be with our own families at Christmas,' she'd said, which was to be expected and he had understood.

He hadn't enjoyed that leave, longing to get back to her. Nor had she it seemed, her relief at having him back almost painful to see, and it was maybe then that he'd really come to realise that things between them were becoming that bit more serious. Now he knew that when the time came he'd be able to propose to her without any fear of refusal.

Already he had it in mind for next month on her twentieth birthday in April. What she would think was an ordinary birthday present would instead be an engagement ring, and as she stood breathless with surprise, he would slip the ring on the third finger of her left hand as he popped the question. It would be romantic and he could hardly wait.

He'd been putting money by for months and soon there would be enough to buy a tolerably decent ring. She'd understand that a corporal's pay could never extend to a huge solitaire. But a decent band of three diamonds would make it look much larger than it was. She would accept and he'd vow to make sure that when they could finally marry she'd still be as pure as she was now, despite his almost painful need for her as the weeks went on, compelling him to keep tight control over his natural needs. As small a thing as a goodnight kiss and cuddle usually left him aching, sure that if she would just let him touch her he'd feel better. She might even respond and surprise him, but he dared not risk it in case she took it wrong, ending in a row, even a break-up.

One thing he could do was prove himself a bit of a dare-devil, make her proud of him. She'd said often enough that she was proud of him, though he'd never really done anything to be proud of. But what if he managed to steal her into camp to take a peek at the chandelier that still drew him? Why it did he didn't know, except he'd begun to feel he couldn't rest unless he took a glimpse at it from time to time. In some strange way he felt it might help melt her heart if he got her to come and look at it.

The more he thought of it the more he became eager for her to see it. To his mind there seemed something very erotic about it and he felt that its influence might help cure her natural reluctance for love-making.

On several occasions he'd spoken to her of the thing, telling her how he'd come to discover it and describing the wonder of it. He'd seen her eyes light up with interest, but when he told her that he could arrange to sneak her into the camp so she could see it for herself, her reply was instant.

'I couldn't. That would be trespassing and that's against the law. The place is out of bounds to civilians.'

'You've nothing to be frightened of,' he assured. 'I'll look after you. It's being done all the time. There's a broken down piece of the perimeter at the back that's not yet been noticed and soldiers are always smuggling their girlfriends in.'

She knew why of course and immediately went on the defensive. 'I'm not *any* girl, Norman. I hope that's not what you have in mind.'

'Of course not,' he told her hastily. 'I would do

nothing to harm or hurt you. Why should I? I love you.'

Somehow it was becoming more and more imperative that she saw it, allowed him to share its wonder with her.

'This is simply to show you the chandelier I discovered. I don't want to keep it all to myself. I want to share it with you. It's such a beautiful thing to look at. It'll take your breath away. I'm chuffed at discovering it. No one else seems to have. I just want you to see it too, darling. You just have to.'

In his eagerness to impart his own pleasure of the thing, almost as if it had taken hold of him, the words poured from him. But her mind was less on what he was trying to describe than on a more basic matter.

'How do you know so much about this break in the perimeter fence?' she asked out of the blue, her faintly suspicious tone immediately quelling his rapid flow, replacing it with a surge of anger.

He stared at her, frowning. 'It's what the other men have told me,' was all he could find to say, the wind taken completely out of his sails.

'But how do *you* know where it is?'

'What're you trying to say, Valerie?' he asked harshly, his anger rising even further. 'What're you trying to accuse me of?'

Surely she hadn't realised what she was saying. She was too innocent a girl to dream him low enough to have enticed another girl over the fence for his own gratification. She must know he was above that sort of thing.

With an effort he managed to curb an outburst

of fury. To lose his temper with her would be to lose her completely. But the sensation took a while to dissipate, leaving him trembling even as he forced his words to sound gentle and calm. He even managed a small, indulgent laugh.

'What a silly goose you are, darling. Naturally the men talk among themselves. But the brass doesn't know or it'd soon be made safe. But if you think I'd use it to sneak in some other woman...'

He let the words die away as her face crinkled with misery.

When he began again his tone was filled with passion. 'Oh, my sweet, surely you didn't think I'd ever dream of doing such a thing? I love you. Why would I ever even want to look at anyone else? You're my world. You must know that.'

Tears were now trickling down her cheeks as she continued to look up at him with her expression of abject pleading.

'I'm sorry,' she burst out in a rush. 'I don't know what on earth made me say that. It just popped into my head from nowhere, just as if someone else was saying it for me. Forgive me, Norman, I was just suddenly so frightened of losing you.'

Her admission startled him. 'Why would you imagine that?' he cried, grabbing her to him to clasp her tightly.

Her head resting limply on his shoulder he heard her tremulous reply. 'I don't know why.'

'I'd never leave you,' he went on, still holding her to him, his gaze travelling past her into the dark, cold March night air beyond, imagining himself without her.

Bloody imagination! Sudden fear ripped through him so that he held her away from him to stare into her face again. Her expression was wan and tear-stained, pleading to be loved so that he drew her to him once more to press his lips to hers in a long, needful kiss. He felt her respond, felt the warmth of her body against his even through his thick army coat and her winter beige one. It felt good as they stood locked together in that kiss.

Finally releasing her, he murmured, 'I'm sorry, my darling. I had no right to cause you all this upset. It was just a silly whim I had. But look, I won't ask you to come and see that blasted chandelier if you don't want to. It wasn't fair of me to ask.'

To his surprise she whispered, 'If it means that much to you, my love, maybe we'll see. The thing is I'm a bit worried. I've never crept into a soldier's camp before.'

It sounded such a very ridiculous statement for her to make that the pair of them suddenly burst out laughing, their voices echoing on the cold air as, still chuckling, he said, 'Oh, I do love you!'

'And I love you too,' she returned, happy again. 'So very, very much.'

This evening, unusually warm for April, he stood alone in the dark beside the broken area of the perimeter fence. Valerie's birthday was tomorrow, but he'd been unable to wheedle a pass just as and when he wanted, so tonight would have to do.

The previous evening he'd got one of his platoon who did have a pass to deliver a note to her home, bribing him with a couple of drinks for his pains, the man willing enough to oblige after that. The note explained why he needed to see her tonight, just before her birthday, that he had something very special to give her, something far more special than any ordinary birthday present. Also that he had something very special he needed to ask her. He was sure she'd instantly guess what it was and that for that reason she would be here, no matter how nervous she was about the meeting place.

There was no reason to doubt she'd say yes, for over these last weeks their conversation had turned to making up romantic little scenes of how life could be when this war was over: weddings and bridesmaids and being together always instead of having to kiss goodbye to each other all the time; some pretty little flat of their very own somewhere and how she would decorate it, the furniture they would buy for it, of closing the curtains to shut out the long, cold evenings to sit together in front of a warm blazing fire listening to the wireless – all very cosy and pleasant. In all this he had not yet made any proper formal proposal, but such was the way many young couples drifted into marriage, so he'd heard.

Tonight he intended to propose, romantically. The engagement ring had been in his pocket for two weeks, he having managed to buy it in some rush in Brentwood. Maybe more sensible to have waited for the two of them to go together so she could have chosen what she wanted, but for the first time in his life he hadn't felt sensible. He wanted to surprise her, see her eyes light up in joy and amazement. He hadn't thought to formally ask her father for his permission, but after all it wouldn't be until next year before they were married. By then she would be twenty-one and able to do what she wanted. Tonight he would slip the ring on her finger in the quiet interior of the outbuilding as they lay together near the chandelier, a perfect setting.

He'd asked the chap to whom he'd given the note to bring back a reply, the price of a third beer making him happy enough to do that extra chore, the man like some secret agent slipping the sealed envelope to him with a broad grin and a knowing wink as he passed Norman's bed space.

Reading it, his heart had at first dropped like a stone as he read: 'Darling, I don't really think I have the courage to do what you ask, so I have sent the man away while I think what I should do.'

Moments later it was soaring like a bird as he read on, the words in an entirely different pencil betraying new eagerness: 'The man came back. It's given me time to think. I'm still scared but I think I know why you want me to meet you to-night. This special thing you have for me, I hope it's what I think it is so I'll do it, darling, meet you there at ten. I love you with all my heart, Val.' She had covered the entire bottom of her note with kisses.

Eighteen

It had been quarter past seven when her brother Sidney had gone to answer the knock on the door.

In the living room Valerie's father had looked up from his evening paper. 'Whoever's that at this time of night?' He looked across at his daughter. 'Are you expecting anyone?'

Before she could answer, Sidney was back, saying there was a soldier at the door asking for her. Immediately all eyes turned to her. 'A soldier?' her mother echoed, then turned to her son. 'What sort of soldier?'

'He says he has a note for Val, from Norman.'

Instantly Valerie was on her feet, already visualising something really dreadful having happened. 'I'll see what it is,' she cried out as she ran from the room.

The man at the door looked awkward and her panic mounted. 'What is it? What's wrong?'

'Nuffink's wrong,' came the reply in a strong Cockney accent. 'Ain't nuffink 'appened. Corpr'l Bowers just ast me ter give yer this note. Says fer me ter take yer answer back to 'im.'

Still imagining something dreadful, by this time unreasonably fearing it to be a note saying he didn't want to see her any more, even though she knew such a thought to be utterly foolish, she all but snatched the sealed envelope from the man, and as he waited somewhat impatiently, tore it open to frantically scan the note.

The relief was overwhelming, yet its contents promoted an instant feeling of something like panic rippling through her as she stammered, 'I can't possibly give him an answer straight away, but if you could come back in say about half an hour, I can give my answer to you then to give to him. Please. Can you do that for me?'

The man sighed mightily. But in his pocket was the price of three free pints of beer, very acceptable to a man on an ordinary soldier's pay. 'I s'pose I could,' he said, half begrudging.

'But you will come back?' she pleaded, her expression so full of anguish in case he didn't that his heart melted. He thought of his own girl back home in London, how she'd feel if she was going through whatever this girl was experiencing. Yes he would come back. Then he'd go to the pub to enjoy his third buckshee pint before delivering the girl's reply to Corporal Bowers. The note could wait that long to be delivered at least.

For Valerie Prentice, labouring in her bedroom over her reply, waiting for the man to return seemed never ending. She was downstairs in the living room again, very much on edge, when the second knock did come and she was off the settee, making for the door before anyone else could move.

She'd told them it had been a note from Norman and needed an answer, the man coming back for it. She said he'd been unable to get a pass this week due to a lot of extra training but wanted to know if she'd be free on Monday.

Having handed her reply in its sealed envelope to the man, she ran up to her bedroom to scramble into a hat and coat, a pair of sturdy shoes and to grab her handbag. Downstairs, out of breath, she put her head round the living room door just long enough to say she was popping out to see her friend Audrey for an hour or so, retreating before they could point out that it was almost nine o'clock. It wasn't until she was outside her gate that she paused, suddenly unsure she had the courage to go through with this.

Like most without a pass, Norman had spent the evening in the canteen, playing darts, cards, billiards and merely nattering. Those returning to camp usually made straight for there as well before retiring to their huts, and Norman had waited on tenterhooks for her reply to his message, irritation then anger gnawing at him when it failed to appear. So he was in no mood for the man's sly wink when it was finally slipped to him as he sat on his bed, despondently cleaning his equipment, aware that it was getting very late for Valerie to come now. He'd slipped that tyke enough for him to get drunk on and he hadn't bothered to deliver until now.

With hardly a thanks apart from hissing that it was about time, he ripped open her reply. His heart should have soared reading it, but all he could think of was the time. Nine thirty, not all that long to post being sounded, but maybe just time for what he wanted.

Muttering to Mac, who was already stripped down to his trunks ready to relax on his bed, that he had a headache and intended to walk it off for a while, he left him grinning, the man's bloody eagle eyes no doubt having seen the folded envelope being slipped to him despite the under-cover move.

Norman ignored him and went out. At the peri-meter fence, where it had become rather broken down but so far unnoticed by the authorities, he stood, his eyes trying to pierce the darkness as he looked up and down the lane with its overgrown weedy verge. There was no sign of her and his heart sank. Maybe she too had felt it was too late now to meet him.

It was so quiet, eerily quiet. Somewhere in the distance an owl hooted, a sharp, 'Wit...' instantly answered by its mate, 'Woooo...' on a much longer, drawn-out descending note. People usually thought it a single bird, but he'd learned long ago that it was two birds not one – male and female.

Several times the calls were exchanged then ceased abruptly, the pair having probably flown off. In the silence he could just hear the low, hardly discernible rumble of traffic on the distant Arterial Road, carried on the quiet night air over the few miles of rolling fields. Most likely military vehicles – these past few weeks there'd been a build-up of movement, no doubt in pre-paration for this possible invasion. Even here training had increased, not a day going by when they weren't being made to clamber through tyres and up nets, swinging on ropes, leaping over ditches, negotiating narrow planks, yelling like banshees at bayonet drill, rifle practice on the firing range leaving the ears ringing, every poor sod constantly being barked at and he himself made to shout his head off relaying the commands Sergeant Price shot at him.

Still the bane of his life, Price badgered him mercilessly, taking a delight in mocking him at every turn, usually in front of the men, making him look as foolish as possible. There were times he would have joyfully liked to put a bayonet through Price. But to show one iota of spirit would have seen him confined to camp, prevented from seeing Valerie. With time running out before they were moved on, he couldn't afford not to see her, so he forced himself to grin and bear it – or at least bear it. A grin seen as silent insubordination might also have found him confined to barracks, even marched at the double before some top brass, maybe losing his stripes, his corporal's pay along with them, and he had needed every penny for Val's ring.

But there was no escaping someone who harboured a special grudge against a person, looking to put him down at every turn. Kit inspection the man's special joy, no matter how tidy his bed, how well laid-out his kit, how clean his rifle or how highly polished his boots, the man took delight in finding something wrong, even if it wasn't, aiming to belittle him before the men. All this he kept from Valerie. The last thing he wanted was to destroy her vision of him.

Where was she? Time was going by. In fact

time was running out in general with the possibility of these invasion plans becoming real. At any time all leave and passes other than embarkation leave could be cancelled. He had to slip that ring on her finger tonight as a firm promise of marriage before the command came for the big push.

He could already see himself with the whole unit aboard one of many lorries streaming through the village to be transported off to some coastal town or other, left kicking his heels with only pen and paper to keep him and Valerie in contact with each other, not knowing when he'd be told to board some ship bound for whatever secret destination across the Channel awaited him.

His stomach churned at the thought, not from fear of battle but because now he had a girl he intended to marry. The last thing he wanted was anything to go wrong now. Where was she? He dared not call out too loud but managed a low hiss, 'Valerie?'

No sound. Doubt took hold of him. She'd gone home after all, though he couldn't blame her. She had been anxious and a little scared. Or maybe she was waiting at another spot. He lifted his voice a fraction, urgently.

'Valerie!'

There came a rustle a few yards from him, then a small, tremulous voice, 'I'm here, Norman.'

Relief was almost like a stab of pain. 'Over here,' he called softly. 'I'm over here.'

Moments later he was lifting her over the trodden-down area of barbed wire, making sure her clothing didn't get caught up on it. Her body was light in his arms, even with the weight of her warm coat. A brief embrace as he set her down, then they were running across the field, shielded from sight by the trees ahead, she one pace behind him, he holding her hand in case she stumbled. It had started to rain. The moisture already on the grass from a morning downpour was damping the bottoms of his uniform and probably soaking into her shoes.

'I don't like this,' she was panting, her voice scared.

He too was beginning to wish he'd not embarked on this folly. What had he been thinking? What if they were seen, were caught? She'd already expressed her worry that he could be in more trouble than she, but it was she he was worried about, the embarrassment, and he to blame, practically forcing her to come. They had left the cover of the trees, were now exposed to any who might be outside. But with the rain getting heavier, who'd want to be out?

Moments later, however, they were by the outbuilding, he taking the key from his pocket while she stood by, shivering now – with cold or fear? Turning the key in the padlock, he fumbled with it until the metal arm was free. In a matter of seconds they were inside, in the dry, in the dark.

She was still shaking. 'Norman, I don't know why I'm here. I shouldn't have come. I'm feeling so scared. I don't like it.'

This wasn't what he wanted to hear. Before showing her the lovely chandelier that so beguiled him, he wanted to present her with the ring he had in his pocket, see her eyes light up with a glow of joy. He turned on the small torch he'd brought with him, trusting that its light would help her fear go away, but she was still on edge.

Her voice tremulous, she pleaded, 'Let's go, Norman. I should never have come here. I think I ought to go back home.'

For answer, he took her in his arms, holding her gently. 'But you're in here now. You can't go without—'

'I don't care any more!' Her tone had grown sharp. She sounded as if she was on the verge of tears as she made to move away from his effort to reach out to her, seeking to calm her. There was nothing for it but to fish into the breast pocket of his battle dress and bring out the plain little cardboard box, expensive velvet engagement ring boxes almost a thing of the past in wartime.

'Valerie, look, I've got your birthday present,' he burst out as he pressed it urgently into her hand. 'It's special.'

He heard her give a little gasp, her fear brushed away.

'It's the one I told you about in my note. Go on, love, open it.'

He watched her lift the lid carefully, and as the three small diamonds flashed and flickered in the torchlight, heard her gasp again.

'An engagement ring,' he supplied before she could speak. Plucking it from its cardboard niche and catching hold of her left hand, he slipped it neatly onto her third finger in one smooth movement. He had got the size right, it was a perfect fit.

'Valerie ... darling...' he began, feeling oddly out of breath. 'Will you marry me?'

He waited, hope faltering in the silence that seemed to go on and on, though it could only have been seconds before she spoke.

When she did, the words burst from her as if unable to be contained a fraction of a second longer.

'Oh, yes, my darling, yes, with all my heart!'

His joy springing unbounded, he drew her to him, held her tight as they sank together onto the rough wooden floor, her lips on his, her arms holding him as though never wanting to let go. He had no thought of anything but that he was holding her, fondling her, she letting him. In a moment he knew they would make love right here, but then suddenly she tensed, dragging her lips from his.

'No, Norman! We mustn't!'

He moved back from her instantly, fearing rejection of his proposal of marriage. He heard himself mumbling an apology, saying sorry, he was sorry, he was very sorry.

'No,' she said breathlessly as she sat up. 'No, darling, it's not your fault, but I can't ... not until we're married.' Her voice was trembling. 'One or two of my friends have boyfriends who they ... you know, but my family would never forgive me if I found myself ... you know. They're very strict in that way. I think I frightened myself because I wanted to ... I wanted...'

Unable to help himself, he laid a gentle hand over her lips to prevent her saying any more. 'I do know. Believe me I wouldn't do anything to hurt you. I do understand.'

He did understand, knew just how she'd felt for he'd felt the same, gripped now by this miserable frustration of his own natural instincts. Yet his own upbringing had been similar to hers, maybe even stricter. When their relationship had matured a little it might be different. He just had to wait and see.

Slowly he got to his feet, helping her up. Retrieving the still-lit torch he took a deep breath. Passion had passed but she'd said yes to his marriage proposal and elation returned. All that was needed now was to inform their respective parents, he taking her to meet his and finally setting the date. That of course would be totally dependent on present circumstances. If only this bloody war would let them carry on as young people had done in peace time, he thought seedily. None of them knew how lucky they had been then.

They were both still feeling strained, and to dispel it he returned to his other reason for bringing her here. Time was passing. He'd begun to fear discovery, and post would be sounded soon and he still had to get her back through the fence without detection. Perhaps he should not bother to show her that marvellous chandelier that so fascinated him. In fact its fascination had begun to play on his mind so much lately that sometimes he felt he was going a little insane trying not to think about it. He even found himself dreaming about it in his sleep. He needed to lay the ghost to rest, so to speak. So he said,

'Before we go, darling, there is one other thing I wanted to bring you here to see – the thing I told you about. Look!'

Lifting the edge of the dust sheet before she could say anything, he shone the torch on the crystal embellishments so that they glittered like the diamonds on the ring now nestling on her engagement finger.

'Hey-presto!' he declared in triumph, his earlier frustration forgotten.

For a moment she stared, then in an odd tone said, 'Is that what they say once hung in the ballroom of the big house?'

He shrugged, faintly disappointed at her lack of wonder. 'I suppose so,' he offered. Why hadn't the magnificent thing thrilled her, made her gasp as it had him that first time he'd seen it?

There was a further moment of silence then to his amazement she shrank back. 'Cover it up! Quick, cover it up! I don't want to look at it!'

'What's the matter?'

'Don't you know?' she said as he let the cover drop. 'It's haunted. You must have heard. In the village they say there's a ghost in that house that made the people there do terrible things. People say it has something to do with this chandelier.'

'Oh, come on!' Norman scoffed, strangely angry.

She was backing away from the unevenly shaped dust sheet.

'It's true – the people living there in the early 1930s, they say, brought that thing with them and it gave them nothing but bad luck. The tale goes that the wife left her husband over a woman, then the woman disappeared and the husband drowned himself.' She was beginning to gabble. 'And then the next people that came to live there, the wife killed her husband and said she was told to do it by a ghost in that room. And there were tales about it being something to do with that chandelier, about a woman hanging herself from it way back in the 1920s.'

Norman would have burst out laughing but she seemed so scared that he kept a straight face out of concern for her.

'That's a load of Tommy-rot, darling,' was all he could find to say.

'It isn't!' she shot back at him almost vehemently. 'I had the same eerie feeling looking at it just now – a horrible feeling. I don't like it. I want to leave. I just want to go home!'

The fear in her voice pierced right through him, his heart beginning to pound so fast it seemed to be strangling him. Without a word he hurried her outside. The rain had stopped. He began to breathe easier, though she was still panting from panic as he turned, snapped the padlock shut and pocketed the key. He knew she would never set foot in there again.

No good trying to calm her by scoffing. The best thing was to take her back to the fence, climb over it with her and conduct her to the end of the dark lane. There he would have to leave her to go the rest of the way home by herself. He knew he'd be taking a chance of being seen out of camp, but he couldn't leave her to negotiate that dark lane alone. He would have worried himself sick until he heard from her again –

if he had.

When he got back to the hut, Mac would no doubt ask him if he'd enjoyed his walk in the rain, if his splitting headache felt better, a knowing grin on his face as he put two and two together. Tomorrow he'd probably make some comment on how love wasn't just blind but quite obviously oblivious of discomfort as well.

He just hoped most of the platoon already had their heads down or were reading, uninterested in his comings and goings as he got out of his damp uniform and into bed to close his eyes and try to forget how Val's words about the chandelier had thoroughly shaken him, spoiling the joy of his surprise birthday present to her.

Nineteen

'Hear you've managed to find yourself a nice little bit of stuff, Bowers,' Sergeant Price whispered in Norman's ear as he came off detail one afternoon. 'Had her yet, or haven't you got the guts to go for it?'

Norman said nothing, keeping his gaze lowered. To have met Price's taunting grin with a glare would have just been asking for trouble. He was meeting Valerie this evening and Price could have stopped his pass in the blink of an eye.

Getting one was becoming more and more difficult. It was well into May and something was definitely in the air. Training had been stepped up, with further talk of an imminent second front, many having noticed an increasing amount of troop movement; there were whispers of embarkation leave soon to be granted, someone having heard from another who'd heard of someone having seen it in orders – nothing positive, but rumour had a tendency to possess more than a grain of truth and Norman found himself dissolving into quiet panic.

If he was lucky enough to get a twenty-four-hour leave, he intended taking Valerie to see his parents. He'd written to them about her, had had a letter from them saying they hoped he knew what he was doing, which had immediately riled him, as if he were some child to be guided and advised.

Her parents had smiled on their engagement, yet he couldn't help feeling it had politely covered up a wish to have been asked first. 'I do hope you're not both going to rush into marriage,' her mother had said anxiously. 'What with a war on and all that.'

But it was precisely war that was driving couples to get married as soon as they could lest they never saw each other again.

'Valerie's only just turned twenty, far too young to get married. She's hardly seen anything of life yet.'

To which her husband had nodded sombrely as she went on, 'We were so worried when she had to register for National Service last year. She has never been away from home. Fortunately they decided that the work she was doing in Brentwood Main Post Office was essential.'

'We won't be getting married for at least a couple of years,' he told them, wondering if Valerie might have liked the adventure of going into one of the women's services. But then he might never have met her.

But it showed how much her parents coddled her, and when they did marry he could find her mother forever interfering in their marriage, clinging to her daughter like she was a baby.

Being in the army these two years he'd become independent and free of his own parents' overprotective notions of parental guidance, as he now saw it. If he were sent overseas, neither of them could ever tell him what to and what not to do. He'd made up his mind about that. He might even be able to marry Val by special licence beforehand if she consented, and he was sure she would.

Sergeant Price was right in one way, he hadn't imposed himself on her and had no intention of doing so without her agreement. Even then he was prepared to respect her, which he bet Price would never have considered with a girl. Anyway, sod Price and what he thought! Outside barracks he was his own person.

That evening he stood outside the Baker's Arms, the place where he and Valerie always met. It was early and still light. He had until 23:59 to be back in barracks and he was taking her to the pictures in Brentwood. The bus returning to the village passed the camp gate around eleven, plenty of time to say goodnight before leaving her. Valerie was slowly growing bolder, letting him touch her in some dark corner of one of the lanes. She would sigh with pleasure at his touch, confident now of their love with his ring on her finger. But he still felt he needed to treat her gently, still fearing resistance from her.

Given time she would eventually let him make love to her properly. That was if he was still in this country by then, which, the way things were rushing ahead, didn't seem likely. So little time left, it seemed to him, but he was not prepared to force her. In that, he *was* his own person, say what Sergeant Nigel Price liked.

A bus from Brentwood passed, pulling up at the stop further down the road. Norman glanced at his watch, six thirty already. Hardly time to go to the pictures if she didn't come soon. The one to Brentwood would be passing any minute; if they missed that it would be too late to go to the pictures.

Then he saw her, coming towards him at a run. He noticed she was in the same suit she usually wore for work, clothing coupons allowing for very little daily change of such garments.

'So sorry I'm late,' she gasped as she reached him, lifting her face to his to give him a kiss, her lips soft, making him feel warm inside. 'Left work late and missed my usual bus, had to wait for the next one. No time to even go home and change. Hope you don't mind.'

Of course he didn't mind, he merely felt deep relief. He said so and had her reach up and kiss him again, her arms about his neck, no care for passers-by seeing them in close embrace. But he was rather concerned at her not going home before they left, knowing how protective her parents were of her.

'You ought to let your parents know you're home,' he said sombrely. 'Surely they'd expect you to, just to know that you're all right.'

But she was in a frivolous mood. 'Too late! The bus will be here any minute. And they do know I'm going to the pictures with you this evening.' Just lately she seemed to have gained new independence, which he took to be due to her newly engaged status.

'Have you had anything to eat?' he asked and saw her smile.

'No, but I'm not hungry. I just needed to get

225

back here and see you.'

A thrill of possession went through him that in order to see him all the quicker she was prepared to sacrifice even a tiny cheese sandwich or a plain bun, often all there was to buy from a cake shop in these days of rationing, unless one went into a café or restaurant that enjoyed special treatment.

'The main film doesn't start until gone eight,' he said, now feeling in complete control. 'We'll get something to eat in that café opposite before going in.'

'I'd like that,' she said, planting another kiss on his cheek.

Catching sight of their bus coming into view, he asked, 'Do you still want to go to the pictures?' feeling that he should at least allow her an opportunity to make a decision for herself.

He saw her nod emphatically and felt glad. It would be a while yet before it got dark. But in the back row of the cinema, enveloped in darkness, he could sit with his arm around her, his free hand gently caressing her knee as it had done the last time they'd gone. Then she'd made no effort to push it away and he was sure she had enjoyed his touch, though if he had let the hand travel upwards she might have stopped it.

This time he planned to let his hand move slowly and gently upwards, and if she eased herself away before he reached the part he most yearned to rest his hand on, he would know it was a silent hint that he'd gone far enough for the time being. Or maybe she would not – he would never know if he didn't at least attempt it.

It wasn't for carnal pleasure that he needed to have his hand lay on that secret place, but a real need to be as near a part of her as possible.

If she did ease his hand away he would understand, not become too impatient. Difficult not to though, with the imminent threat of his unit being transported far away, tearing them apart, possibly forever. Perhaps this evening, if he explained, which as yet he'd not done, fearing to upset her when it might only be a threat after all, she might even consent to being made love to properly. He would just have to wait and see.

It proved a longish wait, standing in the queue, moving forward in slow erratic paces before finally being let in, and he was glad they'd had a quick meal. Finally allowed inside the foyer, dingy from blackout shielding, by a uniformed elderly commissionaire, younger men mostly in the forces, he bought their tickets by the light of a dim torch and, taking Val's arm protectively, followed the usherette to their seats inside the almost full, darkened auditorium. But detecting two empty ones in the back row he made for them instead, bringing a knowing smile to the usherette's lips as she left them to assist other patrons.

The film was one that Val had been aching to see: *Meet Me In St Louis* with Judy Garland and little Margaret O'Brien, at which she ooh'd and aah'd most of the way through, shed a tear or two in the sadder parts, caught up by Hollywood's opulence compared to Britain's present austerity. She hardly seemed to notice his hand caressing her knee.

With the second feature, which they had come in halfway through and were not overly interested in, she soon became more aware of his hand on the flesh of her upper leg. For a moment she let it linger, but only for a moment before easing the hand away. In the flickering white glow from the screen he saw her glance about at those seated nearby

'No, Norman, not here,' she whispered, but it was said mildly. She wasn't rebuking him. Indeed it seemed to his ears almost reluctant. 'There are people standing behind us.'

For the first time he realised that with the theatre full, any overflow of patrons were required to remain standing at the barrier behind the rear row to watch the film, while waiting for seats as they were made available by others leaving at whatever part of the film they'd entered. Suddenly embarrassed, he hastily moved his hand, she quickly straightening her skirt, still glancing furtively around.

'This is where we came in anyway,' she whispered, pulling her jacket around her and gathering up her bag with exaggerated care while he busily retrieved his forage cap from its shoulder strap and put it on.

Hardly had they risen from their seats, obliging other people to get up to allow them to get past, than two from the queue at the barrier hurried past to occupy them.

On the bus home they sat in silence, each with their own thoughts, while he watched her constantly fingering her engagement ring, twisting it round and round on her finger with her other hand. What was she thinking?

He said nothing but through his mind flowed one sense of regret after another: he shouldn't have tried to touch her like that; maybe he shouldn't have rushed her into this engagement; maybe she was silently regretting it; had he been wrong to have made her steal into camp that night like some cheap tart so he could show her that bloody chandelier – he could have chosen somewhere far more suitable to propose.

She'd never mentioned that night, but he couldn't help remembering the way she had reacted to the sight of the thing, feeling that even now it still haunted her, yet he dare not ask.

Glancing up she noticed him watching her silently and she smiled, ceasing to fiddle with her ring and clutching his arm instead.

'I do love you so,' she said in a voice hardly audible, sending an instant flood of relief through him. He had no need to blame himself for anything. She loved him.

'I love you too,' he murmured back and had her cuddle even closer, no longer caring who noticed.

Arriving at their stop, she said quietly as they stood together for a moment, 'I think I should go straight home.'

It was uttered with a certain amount of significance and he knew immediately what she meant. His hand on her thigh had disturbed her, but in a way that he now knew had made her frightened to trust herself. He had to honour that.

'Maybe it's best,' he said. 'I'll just walk you back.'

229

The last thing he wanted was to push her and have her loathe herself because of it. Once they were married, he knew she would give him all the love a man could want, but for now he must allow her time to take things at her own pace. That was how it should be. But time wasn't being kind to him.

Panic would make itself felt every time it came to mind that any day the whole unit could be ordered out. The first sign of course would be being given embarkation leave, and he vowed not to waste all of it going home to see his parents, but to spend part of it taking her somewhere nice for a few days, with only one day to visit his parents and introduce her to them.

Off alone together, how would it be? That was if her parents would let her go off alone with him. How would she react if they tried to stop her? Knowing he might be sent away from her for God knows how long, surely she'd want to spend what time there was with him, rather than bend to their will like some child. If she did, what chance was there for them?

Even if she did defy them, come away with him, would she let herself behave like a married couple? He would have looked forward to finding out if it wasn't that at the conclusion of their time together he was to be taken away from her for God knows how long. So much could happen in that time. He could be killed. He could be wounded, to return broken and crippled. Could he ask her to spend the rest of her life nursing him? Or maybe in his absence someone else would come along to sweep her off her feet ...

God! That would be unbearable. It was this that plagued him as he kissed her goodnight on her doorstep, refusing to come in. To do that would have been to break the spell of their being alone at this moment, kissing her ardently before leaving, she standing waving until he was out of sight.

It was still only eleven o'clock as he passed the Baker's Arms, hearing the faint music of the jukebox from inside. He felt less like going in there than jumping into that lake hidden by the small circle of trees some way off – the lake, it occurred to him, where Valerie had said some previous owner of the big house had drowned himself. Neither did he feel like going back to his Nissen hut or the NAAFI. Instead he wandered across to the outbuilding where he and Valerie had lain in each other's arms in the cool darkness.

The memory was sweet but he wished now that he hadn't shown her that chandelier. To his mind it had spoiled everything. Why the hell had he been so enamoured by it? It no longer mattered, yet he wanted to go inside the building just once more to relive the moment he'd held her close and had begun to fondle her. She'd been almost on the verge of letting it happen, he'd been sure. If only he hadn't made that one silly move.

One more look inside to recapture the moment, then he'd never go in there ever again. Taking the key that still lay in his pocket he inserted it in the padlock. To his surprise it didn't turn. He tried again before realising the padlock had been changed; his key was useless. Perhaps it was just as well. He shrugged and turned away. Lifting his arm he swung it like a fast bowler, in the dark imagining the key describing a wide arch to land ... God knows where, but he didn't care. He wouldn't need it again.

He was walking away when a movement caught the corner of his eye. Faintly he heard his name called, or so it seemed. Turning, he could just make out the slender figure of a woman standing by the door of the building in the darkness. For a second he froze then found his voice, keeping it to a whisper lest he alert other ears.

'Valerie?' Surely it couldn't be her. How had she got here so quickly? 'Valerie!'

What was she doing here? He started towards her but she had already moved away to the edge of the building. As he went after her she turned the corner of the building. It was her. He knew it. But reaching the corner there was now no sign of her.

Where had she gone so quickly? Racing along to the back of the building he called her name again and again. There was nowhere she could hide. It was open ground from here all the way to a clump of shrubbery half a field away. She could never have made it that quick. What on earth was she up to? After a complete circuit of the building, ending up where he had started, he turned slowly round on the spot, his eyes trying to pierce the night, completely at a loss.

It was then he saw her again, a shape rather than a figure, shadowy in the darkness, about thirty feet from him, now well away from the building and to one side, but so indistinct that he could hardly make her out.

He felt suddenly furious with her. 'What the hell do you think you're playing at, Val, coming here...'

A raised hand cut him short, but the voice didn't sound like hers, unless she was disguising it, playing games. But what he heard wasn't funny at all. In fact it made him feel all the more angry.

'The lady you love is playing you false.'

'What?'

Instead of repeating what she'd said, she turned and began to walk towards two officers who were now approaching along one of the footpaths. In moments she would be directly in front of them, unavoidable. He glanced quickly towards them then back at her to warn her, but there was no sign of her.

The two officers were almost upon him. Seeing him, they stopped, instantly aware of his tense posture as he stared at them.

'What's the matter, Corporal?' demanded one, his tone sharp and suspicious. 'What are you doing here?'

Recovering himself, he came to attention and saluted. 'Sorry, sir, I thought I saw a civilian.' Why had he said that? If they searched, Valerie could be in trouble – if it was her. But who else could it have been?

The officer, a captain by his three pips, gave a frown. 'I saw no one.' He turned to the lieutenant, his tone almost flippant. 'Did you see anyone?'

'Not until this man hove into view,' was the

reply.

The captain cast Norman a look of controlled amusement. 'Well, there doesn't seem to be anyone here now, Corporal. Had a few drinks, have we?'

'No sir!' Norman said smartly, with an inner sigh of relief that she must have got away, yet he was puzzled. Why hadn't they seen her? Just yards away, in plain sight, they couldn't have missed her. Obviously they had and he thanked the Lord for that. But he'd have to have a serious word with her, creeping into camp like that. What on earth had possessed her?

'It must have been some trick of the light. Me coming straight out of the canteen – some shadow or other. Very sorry ... sir!' he added hastily, recovering himself enough to remember the man's rank.

The two regarded him with unsettling gazes for a moment, then the senior officer gave a crooked grin, although it didn't exude friendliness or any deal of indulgence.

'Very well, Corporal, I suggest you go and get some sleep.'

It was more an order than a suggestion. He might as well have said 'sleep it off', and as Norman saluted, they moved on, picking up the conversation they'd been having before coming upon him.

Twenty

The rest of his week he spent pondering on the incident, slowly becoming convinced that it could only have been Valerie he'd seen, yet not knowing what to make of it.

He'd have to tackle her on the stupidity of going down that dark, lonely lane all on her own, to clamber into camp through that broken part in the perimeter fence. She must have realised the trouble she would have been in had she been discovered. So why had she done it?

When he was finally able to meet her, he hardly kissed her before bursting out, 'You know, darling, you scared the living daylights out of me the other night. What made you do such a thing?'

He was trying not to sound angry. He loved her too much for that, yet he *was* angry, and frightened and deeply concerned by such odd behaviour on her part.

'What other night?' she asked easily, smiling as she tucked her arm tightly through his, obviously anticipating them walking on slowly as they normally did. But he stood stock still, staring her in the face, his expression grim.

'You know what other night, when I took you home after we'd been to the pictures. I said goodnight to you. I thought you'd gone indoors.

But you hadn't. What on earth did you think you were up to, sneaking into the camp like that?'

Her smile had become puzzled. 'What are you talking about, Norman? We said goodnight and I went indoors and straight to bed. Why would I want to sneak out again – and into your camp without you? It was scary enough that last time when you were with me. I wouldn't want to do it again in a hurry and certainly not on my own.' She too was beginning to sound huffy. 'I don't understand!'

'But I saw you. You were standing by that outbuilding I took you to.'

'No I wasn't.' Even with the blackout he could see she was looking annoyed. 'I don't know what you are talking about, Norman. You took me home and we said goodnight. Why would I want to go out again that time of night and on my own? Why should I? Honestly, I don't understand you, Norman!'

Her tone had grown so sharp that he feared a full-scale quarrel, their first one ever. She began walking away from him, her pace quickening. For a second or two he watched her, unsure what to do. Then he started after her, in a few steps catching her up to swing her round by her arm to face him.

'Stop for just a minute!' he demanded, his voice raised.

'Don't shout at me, Norman!' she cried back at him.

Even in the stygian darkness of the main road, silent but for the faint music issuing from the Baker's Arms just along the way, he knew she was glaring at him. This was threatening to become a real row. He couldn't let that happen.

'Look, I really am sorry,' he said quickly. 'But I had such a strange experience the other night after I left you at your door.'

Hastily he explained going back to camp with an idea of taking a peek into the outbuilding where the chandelier was stored for a last look at it. But as he mentioned the thing he felt her shudder and hurried on to explain that he hadn't, that he'd thrown the key away. That was at least half true. 'That was when I saw this figure, this woman, just standing there. I don't know why I should have thought it was you. Obviously it wasn't.'

'Then who was it?' It was a relief to see she had calmed.

'I don't know.' All he wanted now was to have the subject drop. 'Probably another bloke's girl, but for a moment I really thought it was you. Please don't ask me why and please, my darling, forgive me. It was silly of me and I suppose I should have known you wouldn't ... It was dark and—'

'Did she say anything when you saw her?' Valerie cut in.

'No, she didn't.' It was a lie. Whoever she was she'd said something so odd that he still didn't know what to make of it, only that it had sent a shiver down his spine and did so even now as he recalled the words. But the last thing he intended was to relay them to Valerie.

'She didn't say anything,' he continued the lie, 'and when I called out to her she vanished round the side of the building. I went after her, still thinking it was you. I didn't want you to get into trouble.'

Even as he spoke a strange sensation rippled through him at the recollection of those brief words that at the time he had almost put aside during his uncomfortable brush with the two officers. Now they came back, so starkly vivid that it made him shudder: *'The lady you love is playing you false.'*

It was like some bad dream that persists into the next day to spoil the waking hours. But who was she, the woman? What had she been doing there? Had he really seen her or merely imagined he had? Yet he was sure she'd been real, that he wasn't going off his head.

Her words had become imprinted on his brain. All this week they'd been dancing inside his head like tiny invisible wraiths, but he wasn't about to repeat them to Valerie, not now or ever.

'She ran off when two officers came along,' he said instead, wanting only to have done with this awkward subject. 'I'm really sorry to have upset you. It was stupid of me to think...'

He broke off, aware that he could be digging an even deeper hole for himself. He gave her as bright a smile as he could manage, hoping it would help to make her relax a little.

'Look, darling, I was just being a bit silly. Let's forget it, shall we? Do you fancy a drink?'

He heard her give a huff, but at least she had taken his arm, the huff turning to a subdued, slightly begrudging, 'Yes, if you like.'

Relieved, he gave her hand a loving squeeze,

totally overjoyed to have her respond with her own squeeze as they turned toward the pub, a loving couple once more.

Something was in the air – more than something. It was the middle of May and men began to find themselves in line for seven days' leave, which could only be interpreted in one way – embarkation leave, or as Mac exclaimed excitedly, 'This is it!'

Norman ignored his lance corporal's enthusiastic prediction, even though he recognised the truth in it. His main concern, that his parents would automatically expect him to spend most if not all of his embarkation leave with them. How could he not, they as parents needing to squeeze as much of their one and only son's time out of him as possible.

Sent overseas, when would they see him again, if ever? He refused to think about that last bit. Of course they'd see him again, no question about it, he told himself.

Even so, he had no option but to spend time with them, when what he really wanted was to spend the entire time with Valerie. She was the one who mattered most. He had written to them all about her, had sent them a snapshot of her, one which she'd given him for that purpose – a rather distant shot amid a huge area of countryside that failed to show her in full light. He knew why she'd chosen it, so that any faults she harboured about her appearance wouldn't show up, though that was silly. She was a lovely looking girl. Her only fault was a tendency to have a low opinion of herself and her looks, no matter how many times he'd told her she was wonderful and beautiful.

She had a lovely nature and a smooth temper. Only once had she lost it and that had been the previous week when he'd unjustly accused her of sneaking into camp, mistaking that woman he had seen or thought he had seen, whoever she was, for Valerie. But even that unusual show of anger had been short lived. And it had been more hurt than anger; he still felt deeply sorry whenever he thought of it. He knew he should count himself lucky to have found a girl like her.

He'd tried to put the incident behind him but it kept coming back. Who was that woman? No matter who she was, why had he behaved so badly towards Valerie? He loved her dearly and she hadn't deserved to be upset like that.

Another thing that riled him was his parent's reaction to her, even before they'd met her, writing back to say she looked a bit too young to be getting engaged and did he really know what he was doing. How dared they? Their letter had made him so annoyed that he hadn't answered it. It still annoyed him every time he thought about it.

Now of course he was going to have to scribble a note to them about his embarkation leave, when it was known, also that he'd be bringing Valerie to meet them. What he wouldn't say was that their visit would be for one day only, two at a pinch. After their remarks about her age and what he could only see as a censure on whether he was doing the right thing, he meant to spend as little time with them as possible, if only to save her from any embarrassment. The rest of his leave he would spend elsewhere with her, just the two of them alone.

Wild thoughts went through his head that if he could persuade her to go away with him, spend the whole of his leave with him, they might even get married by special licence. That was if she would agree. It was a big if, but if she did agree, how would her parents react? She was still under-age and they were, if anything, over-protective of her. What if they forbade her – would she take notice of them, submit to their wishes and be the obedient daughter, or would she defy them? If she did, would she make an enemy of them? Would it make him the enemy? There was no getting away from the fact that they were nice people and had most certainly been decent enough about them getting engaged so quickly, though her father's faint consternation at not having been spoken to first still lingered. How would they react to their daughter running off to get married in virtual secret? In their old-fashioned way of thinking, as with many of the previous generation, an engagement went on for at least a year or more, preparing for the wedding and all its trimmings, certainly not some brief register office thing.

In peace time long engagements were all very well, but this wasn't peace time. The whole country gripped by growing tension, the allies waiting in the wings for the lights to go up, the orchestra to begin, the curtain to rise on the stage that was Europe – or as Mac put it more succinctly, 'Any minute now the balloon'll be going up!' – a spate of hasty engagements and hurried weddings was breaking out everywhere. Would Valerie agree to join the rush to get married before the balloon did go up?

That evening Norman made his way to her house with a desperate need to talk to her, to ask her to go with him to meet his parents. He prayed she would. But would her parents see fit to let their daughter, who had only just turned twenty, go away alone with a man, even though they knew him? And if they didn't see fit to allow it, would she have the courage to defy them? Several times she'd said she wished she was of age and able to do what she liked, but could that mean that at the moment she wouldn't dream of going against them?

It also gave him the feeling that even when she did reach twenty-one, she'd still need to ask their blessing before attempting anything they didn't entirely approve of. It was the way she'd been brought up, though even now she might surprise him. That little show of temper of hers the other day had proved that she did have spirit, and maybe when they eventually did marry she would become more independent of them.

Meantime, what he was about to ask her threatened to raise all sorts of difficulties – would she be too frightened to offend them? What about offending him? What about how he felt? And what would he do if she did say no to him? It was something he couldn't bring himself to contemplate.

By the time he reached her door his mind was

in turmoil, almost dreading her reply: 'No, I can't. It wouldn't be right.' All sorts of fears were going through his head as he lifted the door knocker. He would not go in. As soon as she answered he would ask her, demand if necessary, that she take a walk with him here and now. They needed to have a long talk tonight, away from everyone else who might feel fit to put their oar in. There wasn't much time to come to a decision. Within a week or two he would be with his parents. She had to be there with him, even though she'd probably feel scared at the prospect of meeting them. But he would be with her to support her, make sure she overcame her fear. His parents weren't that daunting, even if they did feel that their son could be marrying in haste.

Of course she'd agree to take a walk with him. It could be their last time together and she'd want to have him all to herself. Would she want to have him go without some precious time together? He couldn't see her letting that happen so things might not be as bad as he imagined. More sure of himself now, he let the knocker fall twice, gently, trying not to make it sound too loud or urgent, and waited.

It was some time before it opened. Normally she would have been watching for him from the window and would run to the door hardly had he reached it. Instead, after what seemed an interminable wait, the door was opened just a fraction. But it was her brother Sidney who stood there. Usually if anyone other than Valerie answered he'd be invited straight in without hesitation. But this time Sidney didn't budge, almost as if he was deliberately blocking his entrance.

'Valerie?' he heard himself query inanely.

'I'm sorry, Norman.' Sidney's voice was grave. 'Val's not at all well. She's in bed. She won't be able to see you tonight.'

Alarm clutched at his heart. 'What's wrong with her?'

'She's got 'flu – has got it really bad. The doctor came yesterday and said she must stay in bed for at least a week and she certainly mustn't go out. Not that she's well enough to want to go out.'

'Flu! He felt himself relax a little, though he was still concerned and worried for her. 'Can I talk to her?'

'She's asleep, been asleep most of the day and all yesterday. She looked proper wretched, poor Sis.'

'Then can I pop up and see her?'

Sidney looked flustered. 'Mum and Dad's out. They popped round to see my aunt and uncle. They asked me to stay in and keep an eye on her in case she wants anything. They wouldn't like it very much if you went up to her bedroom. It's not right.'

He'd never been allowed up to Valerie's bedroom, even though they were engaged. According to her parents it wasn't done. But Valerie was ill and most likely feeling wretched. What did they imagine the two of them were going to get up to? He felt himself growing angry as he voiced this opinion.

'And anyway,' he concluded, 'she *is* my

fiancée.'

But the boy's face held a stubborn expression. 'It's still not right. And they could be home any minute now and if they found you upstairs in her room, they'd be most upset and they'd blame me for letting you go up there.'

Norman stared at him in anger. 'What the hell do they think the two of us would get up to when she's ill? All I want is to see her to try and cheer her up. She'd want to see me. You can come up there with me to make sure there's no foul play!' He ended on a deliberately sarcastic note.

The lad remained adamant. 'I'm sorry, Norman.'

'All right, so I'll call up to her, talk to her from down here.'

Sidney was looking flustered. 'She's asleep. Best she's not woken up.'

Nothing more seeming to be forthcoming, it was like trying to push through a brick wall, the two staring silently at each other, the boy two steps above him, he on the path below, making him feel small.

He began to hate Valerie's brother, but there was nothing he could do other than mount the two steps and barge past him and he wouldn't do that. For all his youth, the boy was the bigger build, and how could they indulge in a tussle on the doorstep, he knowing he'd be in the wrong, no matter how he felt? There was nothing he could do.

'Tell her I called,' was all he could find to say, 'and that I wish her better very soon.'

'I'll do that.' Already Sidney was beginning to

inch the door closed, indicating an eagerness to have him go. It was then Norman heard a small, high, querulous female voice emanating from within the house.

'You going to be much longer, Sidney?'

It wasn't Valerie's voice. It came from downstairs. The lad had a girl in there. A surge of anger went through him. If this bloody young monkey could have a girl in, any old damned girl, why was he forbidden to go upstairs and see his own sick fiancée? And did the boy's parents know that he had a girl in there?

He should have argued, but what was the point other than to make himself look a fool? 'Tell Valerie I hope she'll be better soon and I'll see her as soon as I can...'

The door was already closing, making him even angrier. He'd have dearly liked to mount the two steps and hit the boy on the nose. But he'd never hit anyone in his life. His voice sounded hoarse.

'Tell her...' He was about to say, 'that I love her', but he wasn't going to give a message like that to this lout. His unfinished words of love on his lips, he turned sharply on his heel and went back down the path. Behind him he heard the sharp click of the street door closing.

In some strange way the sound brought all the fury in him rising to the surface, and with his clenched fists he hit the top of the wooden gate several times very hard, painful on his knuckles.

Twenty-One

It was too early to go back to barracks. At a loose end, he found himself turning into the Baker's Arms. Not that he was looking for company, but he was desperately in need of a drink.

The pub was busy. As usual the local people were gathered together under the blacked-out windows, taking up all the hard leather settles and wooden chairs at narrow, beer stained, dark wooden tables. Sipping their drinks, they chatted closely, while soldiers stood in groups, their voices loud, their talk of home, girlfriends, conquests, or else beefing about whatever or whoever had got under their skin during the day, while their minds played on the imminent transportation by truck and train to the coast to await embarkation orders to ... where? No one yet knew except that it was on the cards.

Norman shouldered his way to the bar and with what he would have spent on Valerie managed to get himself a whisky, a precious favour in these times of austerity, to help alleviate a somewhat unjust sense of betrayal and lonely disappointment, following it with a pint for good measure. Not feeling much better for the whisky, he sipped his beer, his thoughts on Valerie.

They should have been in here together tonight

after having taken a quiet stroll. She having listened to his persuasive arguments might have agreed to spend his seven days' leave with him, cementing that agreement with a long, ardent kiss, maybe allowing him a little more licence with her yielding body than she normally would, the promise of things to come.

They would have celebrated her promise in here, seeking a corner to talk over their plans. He would have told her more about his family, soothing any fears she might have of meeting them; she in turn would have given him a promise to overcome her parents' objections to her going away with him, just the two of them alone together. But that had not happened.

He cursed the loss of tonight's hopes even as he felt concern for her in her miserable state, silently praying over and over again for her quick recovery. But most of all he felt anger against her brother. Who did the boy think he was? Damned cheeky young sod, standing there refusing to let him in, barring the door against him like some bloody sentinel, forbidding him to see his own fiancée, saying it wasn't right when all the time he'd got some girl in the front room, probably without his parents' knowledge, Norman could bet his last ha'penny on that.

In fact he had half a mind to tell them of it the next time he was there – if there was a next time. By next week he could be on his way to his parents' to say his farewells to them, Valerie still not well enough to come with him. The thought made his blood chill. She had to be with him. It could be the last time they ever saw each other.

A loud burst of laughter took his attention from his thoughts and he turned automatically towards the sound. Several servicemen had entered and were shouldering their way through towards the bar. Without much interest, Norman took in their half-visible faces between the knots of drinkers, to have his attention arrested by the sight of Nigel Price among them.

Quickly he turned back to the bar, hoping Price wouldn't notice him. The man would grasp any opportunity to ridicule him, taking an avid delight in it. Why, Norman had no idea, except that some men delighted in picking out a scape-goat from among a group to torment. He was quite aware that his own naturally withdrawn nature was a magnet for such men. Quiet types always were to bullies such as Price. But quiet types could smoulder for years until, like a dormant volcano, they could suddenly erupt with often disastrous results. Although he told himself he was not one of those and would no doubt continue to smoulder until Price finally moved on, he could sometimes detect a little of that weakness even in his own breast.

Unluckily Price had seen him and was making a beeline for him. The next thing he knew, there was a hearty slap on the back, compelling him to turn and face the man.

'Well, if it isn't our corporal and all on his own too. Now why's that?' Giving Norman no time to answer, he went on loudly, commanding the attention of the others with him, 'So where's the little lady tonight? Stood you up, has she? Had enough of you, has she? I can truthfully say I don't blame her. If ever there was a wimp, this one is!'

Norman turned back to his drink, controlling an urge to retaliate. 'If you must know, she's ill – gone down with 'flu,' he said, evenly as he could.

Price guffawed. 'That's what she told you, is it?'

'She was too ill in bed to tell me anything. Her brother told me.'

'Oh, we've heard that one before. Didn't want to tell you herself she'd had enough of you and have you burst into tears – bloody embarrassing!' He turned to those around him, but his resonant tones boomed across the entire room, making several people look up. 'Here that? This man, if you can call him that, has got himself stood up by his girl. She's probably found herself a real man.' He turned back to his quarry, his voice still resounding across the room. 'If you ask me, you'd be more suited to finding yourself a nice bloke.'

As those with Price chuckled at the quip, Norman stood silent for a second, striving to control himself, but it was no good. Lifting his half-empty glass, he made to aim it at his sergeant, but Price was ahead of him.

Catching hold of his wrist he held it firm, his face thunderous. 'Throw drink at me, would you?' he challenged, his voice dropping to a whisper while behind him his mates stood chuckling. He continued to glower, holding Norman's gaze. 'If you think I'm going to start a brawl in public, you've another guess coming,

Bowers. But don't think I'm forgetting this. You know what I mean. Your life's due to get quite a bit hotter, if you get my meaning.'

A smile beamed on his narrow face as he turned back to his mates. 'Right, what's everyone want to drink? First round is on me. But I won't be staying here long, because guess what little girl I'm seeing in a quarter of an hour from now? The same little girl our friend here has been courting all this time. And he didn't know it. While he was in barracks, I was with her. Didn't she tell you, Bowers?' He rounded on his victim, grinning. 'Pity...'

He got no further as Norman's fist came up in an effort to land it on the taller man's chin. At the crowded bar there was no room for a good swing and the blow glanced off, but Price's expression became like granite and he brought up a hand to stay his assailant's.

'Careful, Bowers, I wouldn't if I was you.'

As he spoke, he brought the held arm sideways to swiftly guide it towards Norman's half-full glass, deliberately knocking it over. The spilled beer spread across the bar, the publican serving behind leaping to catch the rolling glass before it fell to the floor.

'Watch it, you two!' he blurted as he whipped a cloth from under the bar to begin mopping up. 'Any trouble and you're both out! This is my pub and I'm having no fighting. Rank or no rank, I'll aim you and him out on the pavement.'

Price shot him a tight smile. 'Don't worry, landlord. I'm off anyway.'

Reaching into his pocket even as Norman

stood glaring at him, he dragged out a couple of screwed-up pound notes to slap them on the damp bar. 'But I want to stand my mates a round or two, and him as well,' he indicated Norman with a sharp tilt of his head. 'Give them whatever they want. I know liquor's in short supply but I'm sure you've sufficient there behind your bar to serve these bloody poor heroes who'll soon be leaving these shores to finish this war for you! Although him...' He tilted a chin at Norman, still standing tight lipped and fuming, 'I'm not so sure about.'

Before he could retaliate or burst out that he didn't need his bloody handout, Price was already shouldering his way through the knots of customers, leaving Norman to stare balefully after him while the men he'd entered with had already begun giving their orders, huge grins on their faces despite the publican protesting that to serve them shorts while having to refuse everyone else who asked on this busy evening would not do.

In the end, put in a good mood by two quid's worth of free drinks, they settled for as many pints of the copiously diluted stuff as they could drink, which was quite a bit at the current price per pint. Cheering their now absent hero for his generosity, Norman and his brief ruckus with his sergeant was forgotten.

Preferring not to join their buckshee binge, he bought his own pint and went to stand as far from them as he could in a quieter corner of the pub. Brooding as he sipped, he let his thoughts go over everything Price had said. The man was lying of course with his talk of seeing Valerie. But what if ... Quickly he shrugged away the idea of her and Price as ridiculous. Yet there came into his head an echo of a woman's voice, which in retrospect now seemed almost spectral.

'Your lady ... she will betray you...'

He wasn't sure of the exact words, but the disconcerting quality of it still haunted him, that and the woman's strange disappearance at the approach of those two officers – a disappearance that had been almost uncanny in its suddenness. Even now as he drained his beer, he felt a shiver run through him at the recollection, despite having shrugged it off as some stupid trick of the enforced darkness everyone was compelled to endure.

Yet thinking of those words, a seed of doubt was beginning to make itself apparent. Valerie hadn't complained of having had a cold. Usually 'flu would start with the onset of a rather vague if somewhat persistent chesty cold, and that last evening he'd met her, only a few days ago, she had seemed as right as rain. And that call he'd heard from downstairs in the house when Sidney had been talking to him, had it been a girlfriend or Valerie herself?

The awful thought that he was actually mistrusting the girl he loved brought him up sharply. Why should he think that? Why after all this time would he have reason to mistrust her? Standing here pondering wasn't going to solve anything. He needed to go and have this out with her brother.

Maybe his parents would be home by now.

They wouldn't lie. If Valerie wasn't there, they would tell him so. And if she was indeed ill, who knows, being her fiancée they might let him go up and see her for a little while, just to cheer her up.

Depositing his empty pint glass on a window sill, he made his way out, turning in the direction of her house. But halfway there common sense clicked in. What the hell did he think he was doing? If Valerie knew his thoughts at this moment she'd never forgive him. It was that bloody Price putting evil thoughts into his head.

But of course that had been the man's sole aim, to goad him into putting a spanner in the works. He took delight in seeing his corporal squirm, make a mess of things, a corporal he knew to be more intelligent than he and so needing to pull him down a peg or two. Well, he wasn't going to allow Price to humiliate him this time.

His watch told him it had been well over an hour since the confrontation with Valerie's brother – still time to try once more to see her before he needed to be back in camp. Perhaps being more insistent this time would force her brother into letting him in. What right had the young beggar to prevent him seeing his own fiancée? Yet again the doubts came. What if she wasn't ill at all and had gone out with a girl-friend, leaving him to cover for her? And if she'd gone out, why that concocted story of being ill? Why not be truthful? Why hadn't she wanted him to know? Was there someone else? Surely not! He'd have known. There'd have been signs long before this.

He'd come to a standstill without realising it. Coming to his senses he scolded himself for the doubts that had been going through his head and began walking back towards barracks. Of course she wouldn't be untrue to him. He knew her well enough by now to have known that. But it didn't solve the problem of that most important question he'd gone there to ask her. Soon he could be sent abroad – he might never see her again. Talk of imminent allied landings on French soil, though where was still undisclosed, was no longer just talk.

His mind in a whirl, he reached the camp gates, but loath to go on he stood a short way off, reaching into his pocket for his cigarettes and lighter. Flipping up its cap with his thumb, he flicked the wheel against the flint. The flame leapt, strong and bright.

Instantly there came a low shout from the soldier on guard duty: 'Watch that light, mate!'

Hurriedly, he shielded the flame with his hand, quickly letting the cap fall. The cigarette lit, he drew in a much-needed lungful of smoke. Maybe he still had time to get back to Valerie's ... He'd half turned to retrace his steps when a quiet laugh came from one of those on guard duty.

'Are you comin' through or stayin' there, soldier?'

Prompted, he realised the stupidity of going back and causing a scene, delaying his getting back to camp and thus being put on a charge. All thought of her and someone else evaporated. She loved him. All he could do now was to write what he'd wanted to ask and hope she'd reply with a yes. Except that it could take time to persuade her if she was in doubt, and there was no time.

Even so, she must know that she might never see him again and surely she would move heaven and earth to be with him before he was torn away from her for God knows how long? He'd have to word the letter carefully, poignantly, putting all his heart into it so that her own heart would break enough to compel her to say yes. He'd write tonight, post it first thing tomorrow.

Yet once through the gate, misgivings came flooding back. He should have gone back to her home, should have argued. He glanced at his watch, in the dark holding it close to his face and drawing fiercely on his cigarette to see the time, surprised to find how long he had been standing outside the camp. No wonder those on duty had laughed at him.

Not wanting to go to his sleeping quarters yet, he was at a loose end. Most would be in the canteen, but he was in no mood to join them. Instead, lighting up another cigarette, he wandered on past the big house and over to the quiet of a small copse, hoping not to meet anyone, particularly any nosey parker officers who'd want to know what he was doing out here on his own. Though they were probably all in the house, from where came the distant sound of a party going on, maybe someone's birthday or celebrating the imminent prospect of leaving behind this back-of-beyond place and actually going off to war, becoming part of the excitement of invasion, eager to get at the enemy and give him a good bashing.

Not sharing their enthusiasm, he wandered as far as he felt was worth bothering with. Finally, lighting up yet another cigarette, he turned to begin wandering back, taking his time. He needed to be alone a little while longer, not relishing the thought of going to his hut with men yapping away and swapping wisecracks as they prepared for bed.

Passing the outbuilding that housed the chandelier which had once intrigued him so, he wondered if it was still there, grinning to himself as he thought about it. What a bloody fool, letting himself become so besotted by it. Yet it was in there that he'd put the engagement ring on Val's finger and she had kissed him so ardently. It had been wonderful – until he'd been daft enough to show her the chandelier, mucking up his chance to make love. Idiot! No wonder Price took the constant mickey out of him.

Thoughts of Price sobered him and resentment flooded back as he made his way past the outbuilding, putting on a bit of speed, and in a few moments the rear of the big house came into sight. He didn't want to think of Price, he wanted to think of Valerie, but nothing would come. He slackened his pace in an effort to concentrate on her, but his mind seemed to have gone completely blank and he didn't like it.

The sound of raucous jazz music coming from the house was louder now. They really were having a good time in there, those well-turned out, normally sober officers more like a bunch of navvies behind the blacked-out windows. From where he stood he could see the side of the house and the conservatory beyond, all blacked out too. Outside was completely dark, or nearly so except for the pallid gleam of the moon just rising.

Listening to the din of the officers supposedly enjoying themselves, he smirked sourly to himself against every rank over that of corporal. Seconds later the smirk died on his lips as the ripple of female laughter came to him, high and musical.

It was Valerie's laugh, no mistaking it, that laugh he so much loved to hear. It had come from the rear door of a passage leading to the kitchen and the two rooms that served as the officer's mess halls. He had been in there several times in his duties, taking and delivering messages and the like.

Catching his breath in shock and disbelief, he turned sharply in the direction of the laugh. The moon was casting an eerie glow, though to those used to the blackout, luminous enough, and by that faint light he could just make out two figures standing by the rear door. Again the light laughter came and this time he knew. She'd lied to him. *'Your lady is playing you false...'*

The voice seemed to be speaking into his ear now, as if were he to reach out he would touch whoever was speaking. But he had already galvanised into action, sprinting towards the couple, a wave of blind fury enveloping him.

Twenty-Two

In his whole life he'd never let his temper get the better of him to any excess, but now a flame seemed to explode inside him. The next thing he knew he had cannoned bodily into the tall, slim frame of the man, the impetus almost knocking them both off balance.

'What the bloody hell...'

The yell from his quarry merged with a high-pitched shriek from the woman. He vaguely recognised it as Valerie's voice as she fled in panic. But there was no time to think. With the man now flailing into him, it sent the two of them crashing against the rear door where the couple had previously been standing.

Under the impact the door gave, bursting open, sending both men falling through it onto the floor of the rear passage, knocking over a pile of dirty kitchen towels and a bin of kitchen waste from the day's cooking put out for collection some time in the early morning.

Amid the strewn refuse, fists flying, the heavier of the two had instantly gained advantage and Norman Bowers knew he was in trouble. Desperately he fought to twist his head away from the blows raining down on him, wildly feeling for something to serve as a weapon of defence.

The first thing his groping hand found was the lip of a large metal can. Grasping it he brought it up sharply and swung, catching his assailant a hefty blow across the face. A flood of stinking oily liquid showered them both and the man gave a grunt, tumbling aside. Released, Norman scrambled to his knees, the can still in his grip. Automatically he swung it with all his might again and again at the other's head, how many times he had no idea. The can was large and heavy but an instinctive need to protect himself gave him strength as he repeatedly brought the thing down with as much force as he could muster.

Even when the man lay still he continued to beat at him with the idea that he might spring up again and get the better of him, but there was no movement.

Clambering to his feet at last, exhausted and out of breath, Norman stood swaying over the silent form. From the big room on the other side of the passage wall, sounds of high jinks were still going on. Obviously with all the noise they were making in there, no one had heard the up-heaval in the passage the other side of the wall.

In the deep darkness, even though he bent over the form lying amid the kitchen rubbish now strewn around them, it was impossible to identi-fy who the man was. To see better, he fumbled for his lighter, flicking the top up. With his hand trembling, he was forced to strike it several times before he could get a flame. Holding it close to the man's face, he recoiled with a terrified gasp.

The man was Sergeant Nigel Price.

'Oh dear Jesus!' The epithet tore itself from him. He was in trouble. Panic filled his whole being, his immediate thought to make off before anyone discovered him. But he couldn't leave the man here. The strong flame heating up the lighter, the metal was beginning to burn his hand and he let the cap drop, plunging the place again into darkness.

The rancid smell of spilled cooking oil was making him feel sick. His face hurt where he had not quite dodged some of Price's blows, but he thanked God for the heavy can of cooking oil. But for that he'd have ended up being pummelled into a pulp himself, a smaller man than Price, giving Price the greater advantage. He'd never have stood a chance.

Yet instead of making a run for it, he bent down to take another look at the man, flicking the lighter flame on yet again. Price was spark out, his face bloody. Had that can he'd wielded done all that damage? Wondering, he leaned closer for a better look then recoiled. The man's eyes were open, just staring up at him from out of what seemed a complete mask of blood.

Cold with sudden horror, his paralysed grip on the cigarette lighter with its still flickering flame, seeming unable to let go, he sank to his knees in a desperate but futile attempt to shake Price back to his senses. It was then he realised that Price wasn't breathing.

For a moment his own breath seemed to have stopped, stifled by the dismay gripping him at what he'd done. He shook the limp body with all his strength, crying out as his own breath came back to him in a sudden gush, 'Wake up! Wake up, Price! For God's sake, wake up!'

He let the lighter fall from his hand. It lay on the floor amid the kitchen waste, the spilled cooking oil, the cloths that had been put out to be taken for laundering, now all soaked in it.

Still gripped by shock, he hadn't noticed that the top of the lighter was still up, allowing the wick to continue burning, until he became aware that the flame had caught some of the oil-soaked cloths and, to his instant fright, the oil-soaked bottom of one of his trouser legs as well.

Leaping up in alarm, the first thought should have been to drag Price to safety or perhaps try to stamp out the fire, but the only instinctive reaction that came was of self-preservation, to run outside as quickly as possible and douse his own smouldering clothing before it became seriously worse. Forgetting the other man, he fled through the open passage door and once outside began frantically slapping out, not a moment too soon, the small flame that to his horror was starting to spread.

Extinguished in a matter of seconds but it could have been bad. That thought made him turn with some idea of going back to drag Price to safety, but oily black smoke was already pouring from the doorway. To go back now would probably choke him before he got anywhere near Nigel Price.

He had to run for help. But it came to him with renewed shock that Price was beyond help. The memory of those sightless blue eyes staring up at him quivered in his brain like a wavering spectre. He had killed him, not intentionally, but who'd believe him? If he ran off now no one would know he'd been here. But his own bruised face would raise questions of how he'd come by it. And there was Valerie, she'd seen him. Where was she now?

Staring at the smoke, he knew he had to go for help, in panic sprinted towards the front of the house, yelling, 'Fire!' at the top of his lungs.

But already men were streaming out through the main door, smoke obviously having begun rolling down the back passage and into the big room used for officers' recreation. Through the open door he saw others pouring down the wide staircase, smoke already rising up the back stairs from the passage, cutting off any retreat in that direction.

'It's round the back!' he shouted rather un-necessarily at two officers hurrying past him. 'I saw it start,' he began, then realised immediately that it was the entirely wrong thing to say as they pulled up sharply while others carried on stream-ing past.

'What do you mean, you saw it start?' demand-ed one.

'Just that...' He broke off, cursing himself silently, while one of them said, 'Come with us,' he finding himself being conducted along by them. It was then he saw Valerie standing a few yards off. For a second he stared in disbelief as they made to pass her. Then a raging fury caught hold of him.

'You bitch!' he screamed. 'What've you done?'

The officers paused at his shout. 'Who're you yelling at, Corporal?' one asked sharply.

'It's her!' he yelled, pointing towards her. 'It's her fault!'

The man's eyes followed the pointing finger. 'What are you talking about, man? There's no one there.' Looking back at him he noticed for the first time the pummelled state of Norman's face. 'What happened to your face? Have you been fighting?'

Frantically, Norman pulled away from him. 'She made me do it. She made me hit him. It was her!' Even as he looked at her he now realised it wasn't Valerie but the woman he'd seen before, smiling at him, taunting him.

'Who the devil are you?' he screamed. 'What d'you want with me?'

He tried to make for her but the officer's grip on his arm tightened, drawing him back forcefully while men streamed past them to where choking black smoke continued to billow through the open rear door.

'What's the matter with you, man? Who're you talking to? There's no one there.' He looked accusingly at him. 'Have you been drinking, soldier?'

Trying to pull away, Norman looked back but the woman had disappeared. She seemed to have totally vanished.

'Where's she gone?' he yelled at the second lieutenant, who still had him by the arm. 'She was there just a moment ago.'

The man gave a mocking chuckle then grew serious. 'Enough of this, Corporal, there never was anyone there. I reckon you've had a skinful.'

The lieutenant with him wasn't quite as amused. 'More than a skinful,' he growled. 'Your name and number, Corporal?'

Confused, Norman didn't reply, tightening his lips.

'I asked you what is your name and number?' demanded the man, while the second lieutenant's grin faded.

'Corporal, answer your officer!'

'I don't know who she is...' Norman began, but the shouting and urgent activity from the direction of the fire was diverting the lieutenant's attention.

'We should see what's going on,' he said urgently. 'They may need some help.'

But his companion's face tightened. 'Do you think we should leave him, sir? It looks as if he's been in a fight and probably drunk, and the way he's acting he could have had something to do with that fire.'

'Maybe,' agreed the other as the din of the fire alarm reached them. 'Right, bring him along.'

With an officer on either side holding him firmly as they made towards the commotion of fire crew and helpers, Norman began yelling at them to listen to him.

'She was there, I tell you! She was there!' He began to gabble in a torrent of only half intelligible words. 'It was a woman. She keeps appearing to me, telling me my fiancée is having it off with someone else. Then she disappears again. I don't know who she is, what she wants, but she's haunting me! It's not Valerie. I don't know who she is.'

'That's enough!' came the order. 'Be silent!'

He hardly heard them, raging desperately on. 'I'm telling you, she was there! Let me go! I have to speak to Valerie, say sorry to her for not trusting her. She's down with the 'flu. She was telling the truth, I know it now. I've got to see her and—'

'Shut up, will you!' The command was sharp and agitated as they turned the corner of the building to see smoke still billowing from the rear doorway, small orange tongues of flames now flickering within the rolling, black pall.

The sight took away all thought of Valerie, the mysterious woman, the failure of those who held him to believe him. He thought of Price – should have tried to get him out, but what if the blow from that metal can had already killed him?

The thought overwhelmed him while all around the commotion of those trying to douse the fire filled his ears. From the NAAFI canteen men were flooding out to see the fire, to offer help if needed. Helpless, he let his body sag between the two officers holding him, hearing himself saying over and over as if someone else was speaking for him, 'I didn't mean to kill him. She made me.'

It was enough for those holding him – an open confession amid the chaos. Taken to the guard-house, hardly comprehending what was happening to him, everything became a nightmare of confusion. Hour upon hour of unbroken interrogation by military police, hearing himself trying to explain the mysterious woman who had goaded him into doing what he had done, hardly aware that by his statement he was sealing his own fate, later seen as either a pack of lies or the ramblings of a man out of his wits.

The sight of his own face bruised and swollen, evidence enough of an obvious fight, was pounced on, he was accused also of setting fire to the place in an effort to conceal the evidence. Worn down, hardly aware of what he was saying, he tried to explain the cause of the fight, having to defend himself from the heavier man, all the time turning to the mysterious woman, managing only to incriminate himself even more as his interrogators began to see him as out of his mind.

Even trying to explain how the blaze itself had occurred, the cooking oil catching fire as he used his lighter to see if Price was okay, then accidentally dropping it among the oil-soaked rubbish.

'And how did that rubbish come to be soaked in cooking oil?'

No longer sure of what he was saying, his garbled story that one of the large cans containing used cooking oil must have spilled was instantly taken as pathetic prevarication.

Asked why the man's skull had been fractured by what appeared to have been some heavy object, in his agitated state he broke down, admitting that the can had been the only thing he could find to defend himself with against the bigger man who'd had him pinned down and had been punching him repeatedly in the face.

Asked how he could hit someone with something so heavy while being pinned down, before he could give a reply, they switched tactics.

'Did you start the fight intentionally?'

The sudden question took him by surprise. He blurted, 'No, I just saw him with the woman and I thought it was my Valerie!'

This brought a smirk of disbelief to his inquisitors' lips. 'There was bad blood between you and him, wasn't there?'

'Not from my side.'

'You were being badgered quite a bit, quite unfairly you said.' He couldn't remember telling them that, but maybe he had. 'Why would anyone in that situation not look for revenge the moment an opportunity arose?'

The question was unfair. His heart beating with huge heavy thumps made him feel sick. To the evidence being deliberately stacked against him as he saw it, all he could say was, 'I wasn't looking for revenge.'

'But you started the fight.'

Confused, tired beyond endurance, almost ready to give in, let them have their way, he could only deny any idea of seeking revenge; rather that when he thought he had found Price with a girl who at the time looked to him to be exactly like his own fiancée, Valerie Prentice, he had lost his temper, so probably he must have started it. 'But I realised later it wasn't her. It wasn't Valerie. It was this other woman.'

'What other woman?'

'The one who kept turning up, smiling at me, taunting me. I'd seen her before, always there, taunting me. Like a sort of apparition, she'd appear then vanish again, you have to believe me!'

They didn't. His tale so garbled that even to him it sounded as though he'd totally lost his mind. The bemused look on his interrogators' faces said it all. He needed for them to see that he had been in his right mind, that the woman he saw had to be real, though even he was no longer sure.

'Do any of you believe in ghosts?' he challenged out of the blue. He saw their grins change to scowls.

'Don't start being funny!' one of them growled, taking delight in thrusting his large face into Norman's. 'I hope you do realise the seriousness of what you're being accused of?'

He did, but had the girl with Sergeant Price been Valerie or not? He was no longer sure. The girl he'd seen previously hadn't been Valerie. But had it been Valerie or this other one who'd run off when he'd caught her with Price? Exhausted while his interrogators remained fresh and eager for answers, he was no longer sure of anything that had happened.

Finally transported to Colchester to await a court martial, he was accused of having attacked and killed a senior NCO. Examination of the body proved beyond doubt that Sergeant Price had died from blows to the face and head with some heavy object, the fracture to the skull not the fire being the cause of death. Corporal Norman Bowers, having murdered his sergeant, whether insane at the time or not, was sentenced to hang.

Enquiries had proved his Valerie to have indeed

been confined to bed that night with 'flu, although that only made his insistence that she had been there sound all the more rambling.

Knowing how confused she must be feeling by all she'd learned, her pain and confusion all his fault, he wept in mortification, giving himself up to his fate, hardly caring any more, wanting only to hold her close and tell her how much he loved her, a wish denied to him.

He was all Nigel Price had said he was – a useless apology for a man. To him it seemed it was happening to someone else. All he knew was that instead of going to fight for his country, perhaps die for his country, his dying would be ignoble and that grieved him. There would be no embarkation leave, no visiting his parents, no marrying Valerie – just as well to be hung.

While convoys of troops rattled the streets of southern England, few hardly noticed a briefly worded report of a corporal hung for murder, except the man's grief-stricken parents and a grieving girl called Valerie.

Twenty-Three

Clearing up from the fire was being carried out with a sense of urgency which had more to do with the fast-approaching allied invasion – no longer hush-hush, though the exact date was still secret – than any concern for the actual owner of Crossways Lodge, living in Canada in a private nursing home for the aged.

The house, like so many other vacant properties – business premises, shops, schools – had been taken over by the army preparing for the coming invasion. Returning it to its owner required it to be as near as possible to its condition prior to being commandeered.

Fortunately the damage was confined to the passage. The wall of the big room used by the officers had been blackened but still remained intact, although much of the pine cladding had been burnt away. The doors to the two rooms further along needed to be replaced, the rear door and kitchen door were completely gone, though the one at the far end of the passage survived.

What was a surprise was a small door discovered across from the kitchen. Protected by the pine cladding that had once concealed it, it was merely scorched. Quickly forced open, a tiny cellar was found. A few shelves with a few empty wine bottles gathering dust proved it to most likely have once been a wine cellar. More interesting were twin mounds of earth side by side, looking suspiciously like graves.

Obviously not a military matter, the police instantly summoned, excavation did indeed reveal each to contain a partial skeleton still with some dry flesh and skin adhering.

Estimated by the police to have been there around twelve years or so, the exceptionally dry cellar accounting for withered flesh and skin still remaining, the odd thing was that there was no sign of any clothing on either body. The pelvic bones at least showed one to be male, the other female, a fact eagerly picked up by local newspapers, to be read with horror by those living in Wadely, a stone's throw from the terrible deed.

'Twelve years!' exclaimed Mrs Dunhill, who had cooked for the Butterfields when they had Crossways Lodge at that time. She now looked after the village hall, held the key and helped run the Women's Institute, consequently had her finger on every pulse.

'I remember him,' she told several neighbours. 'Butterfield. Horace. His wife, Millicent I think it was, left him when he took up with a young bit of stuff. What was *her* name? Cecily? Celia? Yes, that was it, Celia, a really stunning young woman but a gold digger – eventually left him for someone else as I recall. Just ... went off, vanished. *That* was around twelve years ago. I remember him moping around the house, drinking himself silly. Then they found him in his own lake, drowned. Probably drunk. Some say it was an accident but others say it was suicide. Makes you wonder though.'

It did, and produced a lot of thoughtful nods. What if the two bodies turned out to be those of the young woman and her lover? What if they hadn't run off ? What if Horace Butterfield had murdered them? It was possible. At the time some had suspected him to be a bit of a criminal who'd come into money, and criminals often did that sort of thing, didn't they?

They waited with bated breath to find out what more the papers had for them, along with the other equally exciting and horrific story that had taken place again on their very own doorstep, of the army sergeant killed by a corporal who'd apparently left him for dead, hiding his dreadful deed by setting fire to part of Crossways Lodge.

He'd been court martialled and put under sentence of death and now Crossways Lodge lay empty, the entire army unit having left a week ago, among thousands of allied troops now landing on Normandy beaches.

Norman Bowers wasn't one of them. Valerie Prentice would never see him again. Her family told her she was lucky to be rid of him.

'But I did love him,' she wept pitifully.

'Of course you did, dear,' said her mother. 'And we know how hard it must be for you. But it would have ended up a life of misery. We wouldn't have wanted that for you. Even if what happened hadn't, heaven knows how he would have turned out had you married him.'

'I have to say I never completely took to that

young man,' said her father, his tone cautious as she faced him with reddened eyes. 'You have to admit he was a bit strange at times. He never really spoke much to us, as if he was never at ease with us, almost as if we weren't good enough for him.'

'He never ever said that,' she sobbed. 'He was just naturally shy with people.'

'Well, he shouldn't have been, not with us, his prospective in-laws.' Her father looked awkward. 'To put it bluntly, love, if you don't mind me saying, I always felt that he was looking down at us, so to speak.'

She burst into fresh tears. 'That's not true, Daddy. He never said a bad word against you. He always said that you were nice people.'

'And don't you think that says it all?' put in her mother, laying one hand on her husband's shoulder as if to help cement his words. 'If he'd said he liked us very much, that might have been more normal. But *nice people*? Who did he think he was? *Nice people*!'

Her lip curled disparagingly, making Valerie cringe in support of what she'd thought an innocuous remark on his part, wishing she'd never relayed it to them, thinking they'd be pleased.

'You always said you liked him, Mummy.'

'Yes, we did say that. But I object to the *people* bit. *People*! As if we were *below him*. But he was your choice, you were in love with him and I suppose he was in love with you. Even so, I was worried for you. Now I know I was right to have been. I can now see there was something more to him than we realised. Personally, I think you've had a narrow escape. You should thank your lucky stars for that rather than moping. One day you'll meet a nice young man who'll truly be the one for you and you'll forget all about this.'

In the end, having cried for days, she took their advice, and when it was all finally over, she had to agree that they were right.

The letters he'd written to her almost every day until the end had proved that he'd become strange, ranting and raving about having been haunted by the ghost of a woman he'd taken to be her at first, his letters filled with apologies for having believed it. Not that she'd read all of them, her parents made sure of that, aware of how much distress they would cause her. Valerie had let them open the letters and scan their contents, reading aloud parts of them enough for her to realise how unstable he had become. At first they were filled with words of love, pleading for her to stay faithful, begging her to reply, but on her parents' advice she refrained from doing so. Demanding to know why she didn't, they soon turned to words of anger, accusing her of cold-heartedness, of having no pity; that he never thought she'd turn out to be that kind of girl, whatever that was, all of it deemed too nasty for her to read. Finally they became filled with self-pity, going on about ghostly visitations, at the same time condemning her for thinking so ill of him, and so erratic that she could see the wisdom in her parents' advice to stay well clear of him. Whether it was the fate that faced him or some hovering, deep-rooted fault in his nature coming to light, she could feel herself being tormented by him until she thought she too was going mad.

It was almost a relief when his letters stopped, showing his life to have ended. It felt almost sinful to finally be free to get on with her life.

It was a long time before Valerie Prentice stopped having dreams of walking along a street and seeing him coming towards her. But slowly they faded. She was eventually to meet a nice Air Force chap, actually meeting him while walking along a street, in fact accidentally cannoning into him as she turned a corner. Two years later, the war over, they married.

With accounts of the trial and execution of the corporal accused of killing his sergeant coming on top of the discovery of two bodies buried in a cellar at Crossways Lodge, it didn't take long for both events to be coupled together to make a whole, proof that there were indeed strange and unexplained occurrences at the house.

'You can't wonder at stories of that place being haunted,' Jennifer Wainwright remarked absently to the next in the queue lining up for their various pensions, allowances and stamps at her post office counter.

The elderly woman whose pension she'd been counting out had raised the subject by saying, 'That big house is still empty, you know. I shouldn't think anyone would fancy living in it considering what's happened there in the past. Fancy being told the place you've got your eye on is haunted. I wouldn't want it.'

It had sent Jennifer's mind winging back to when she had known Joyce Johns-Pitman.

At that time the girl had been worried sick by what she had seen or imagined she had seen. Jennifer had scoffed at her then. But in the light of what that condemned corporal had said he'd seen, it now all seemed to fall into place. Maybe Joyce hadn't imagined what she said she'd seen. Whatever or whoever the woman was, she had been right, Joyce's husband had been unfaithful, and in a shock of rage she had stabbed him to death. Terrible thing to have happened, she'd been such a nice girl, a decent friend. But to go off her head like that. Apparently she was in an asylum now, insisting still that she had been visited by a ghost who'd spoken of her husband's infidelity.

Jennifer knew how easily it could happen. Still the village post mistress, she had never remarried after her husband left her for another woman all those years ago. She put no trust in any man, no matter how good and faithful he might appear, and the story of a woman warning of a partner's unfaithfulness had seemed as plausible then as it did now.

Her lips now lined, her cheeks sallow, the corners of her eyes behind her glasses edged by crow's feet, she knew she looked tired, gone the smooth features Joyce Johns-Pitman had known. But for a moment she was young again, listening to the spooky goings on in Crossways Lodge as she handed her elderly customer her week's pension.

'I was once told something strange about that house,' she said as the woman gathered up her pension and slipped it into her handbag. 'People living there then were sure it was haunted.'

'Haunted?' echoed a young woman, moving up to the counter in her turn as the old lady wandered off. On the point of buying stamps for the letter she was sending her husband now somewhere in France, she looked awe-struck.

'I thought everyone here knew,' Jennifer began, then pulled herself up sharply. 'Oh, of course, you wouldn't have. You've not lived here that long.'

As post mistress she knew everyone, but for a second this face had escaped her, forgetting that she was relatively new to the area. The woman was only too glad to enlighten her.

'I rent a couple of rooms down the road,' she explained in a sing-song Birmingham accent. 'My husband being stationed here I come down to be with 'im a bit longer, knowing he'd be moved on during D-Day.'

She was becoming quite chatty to Jennifer's dismay, her queue of customers beginning to fidget, she known for her efficiency in not keeping people waiting overlong.

'Now he's in France with all the others,' the woman continued, 'I'll probably go back home. No point staying 'ere now. Before he left he told me of the sergeant killed by that soldier. What d'you mean by the haunting?'

'Oh...' Jennifer looked beyond her to the queue now joined by yet another customer. She needed to bring this conversation to a close. 'Some talk around here quite a few years ago, that's all.'

'I did read something in the paper about that one what was arrested telling the court of seeing a strange woman what vanished right before his eyes,' the young woman continued blithely, the lengthening queue of no concern to her. But Jennifer was becoming ever more aware of it.

'No doubt to make himself sound insane and be acquitted,' she said, letting the end of the sentence drop as termination to the conversation, smiling sweetly but looking beyond the woman to announce 'Next!' adding, 'Hello Mrs Gordon,' compelling the young woman to move away.

Of course, the corporal's story in court of an apparent apparition had gone around the village like wild fire, as had the discovery of the two bodies.

On their very own doorstep, it was on everyone's lips. Like hungry vultures over a carcass, they devoured every last snippet of whatever meagre information the newspapers gave out about the case, which wasn't much, more being devoted to the progress of the allies in France than home news. It was from local newspapers that they gleaned the most.

Mrs Evans, once cook to those who'd bought the house after the death of Horace Butterfield, the Johns-Pitmans, delighted in telling everyone at the WI how Mrs Johns-Pitman had told her of having been suddenly confronted by the strange figure of a woman.

'The way she described her, I thought at the time it might have been the floozy that man Butterfield had been carrying on with, that maybe she'd decided to come back to him, her not knowing he'd drowned himself. Not that I knew her. But I heard tell of her. Mrs Johns-Pitman wouldn't have known her either, she being before my employer's time, and of course none of us knew then that she'd been murdered. It was merely assumed she'd gone off with someone else.'

The identity of the strange sighting only began to be guessed at after Mrs Dunhill, cook to the Butterfields, was prompted to relate a story Mrs Butterfield had told her about the huge chandelier her husband had bought in some London antique shop for his then newly constructed chandelier ballroom, as he'd decided to call it.

'Great big thing it was – all glittery. I suppose it was impressive and caught everyone's eye, but his wife told me she thought him a complete fool wanting to install a thing like that, acting as if he was lord of the manor. Her words, but I had to agree with her. He loved impressing people although I didn't say that to her face. She said he was completely taken in by the tale the person who sold it to him told about some heiress having owned it.'

As old as she was, Sarah Dunhill could tell a good story and she had the WI members enthralled.

'Well,' Sarah Dunhill continued, sipping her cup of tea, 'this rich woman apparently lost her entire fortune in 1929, during the Wall Street Crash, like a lot of people did.'

Mrs Dunhill was old enough to remember the impact of that terrible time, men losing their jobs, her husband being one of them, out of work for a good few years, leaving them struggling. Her two married sons had also had it hard, they with small children and nothing she and her husband could do to help them. 'It took the outbreak of this war to finally see men back in work,' she added to understanding nods.

'Apparently, the woman became destitute,' she went on, warming to her subject while her audience continued sipping their tea and nibbling their biscuits, their eyes widening with interest. 'And she had a lover who walked out on her when he found she had no money left. I expect he was living off her but she couldn't see it. And she was so devastated she hanged herself.'

Sarah Dunhill paused, aware of letting her story run away with her.

'Or so the tale goes,' she continued stoutly. 'Hung herself from the very chandelier Mr Butterfield bought to put in that big room.'

Pausing only a moment to look around her captive audience with an almost challenging eye, she continued in a mysterious tone, 'And if you ask me, I believe that's where the haunting started. There was never talk of it before he bought the house. It's said the woman, whoever she is, warns the person who sees her that the one that person loves will be unfaithful. I for one fully believe it.'

There were several nods of agreement mixed with a few sceptical mutterings. It was the latter to whom Sarah Dunhill now fixed her gaze. 'You think it's silly? Well, Mrs Wainwright here will bear out my story. Tell them, Mrs Wainwright, what Joyce Johns-Pitman told you about what she saw and how creepy that chandelier made her feel every time she entered that room.'

Pushed into complying, Jennifer Wainwright nibbled her lip. It was one thing to gossip, another to sit in front of a group having to address them cold, especially about the ramblings of a woman who'd killed her husband, albeit unintentionally, ending up in an insane asylum. Where she was now, she had no idea, and would rather not know. It was all in the past.

'Well,' she began hesitantly. 'I was a friend of hers for a while. She was a rather shy person and didn't make friends easily. She did become a member of the WI but never really mixed.'

'But what *did* she see in that house?' prompted one of her listeners, bringing her back to her story with a bit of a start.

Taking a hold on herself, she went on, talking fast, needing to get it over with. 'She always said that she was uncomfortable in that big room. So was her mother. She said her mother was sensitive to such things.'

For a moment she paused, hoping to have said enough, but urgent egging on forced her to continue for another minute or two.

'It was a long time ago now. She did tell me that she saw a woman in the room when it was dark – on another occasion too, when the woman said her husband was being unfaithful. And it was true. He was carrying on with his secretary.'

'I remember that,' someone burst out. 'And she stabbed him...'

'And there's that soldier too,' someone else interrupted. 'After killing that sergeant in his unit, he kept going on about seeing an apparition.'

'Whatever,' Jennifer muttered, and sat back in her chair, glad to be done with her part of the story.

But between them Sarah Dunhill, Florrie Evans and herself had set the members talking, eager to relay it to others around the neighbourhood. And so the story had grown.

'I don't think this ghost has anything to do with the woman found in the wine cellar.'

'I think it could be.'

'No, it has more to do with the one who hung herself, I'm sure.'

'It certainly gives you the shivers though, doesn't it?'

And so it went on; Jennifer Wainwright and Sarah Dunhill's accounts, borne out by Mrs Evans, would be enough to keep people talking about it for years to come, strengthened by the soldier's story at the court martial.

Though the newspapers had looked on what the accused had said as having been concocted by the man as a means of making himself appear insane, in the vain hope of saving his neck, to those of Wadely it was solid evidence of a ghost at Crossways Lodge, probably that of the woman in London who'd hanged herself from the chandelier around fifteen years ago.

Twenty-Four

The war was over. In cities, towns, villages, they danced, cuddled strangers, bunting and Union Jacks appearing from attics, cellars and sheds to be draped from houses or across streets from every support available.

Food hoarded for months for this very occasion was now brought out to be laid out on long rows of tables, kids eating more than they would have done in a week a few months back.

The night was lit by bonfires, blackout curtains that had for years draped windows every night burned alongside the wooden bunks from Anderson shelters and any combustible debris from bombed buildings.

Pianos dragged outside accompanied the dancing and singing, while anyone even slightly gifted as a musician went from street to street with whatever guitar, trumpet, clarinet or instrument they could play.

Fireworks produced from God knows where were let off, as if people hadn't had enough of explosions these last five years, prompting squeals from the children and cries of warning from their mothers.

Tomorrow life would return to normal, knowing that no longer would there be cause to be afraid. Only those who held the country's purse strings felt that burden, saddled with the problem of how the country was going to pay for the war now it was over, at least in Europe, conflict still going on in the Far East.

For the time being, however, people celebrated. Their husbands, fathers, sons, daughters would be coming home again safe and sound. Those whose loved ones wouldn't be returning watched the excitement and tried to be glad for them.

In Wadely, Crossways Lodge had been vacant and neglected ever since the army left a year ago, its grounds overgrown with no one going anywhere near the place if they could help it, the word haunted now on everybody's lips. How could it not be haunted when proof of it had been given by so many? Now, even to walk past the gates brought a shiver down the spine, and that was proof enough. Often the eye could glimpse some unexplained movement in the bushes or the ear catch an unexpected sound – a disembodied voice or just the stirring of branches or some small animal? It didn't matter. It was better to keep clear of the place.

'So what *do* you want me to do about your property in England, Ben?'

The tone was more a criticism than a question and Benjamin Lacey glanced up with rheumy eyes from his armchair at the man who'd acted as his solicitor for more years than he could recall, and shrugged as he always did when the house in England was raised.

'I'm informed,' Arnold Hammond went on, taking the shrug as no real answer, 'that since the army moved out, other than half-hearted repairs to that fire damage, nothing has been done Each month it is left unattended it will continue to deteriorate. Last winter hasn't helped matters.'

With a weary sigh old Ben let his gaze wander from a letter Hammond had handed him to stare through the open French windows of this rather exclusive residential home for the elderly, to brilliant sunshine spreading across the Vancouver skyline. Beyond its wide harbour, where ships from all over the world visited, the mountains were shimmering in the heat of a July afternoon.

His mind saw those bleak, British winter days, dimly remembered as a youngster. Apparently its winter this year, 1947, two years now since the war had ended, had been particularly miserable, the whole country gripped by freezing weather, bringing chaos and shortages.

Ben grimaced. Why on earth did his sister want to leave him a property in that Godforsaken country of wet summers, colourless autumns and gaunt winters? Vancouver never had snow. Every autumn leaves would turn gold and russet and bronze, the country transformed by colour.

Hammond was still nattering on. 'All right, so you were compensated for the fire, but the entire property is depreciating all the time you delay the decision to sell it. It'll need more and more work done to it as time goes on and it'll become increasingly hard to sell. Something ought to be done about it. And I would suggest you come to some firm decision about that, and very soon.'

Ben made no answer. He would much prefer not to be badgered into decision-making. He was too old to make decisions. They tired you out. The thought of going through all that bloody rigmarole of having to sell a place he'd not wanted from the start, being asked to sign papers, all the time being pushed by Hammond made him tired even thinking about it.

'Mr Lacey, Ben. Are you listening?' Arnold Hammond's tone was starting to sound a mite exasperated.

'Of course I'm listening. I'm thinking,' Ben returned testily.

'Well, I'd advise not to think too long. Or soon the place will be in no state to afford you any profit at all. Even putting it on the market this very day, it's going to be a job to sell. And you don't want to lose out. If we do it now it'll still make money. If we don't, in the end it's going to cost more than it's worth to put on the market. You'll see hardly any return at all.'

Hardly any return! Ben Lacey gave him a sharp, perceptive glance. He knew Hammond of old. Efficient solicitor, very reliable, he'd been with him for years, but in all honesty, in the end he was only out for the biggest fee he could get. The better the price they got on the house, the higher would be his fee and he'd do his damnedest to make sure of it. How long it took coming to a satisfactory transaction with whatever buyer came along would certainly affect Hammond's pocket. For himself, he had enough money to see him out in comfort for what was left of his years.

There was no one to leave it to when he did shuffle off. All he wanted was a quiet life. Not so with Arnold.

'The longer it stays unoccupied, the worst its condition will become,' Hammond was saying. 'Before long you won't be able to give it away.'

Again Ben shrugged. 'No use to me all those thousands of miles away.'

'We know that. But that's no reason to leave it to deteriorate. I assure you, Ben, once you give me the go-ahead, there'll be no need for you to lift a finger. That's what I'm here for.'

And for your bloody good fee, thought Ben, beginning to feel slightly choleric now. He was too old to be bothered with these things. All he wanted was to sit back in this quiet, comfy, retirement home, his every need taken care of, his food cooked for him, having one of the staff trundle him around the grounds, well-paid staff judging by the fees they charged, having himself helped to bed, knowing there was always some-one on hand should he need extra help, woken in the morning with a cup of tea and a couple of biscuits. It was all anyone of nearly ninety-one could need.

Just the life – if it wasn't for his solicitor badgering him about that bloody property back in England. Well, it was best to get it over and done with. He gave a deep sigh and sank back into his chair.

'Do what you want, Arnold. So long as you don't come bothering me with a bloody mound of papers to sign.' His hand was far too shaky to hold a pen, much less sign his name as he once

288

could, although he had Hammond to witness whatever scrawl he made that would serve as a signature. 'I suppose you're right. You always are. Just stick it on the market. It's no use to me all that way off. Just take the first offer that comes along.'

'If that's what you want?'

A small seed of irritation mounted in him, making him feel suddenly worn out. 'For God-sake, Arnold, just get on and do it!'

As Hammond readied to leave, Ben closed his eyes. He was leaving himself wide open to being fleeced by the man, who'd make sure of a tidy bit for himself, but he was too old and weary to care. Besides, who else was there to leave his money to? No relatives, not even a distant one. He might leave a decent bit to this home. The rest maybe would go to the state – or he might even leave it all to Hammond himself. He didn't blame the man for wanting to make sure his pocket was pretty well lined. He'd been a good, reliable solicitor for years, and once Ben was gone, why should he worry who actually benefit-ed? In a way he almost looked forward to leaving this world. But first, get that blasted place in England out of his hair. He was sick of it.

'Very well, Mr Lacey,' Hammond assured gently.

Until now his voice had been clipped and busi-ness-like, even though he'd spoken to his elderly client in layman's terms he could understand. There was a time when old Ben Lacey had been as sharp as a tack, no getting anything over on him. But now, if one fancied to be unscrupulous, one could do the old chap out of everything he had, and Hammond suspected he wouldn't have noticed so long as he was fed and cared for with all the attention he was now receiving.

Hammond grinned wryly. He wouldn't do that to the man. As irascible as Ben had become and had been in his time, he looked on his solicitor as a friend, and decent people didn't fleece friends, well, not too drastically. No, he'd make sure he took his proper fee plus maybe a bit extra Ben Lacey wouldn't miss. And as Ben himself had often said, who else had he to leave his money to?

'I shall do my utmost to see you're not bothered with too many details,' he said in a soothing tone. 'But you do understand I will have to consult you from time to time.'

'Yeah, yeah, I understand.' The reply was wearily impatient, leaving Hammond to withdraw, his client left in blessed silence other than the low murmur of his fellow residents, most of them sunk down like him into the soft cushions of their high-backed reclining armchairs.

Wadely had begun to notice activity at Crossways Lodge, builders' trucks turning into the driveway and lorries loaded with scaffolding and building materials, the place suddenly coming to life. There was no need to fear walking past it any more, not even after dark, with lights on inside and a couple of night watchmen keeping an eye on all the building equipment.

'Perhaps it's going to be sold at last,' remarked someone while lining up in the village store to be served. 'I wonder who actually owns it.'

'I heard it's someone living in Canada,' supplied Mrs Evans herself from behind the counter. 'I don't know how true that is. It seems to me a long way off to own a house here in a little village like this.'

'Maybe whoever it is intends to come back to live in it,' said the woman about to be served.

'Well, whoever it is, I can't wait to see the place occupied again,' said Mrs Evans. 'I can see it every night from my bedroom window, all dark and gloomy, and I'm sure I've seen something moving about between the trees sometimes. The place gives me the creeps.'

More likely a blessed fox, thought the woman, but kept the thought to herself. She didn't, nor ever would, believe in ghosts. 'I only need my bacon ration for now,' she said aloud, passing her ration books over. 'Streaky, please, it goes further. I'll be so glad when the whole business is done with.'

'You mean the house occupied again?' murmured Mrs Evans as she crossed off the appropriate spaces in the two somewhat scuffed brown ration books, handing them back before slicing off the eight rashers.

'No, I mean this blessed rationing business. Three years since the war ended and we've still got rationing as bad as ever, worse in fact.'

'And going to get a lot worse, I think, the way the country's going,' replied Mrs Evans, rewarded by several nodded heads from the small queue of customers. 'That's a shilling and eight pence. You've still got your tinned meat ration left,' she reminded as she took the money to ring it up.

'I'll save that for Monday,' said the woman. 'Make it go further.'

As the work on Crossways Lodge continued, two people, perhaps in their early forties, were seen driving in through the gates on several occasions.

From her bedroom window Mrs Evans glimpsed them getting out of the car, the man going round to open the passenger door for who she supposed was his wife. They would stand side by side in front of the house, the woman with her arm through his, as they watched the workman busy with the final touches to the place.

'They do appear to be quite a nice, respectable couple from what I can see,' she told those who came into her shop, which was a relief to everyone, the word going around to that effect.

Wadely was soon agog with interest, neighbours seen wandering by the place, just to make sure all was going well, though there remained one concern – would the new buyers find out about the past that house possessed and be frightened off by stories of strange goings on? Some felt it possible, while others smirked at such superstitious nonsense still being kept alive even after all these years, with nothing more ever having been seen apart from Mrs Evans' reports of having witnessed a few mysterious movements from her bedroom window.

'Not lately though,' she enlightened, almost with disappointment. 'Too much going on over there these days, I suppose.'

Most everyone else felt relief that things were looking up at last. They were sick of seeing the house standing empty at the end of their village like some spectre, and just hoped these new people would settle in for years to come.

Even so, it only would take one careless word to put the newcomers on their guard, scare them off, and it was widely thought better not to allude to the past that Crossways Lodge possessed should anyone chance to come into conversation with them, just in case it did frighten them away.

If there was anything odd still going on there, they would find out for themselves soon enough, and without being aware of the stories in the first place, hopefully they'd put anything of that sort down to imagination. If not, it could mean yet another set of occupants vacating the place, with possibly another long wait for new buyers to come along, Crossways Lodge lying empty and eerie once again.

But for now everyone was breathing sighs of relief to see the house being made ready for occupation at last.

Twenty-Five

In the spacious hall the final stages of renovation were being completed. By tomorrow or maybe the next day, any rubbish left would have been taken away, the workmen gone, along with all their tools and equipment.

Even now with all the wallpaper up, woodwork sparkling with new paint, the last of the carpet-laying almost complete, the house had taken real shape. In two days' time the furniture would arrive and once that was in place, the house would feel like theirs at last.

Eileen Burnley squeezed her husband's arm. 'I can hardly believe it's ours, David.' She gave a deep sigh of fulfilment. 'It's taken so long to get it to just how we want, but now it's all done and it's just wonderful.'

He looked down at her, his expression one of love for her and pride for himself. Forty-five, he was still quite good-looking for his age, tall and upright, and could have had his pick of women, but he had chosen her. Eileen was forty and still pretty in a formal sort of way. She had never been married, had been a schoolteacher all her life, dedicating herself to her profession.

When he'd first met her he had thought her rather prim and proper, but at the time he'd been in dire need of companionship of some sort, someone merely to be with, to talk to, to tell his troubles to. That was all it had been and she'd proved an intelligent listener, just what he'd needed.

He'd lost his wife in January 1945 when a V2 had landed on their house in Croydon, totally destroying streets of homes, killing her and a hell of a lot of other people. He'd been told while he was in France and had been returned to England on compassionate leave.

At the time he thought he'd never get over it, constantly bitter that he in the forces had been the one in danger of being killed, not her at such a late stage in the war when Britain was winning. How could God have been so cruel? Never greatly religious, he had turned against it completely, bitterly regretting that they'd had no children, Miriam unable to have any. If she had, maybe his grief would have been less, the thought only making him grow ever more bitter.

But he slowly discovered, not so much that time can be a great healer as some had thoughtlessly told him, but that losing a loved one was a sort of two-year disease. That first year of his bereavement, his mind going over every tiny anniversary he had spent with her, even to small things like simply going out for an evening or remembering a certain time and place they'd had a lunch out together, had been almost more than he could bear. By the second year those recalled events, having already been gone over in his memory, hadn't felt quite so poignant and heartbreaking, even though he wanted them to be.

Come the third year, he found himself able to face those anniversaries with more determination to rise above them and get on with life. Even so, he would never forget Miriam and all the things she used to do. He remained a lonely man, concentrating on taking over as managing director of his father's still thriving paper manufacturing business, allowing his father to retire

Just into his fourth year as a widower, he had been invited to a small gathering given by a close acquaintance of his, a schoolteacher, who had introduced Eileen to him. They had become friends, companions, nothing more at that time. It had been good to unburden himself of his still lingering grief. Having her patiently listen had been a Godsend, he who had kept his grief to himself those past years, and slowly he had fallen in love.

They were married last June, four months ago. It was a quiet affair in a register office with very few guests, mostly friends, she with no family to speak of and he only his elderly father and a brother in Canada. Raymond and his wife had sent their children there for safety during the war, and afterwards had gone out to be with them and settled out there. He hardly ever heard from them these days. He'd written to say he was getting married again. Raymond had sent his good wishes and a gift of table linen, but he'd not heard from him since then.

'It doesn't matter,' Eileen had said as he began to feel annoyed and hurt. 'We have each other and that's all that we need.'

She was right, of course. She was always

right and very certain of being so, probably the schoolteacher in her.

'I think we're going to settle down here very nicely,' she said now as they waited for the furniture to arrive. A good deal of furniture had been left in the house, all good quality so there had been no need to buy much.

'I hope we can merge in with the people here,' she went on as the furniture van arrived and the men began to unload, both she and David conducting the operations. 'I do hope I shall be able to join in with whatever social meetings there are.'

Within a few days she was putting feelers out. 'I'm told there's a social club held in the village hall once a week,' she said to David as she came in after a wander around, taking off her warm autumn coat and gloves, a late November frost still lying in the shaded parts of the countryside. 'They hold a whist drive there once a week and every so often occasional charity jumble sales. They also have social evenings there or in the church hall. There's a local village pub and one a little more exclusive with a rather nice restaurant. We could go there sometimes to eat and chat to people.'

Standing there in the middle of the kitchen, David nodded a little uninterestedly, his mind more occupied with thoughts of maybe having the place redecorated to a more modern style. But warming to her subject, Eileen hardly noticed.

'There is a regular bus service too that goes to Brentwood and to Chelmsford. Both have very good shopping and nice departmental stores.'

This information had already been given to them by an estate agent eager to sell the house, but Eileen having been in the post office today and having made the acquaintance of the post mistress, felt that any information gathered from her must be far more reliable.

'Her name is Jennifer Wainwright. She seems a very nice person. Our sort, I suppose. She's been telling me the history of this house. It's really very intriguing.' She gave a brief little laugh that seldom seemed to convey any real humour. 'Did you know this place is rumoured to be haunted?'

His mind diverted for the minute, he turned to look at her. 'Well, that's piffle! I wouldn't take much notice of that sort of talk.'

'Oh I don't!' She gave another of her small, dry laughs. 'It just struck me as being rather intriguing, that's all.' Putting that aside, she went on, 'Mrs Wainwright, Jennifer, says we really ought to employ someone as a cook and maybe general housekeeper. She said it's too large a place for one person to manage and I suppose she could be right in a way. But I said we'll see how we get on. If it does prove too much for just one person, maybe we could take her advice.'

'That would mean paying someone a wage,' David warned almost tersely, his thoughts turning back to whether they should have the kitchen redecorated just yet. Maybe it should wait until the spring. It would be more sensible.

'And we aren't all that flush at the moment,' he added, 'after having paid out most of what we had on buying this place, reasonable though it was. It has left us a bit short for the time being, you know.' Come spring he might be able to afford to have the whole house modernised.

Although his stationery firm was thriving under his directorship now his father had retired, his old-fashioned ideas having allowed it to stagnate during the war, it was taking a while to see the full benefit of his own more up-to-date methods and it all cost money. One needed to speculate in order to accumulate, as every businessman well knew.

The country now with its sights on a new world, he had installed far more efficient machinery with a team of reps who really knew their job selling stationery, so different to the couple of old chaps his father had employed, who had trundled their briefcases of samples around uninterested outlets. But it still called for ploughing the profits back into the business to return the firm to its pre-war state. Modernising a house would have to take a back seat for a while yet.

'I suppose you *are* right,' she conceded, dragging his mind back to his remarks regarding her new acquaintance's advice. 'But it would be nice to have some help here. Maybe in the spring as funds became less tight.'

Jennifer Wainwright had felt somewhat privileged to have had a chat with the wife of the new owner of Crossways Lodge. She'd been on the point of closing the post office counter for the Saturday afternoon, the CLOSED sign in her hands ready to prop against the grille even as the woman walked up to the counter.

Jennifer was a strict time-keeper in all things and certainly where her post office was concerned. Closed was closed, and no one flouted that rule. But seeing a new face making towards her counter at the rear of the small village shop, she instantly suspected that it belonged to the wife of the couple who'd only recently moved into Crossways Lodge. Being a person who possessed a natural streak of curiosity, she uncharacteristically found herself laying the sign discreetly aside to offer the woman a cautious smile.

'You're only just in time, you know. One minute later and you'd have found the counter closed.'

'I'm sorry,' was the breathless reply. 'I desperately needed to catch the post. Otherwise my letter wouldn't go off until Monday and that might have been too late.'

'Well in this instance,' Jennifer said generously, 'I'll stretch the rule, but remember this post office closes twelve thirty on the dot, and it is...' she glanced up at the clock behind her, '...now half a minute past that.'

The woman's expression divided itself equally between guilt and gratitude, but she didn't give voice to it, instead introduced herself as Eileen Burnley. 'I and my husband David have just bought that big house—'

'Crossways Lodge,' interrupted Jennifer and saw her relax slightly.

'That's right. I was a schoolteacher. I've written to my old colleagues at the school where I taught, giving them my new address. Then I realised today that I'd left out the most important of them – the headmistress herself, would you believe. It was sheer oversight and I feel dreadful about it. She is a most understanding person but she would feel hurt come Monday when everyone but her gets a letter from me. The last thing I want to do is upset anyone, especially her.'

The woman was running on and so was time. Any minute someone coming into the shop area and seeing the counter still open might assume it okay to take advantage, fully expecting to be served after closing time – after all, what was good for one was good for all.

'So what you want is a stamp, Mrs Burnley?' she prompted, perhaps a little too sharply for the woman gave an almost imperceptible start.

'Oh, I'm so sorry, yes.'

Jennifer melted a little. 'Very well. First or second class?'

'Oh, first, please.' The voice was small. Fishing into her handbag she produced both letter and money. 'This is very kind of you. I hope it's not too late to catch the post. When is the last collection today?'

'You've plenty of time,' Jennifer assured her as she took the money and pushed the stamp through the grille. 'But I do close for lunch.'

The woman appeared to wince at the reminder, instantly causing Jennifer to feel like a tyrant, which was unusual for her. Also, her natural curiosity was roused, eager to find out all about this newcomer to Wadely. This time her smile was genuinely warm.

301

'Look, I must close up. I usually pop into the tea shop along the road on a Saturday instead of going straight home. I wonder ... would you fancy coming with me? It would be nice to have a little company. What do you think?'

There was a fraction of a second's hesitation then the prim expression relaxed. 'Thank you, I'd like that very much. It would be nice to get to know a few people here. It's not always easy, is it?' To which Jennifer had to agree.

'Then give me a moment to get my things. It's not too warm out there today. I think we're going to get an early winter.'

It took only a moment to grab her hat, coat, handbag and her warm scarf, swiftly propping the closed sign against the grille as she did so.

Sitting together at a little round table with its crisp, snow-white cloth, gleaming chrome cake-stand, its delicate, blue-flowered cups and saucers and plates, she found Eileen Burnley not as quiet as she'd first imagined, in fact proving to be quite a chatty soul, which was very helpful. Being the ears of the village, if there was anything worth finding out about these new owners of Crossways Lodge, Jennifer would be the hub of interest for a long time to come.

She made it a point not to interrupt if she could, except to prompt her new friend as and when needed, as Mrs Burnley, or Eileen as she asked to be called, warmed to her tale of how she and her husband had recently married – he for the second time, having lost his wife, and she for the first time.

'I'm afraid teaching took up all my time. I was

dedicated to it and had no eyes for the opposite sex,' she said in her rather flat tone. 'Then out of the blue along came David and within a year we were married.'

Listening to her, Jennifer came to the conclusion that rather than the diffident soul she'd first appeared to be, she seemed in fact quite sure of herself, the very essence of what she imagined a good schoolteacher to be.

Slightly dowdy, she was dressed plain, brown hair cut straight about her ears with an equally straight fringe, spoiling what could have been quite pretty features: clear skin, full lips, a small, neat nose and bright blue eyes. A pity really, looking so prim, for she was proving to be not at all as standoffish as her looks would have had one believe. Her conversation was surprisingly animated. In fact Jennifer guessed she could be an interesting and informative conversationalist when she wanted.

'I think we're going to really enjoy being here,' she said as they sat opposite each other sipping tea and nibbling tiny sandwiches.

'I really do hope so,' Jennifer said with genuine sincerity.

Eileen gave a little smile then grew serious.

'The estate agent did say the house had quite an interesting history to it, though he didn't tell us any more than that, other than saying part of it was built in the early nineteenth century and the rest built the beginning of this. I have always had a liking for history – my favourite subject when I taught at school. I would rather like to delve into it if I can.'

Before she could stop herself, the words prompted Jennifer to burst out: 'As to history, I could tell you a lot about that place,' instantly wishing she could have bitten off her tongue as the woman's eyes lit up with interest.

'Oh, that would be really interesting too! I thought I might try the library in Brentwood, but that's quite a way to go. Having it told to me right here would be marvellous.'

'There isn't that much to tell,' Jennifer began evasively, but Eileen was leaning towards her.

'No, please, I would love to hear.' She gave a small flat laugh. 'It isn't haunted is it?' she quipped, then her blue eyes opened wide and Jennifer knew she had seen her brief change of expression too quickly for her to hide.

'*Is* it haunted?' Eileen asked, her eyes opening even wider.

Jennifer bit her lip. The last thing she wanted to do was to scare these people off and see the house lie empty again for God knows how long.

'No, well, not really.'

Eileen leapt on the words. 'What do you mean, *not really*?'

'It's just rumours.' What else could she say? 'Honestly, that's all they are, nothing more.'

Again Eileen laughed, relaxing. 'Well, I don't believe in ghosts, though I wouldn't be surprised if there are tales. Old houses usually do promote such stories. Although I don't wonder at the estate agent trying to keep it quiet. It hardly helps his job of selling properties, does it?'

She was looking quite amused but Jennifer found herself unable to share her amusement as much as she knew she ought to. An unexpected shiver had trickled down her spine as if she herself had suddenly been confronted by a spectre. Almost as if she too had stood in that room staring at the apparition she'd been told about all those years ago.

She remembered the man who'd murdered two people then done away with himself; the woman who'd killed her husband; a soldier responsible for the death of his sergeant, apparently trying to cover it up by setting fire to part of the house, maybe even burning the man to death, raving at his court martial that he'd been prompted by the ghost of a young woman who'd told him to do it.

She found herself giving an involuntary shudder, only just managing to hide it from her companion with what felt like a rather silly, careless grin.

'You're right,' she said lightly. 'But people love to gossip about that sort of stuff, especially about things that happened a mere stone's throw from this very spot, the big room in Crossways Lodge, for instance.'

Her companion frowned. 'What about the room?'

Jennifer hesitated, but having started felt she must go on or make the woman wonder more. She tried to sound casual. 'Just that the people who bought the house in the early 1930s had the existing three rooms and the hallway knocked into one, though the next people rebuilt the hallway wall.'

But Eileen had detected more to the tale than trivial village gossip. 'And?' she prompted, forcing Jennifer to continue.

'Well, the man who'd enlarged it would often call it his chandelier ballroom. He'd acquired a huge chandelier and put it up there. Apparently he loved ballroom dancing and he'd hold parties there. But he committed suicide eventually, drowned himself in that lake of yours.'

That needed explaining, with Eileen's eyes now practically boring into hers. 'You see, his wife left him when he took up with someone else,' she went on. 'And then he caught his fancy woman in the arms of another man and he went berserk and...'

Breaking off, realising she could be saying too much, she gave a little laugh. 'I'm sorry. I've been going on a bit, haven't I?'

'No,' Eileen said readily. 'It's interesting. What happened to them? But I can see how rumours get started. As you say, people love to gossip. Would you like more tea? There's enough in the pot for another cup for the two of us. And do let's eat these cakes we've paid for!'

As they parted company, agreeing to meet again in the tea shop for tea and cakes next Saturday, with Jennifer promising to bring along some newspaper cuttings of the Butterfield case and a few other bits and pieces, Eileen knew she had made one friend at least.

Thinking about it as she walked home, she couldn't wait to tell David all about it. As for ghosts, some people did love wrapping themselves up in such things. But it would help make their new home interesting to friends who came to visit.

306

Twenty-Six

Two evenings later, Eileen was on tenterhooks for David to arrive home.

He seldom left the office before half past five, often after the rest of both office and factory workers had left – unless of course he was at one of his frequent meetings. His company was his whole world, ever striving to bring it up to the standard of larger stationery manufacturers, and there were times when she felt she took second place to it, even though she had told herself often enough that she should be grateful having security now which was something not to be sneezed at.

Had she not met him when she did she might have ended up a lonely old woman after retiring from teaching, a prospect that made her shudder even to think of it, as she thanked her lucky stars for her timely rescue.

To be able to call herself a married woman still struck her as being quite wonderful. David was easy to live with and she loved him in her own way, despite finding the sexual side not easy to get on with. That night after their wedding had been her first ever experience of sex and had proved quite harrowing, for knowing about it had certainly not equipped her to deal with the physical deed itself, though she had tried to make out that she had enjoyed it. It had seemed to satisfy him however. Fortunately he wasn't one to press his attentions on her and for that she was glad. But she did love him and in fact sometimes felt jealous of his association with the several younger women in his office, even though she felt she knew instinctively that he was true to her.

Her thoughts died away to be replaced by the one in hand as she heard his car crunch to a halt in the drive. In seconds she was at the front door, cardigan gripped tightly around her throat against the cold, dank November evening. Impatiently she watched as he parked the vehicle in the new garage he'd had built, and as he came back to the house almost pounced on him, hardly before he'd had time to mount the three wide steps up to the portico.

'Don't take your coat off!' she called out, running down the steps and grabbing his arm to lead him away from the house. 'You have to come and see what I found this afternoon!'

David pulled back a little from the grasp, his tone of surprise sounding faintly rankled. 'What do you mean, found?'

Hit by the cold night air after being in a nice warm car, he'd already anticipated the cosy warmth from the house wafting out to greet him home. The last thing he wanted was to be dragged off into the chill again.

'What's so urgent that you want me to look at whatever it is at this time in the evening?' he asked. 'I'm tired. All I want is something to eat and to sit down in front of the fire afterwards. Can't it wait until tomorrow – Saturday?'

But she wasn't listening. She frequently didn't listen, not in the way that was giddy, but as someone very positive of her own decisions.

'We've not had a chance to look into those two outbuildings of ours yet, have we?' she went on as she practically dragged him along, he giving up to allow himself to be led off away from the welcoming lights of his home. 'We've been so busy with the house,' she went on, 'we've not really given much thought to the outside, the garden, all this ground we have.'

'That's because it's autumn,' he interrupted. 'And it's cold. Come spring we can concentrate more...' But she still wasn't listening.

'It was such a lovely afternoon I thought I'd take a little look at the outside – the garden and the grounds. I also took a peek into those big sheds we have and I got such a wonderful surprise. I'm dying for you to see. Come, let me show you.'

The cold was now getting to her too, she with nothing but a cardigan over her dress, so that by the time she reached one of the outbuildings to pull the door open, she was shivering as she led him inside. But she was determined to have him see what she'd found.

It hadn't felt all that cold this afternoon, but then she'd been wearing a proper coat to go on her small safari, exploring the length and breadth of the grounds they owned. She'd been just like an explorer, free and at liberty to wander in what had felt like a timeless world. But after a while the damp ground had begun to penetrate not only her shoes but it seemed her whole body, her late afternoon tour proving far less pleasurable than anticipated. Well into autumn, what had she expected? Yet despite the persistent chill, there hadn't been a cloud in the sky all day, which she supposed had been rather misleading, and it had been rather late in the afternoon to go wandering about.

As the sun dipped further towards the west, clouds had gathered on the horizon in flat lines, giving a wonderful sunset eventually melting to a colourful, deep red dusk. It would have taken her breath away had she not felt that such glorious colours could also be misleading, not so much as red sky at night shepherd's delight, but the ominous hue that promised a wet day tomorrow.

Just as well she'd done her exploring today. There might not have been another chance for ages. So now she intended to take advantage of this maybe last dry evening to drag David out to show him what she'd discovered. She'd started to hurry past the two outbuildings to get back to the house and warmth, but curiosity had stopped her and she'd gone into each long shed in turn to see what they harboured,

The first had held a mass of gardening tools, plant pots, seed boxes, also several ladders, some old benches, an old oil-driven lawnmower and some drums of unknown chemicals, no doubt to do with soil cultivation. The two large greenhouses that lay a short distance away had seen better days, but once she and David settled in they'd probably restore them and employ a gardener to return the grounds to their former glory.

The other outhouse was less cluttered, mainly various pieces of furniture that had been stored away for years, most of them damp and mouldering. There was even a grand piano, or what was left after woodworm had been at it no doubt, a sin to see such a thing in that state.

It was then she discovered, lying under a moss-covered tarpaulin, the object that was still playing on her mind as she now led David towards it. She'd recognised it instantly for what it was, recalling Jennifer Wainwright's story of a magnificent chandelier that used to hang in the big house in what had at that time been grandly christened the chandelier ballroom.

'Have you got your cigarette lighter on you?' she asked urgently.

'Why?' he asked, the question faintly terse and irritable.

'To see by,' she said in a tone just as terse. When she had been here this afternoon, the sunset had offered some light, but it was now dark, a full moon only just risen, not yet bright.

'Hurry, it's freezing out here!' she urged. 'Use your lighter!'

Without another word he did as he was asked, the small flame affording just enough light as she lifted one edge of the tarpaulin to reveal what she'd brought him here to see.

'It's that chandelier Jennifer Wainwright told me about,' she cried, her excitement now steadily mounting. 'It's still here. It's been here all this time. Don't you think it's absolutely beautiful?'

In this fitful light of the small flickering flame, even after all this time lying here neglected, the object of her attention threw back such a brilliant sparkle that David gave a gasp of surprise. His earlier look of exasperation had been slowly changing to one of faint amusement and she could understand why. It wasn't usually in her nature to air her feelings with such exuberance, but in this instance she couldn't help herself.

From the moment she'd come upon this exquisite piece of illumination, with its two tiers of gleaming gilt arms and its swathes of twinkling crystal, even in what light there had been, a feeling of wellbeing seemed to have bubbled up from the very depths of her body, leaving her in a fervour of excitement ever since.

'Well, what do you say?' she prompted as he continued to gaze at it. But before he could say anything, the flame heating the cigarette lighter case suddenly burned his fingers, making him drop it.

'Damn!' Fumbling in the dark, he found it but didn't relight it. 'It's cold out here,' he said, his unemotional tone suddenly irritating her, all her excitement doused. 'I need to get back in the warmth.'

'Is that all you can say?' she burst out, but she was cold too, freezing. It was hard to keep any limb still.

'We'll discuss all this indoors,' he said in his sensible tone. 'You'll catch your death out here if you're not careful.'

With that he stood up, leaving her with no

312

option but to let the edge of the tarpaulin drop back into place and follow him out, back to the house.

Once indoors he slowly took off his hat and coat, carefully hung both up on the hall stand and went past her into the sitting room, going to the drinks cabinet to pour a small whisky for himself, taking it to his armchair to begin sipping at it, maybe a little too quickly, all without saying a word to her.

Normally he would have kissed her on the cheek before taking off his hat and coat, and asked how her day had gone. It was only as she followed him into the sitting room that she realised that something must have upset him, maybe something at work. She should have given him time to get indoors, get warm and tell her all about it before dragging him back outside. Perhaps that was it.

All in all he was the most even-tempered of men, and in all the time she had known him she had never seen him annoyed. So it took her a while to realise that it was she who must have upset him. Yet she still couldn't be sure. All she could do was ask, 'Is something the matter, dear?' as she sat down in the armchair opposite to sip her own sherry before going off to dish up dinner.

'Is it something at work?' she queried when he didn't reply.

'No, everything's fine at work,' he said without looking at her, his gaze on the low burning fire in the grate in the already warm room.

She thought awhile, her mind turning to the

way she had pounced on him, dragging him out into the cold night hardly had he arrived home. But surely that shouldn't have upset him all this much.

'Then what is it, love? I'm sorry if I stopped you going indoors. I didn't mean to...'

'It wasn't that.'

Now she knew it was she who was guilty. 'Then what?' she burst out.

'It was that thing you showed me,' he said slowly.

'Do you mean that chandelier?'

'Why did you think it so important to show it to me?'

'I know. I should have waited until tomorrow. I didn't think.'

'That has nothing to do with it. It's *why* you should have found it so very important that it couldn't wait until tomorrow.'

'It was just that...' she hesitated then went on, her speech growing rapid. 'Something Jennifer Wainwright, the post mistress, told me. I've had lunch with her a couple of times in the local tea shop. She said that it was something she was told a long time ago by a young couple who'd once had this house and who learned all about it ... the chandelier, I mean,' she hurried on as David shook his head, having lost the thread of her story.

'At the time they made enquiries about it and the wife who'd become friends with Jennifer Wainwright told her all she'd learned. Apparently it all started in London...'

She became aware that he was growing impatient, no doubt wanting dinner. But she didn't want to break off now. Quickly she went over the story attached to the beautiful object as related to her by Jennifer Wainwright, an apparent suicide attempt that went wrong, the poor woman killed by the very thing she'd tried to hang herself from, falling on her instead, thus ending her life.

'That was all years ago, back in the twenties, so Jennifer said. But you know how stories can grow and get magnified out of all proportion.'

'Yes, I do know,' he said, having previously not said a word. He sounded sceptical, almost sarcastic, which wasn't like him.

Eileen gave a little laugh. 'Heaven knows, I don't suppose any of it is true, and anyway, like you, I don't believe in such things.'

'What things?'

Was he deliberately trying to be difficult? She held herself together. 'You know, ghosts and spooks and haunted houses and such like.' She paused then said, 'Nor do I attach anything sinister to what I've just shown you. I merely think it a beautiful object, that's all. That's why I'd like to see it back in the big room where it used to hang. It must have looked quite something all those years ago. I can see it now, all those people Jennifer said who once attended the parties there – men in tails and bow ties, women in long slinky evening dresses and the crystals on that chandelier sparkling off the diamonds they wore.'

She paused, realising that she was rattling on. She smiled at him. 'Well, never mind dear, you go into the dining room. I'll bring in our dinner.'

'I think your Jennifer Wainwright is right,' he said as he went. 'You *should* have someone here to do the cooking. This house is far too big for one person to manage everything. I might look into it in time for Christmas.'

Annoyance flooded over her. He'd not been listening to a word she'd said, or if he had, had chosen to ignore it. Well, whatever he thought, and whether he liked it or not, she was going to arrange for that lovely thing to be reinstalled in the big room to be admired by those she intended to invite just prior to Christmas: her old teaching colleagues, David's colleagues too, of course. And Miss Reade, still headmistress at the school. She would certainly admire the thing. She had good taste.

It was a lovely party, apparently the first that had been held since those who had bought the chandelier in the first place had left. Eileen had also asked a few in the village whom she'd made friends with – Jennifer, of course, and some of those with whom she'd become acquainted from the village's parent/teachers circle which she had joined a couple of weeks previously, with her experience of being a teacher. It had even been mentioned that maybe she might consider stepping in on the odd occasion as a sort of supply teacher. She had said gravely that she would give the matter serious thought even as she hid the excitement the flattering offer brought to her.

All those who'd readily accepted the invitation to her pre-Christmas gathering, more out of curiosity than anything she guessed, were clustered in the big room – she refused to call it the chandelier ballroom, judging the title as utterly silly, even though the chandelier was now reinstated in its old position.

David hadn't been too enthusiastic about that, but she had been so used to having her own way, making her own decisions for so long as an unmarried woman, and he not naturally an argumentative sort of person, and he had to admit it did look splendid now, though it was far more enormous than they had imagined as it hung there gracing the room.

It was a source of pride, though she did notice quite a few from the village giving it more than one cautionary look, trying to avoid lingering under it, a now well-entrenched superstition hard to shift.

Even so, before the evening was out, with everyone standing about nibbling chicken and ham sandwiches, Christmas cake and mince pies, sipping wine or soft drinks as they talked and talked, they were all behaving as if the chandelier wasn't even there. At least the less superstitious had admired it on entering, which was what she had been aiming for.

All in all, her first social evening was proving a great success, she already considering holding something similar when Easter arrived. Mingling, it was enjoyable to recognise those faces she'd known so well when she'd been teaching and had almost forgotten in her happiness of being married; now they sprang back into mind as if she had never left. It was lovely to renew acquaintances, just like old times when they would all gather in the common-room for their own small pre-Christmas get-together once the pupils had gone for the holiday.

Yet one face she couldn't place. She was a woman maybe in her early thirties, quite small and trim, very pretty with short fair hair and wearing a very odd dress; rather shapeless it looked from where she stood, with the waistline far too low as if made for a much taller person. She was standing by the French windows looking rather lost, while everyone else around her stood in groups. Maybe a new teacher at the old school, not yet settled in? But she wouldn't have issued an invitation to someone she didn't know – unless someone had brought her along rather than see her left out. That was probably the answer. But she looked so alone and Eileen's first thought was to go over and talk to her, make her feel more at home perhaps.

As she began to make her way towards her, she was stopped by Mr Tom Eldred, the maths teacher, wanting to introduce his wife.

'I should have done so long before now,' he rumbled in his deep voice. 'But you seemed to have been so occupied by everyone.'

Eileen smiled. 'Oh, don't worry,' she said graciously. 'There are some here I still haven't had a *chance* to talk to yet. As a matter of fact I was about to have a word with that young lady over there by the French windows. She seems to be all on her own. I can't place her. She's not local. Perhaps she's a new teacher at the school?'

He glanced to where she'd indicated. 'Young woman?' he queried. 'There is only Mr and Mrs

318

Chandler over there with some other people, probably local.'

She let her gaze turn to where she'd been pointing. There was now no sign of the woman. 'Oh!' she said, then laughed. 'Well, whoever she was she's not there now.'

They laughed with her at her little jest and she excused herself to continue on towards the French windows. There she asked the English teacher Alfred Chandler and his wife and the two they were with whether they knew which way the woman who'd been standing near them a moment ago might have gone. All four looked mystified.

'Sorry, my dear,' said the rather elderly Mrs Duncan, a long-standing member of the parent/teacher group, while her even older husband stood looking a little blank. 'I've not seen anyone on their own and we've been here some time, haven't we, Kenneth?'

To which the man gave an emphatic nod then an equally emphatic shake of the head, obviously unsure whether she meant standing here or seeing the woman.

Eileen gave up, moving away after voicing the hope that they were all enjoying themselves and to help themselves to more food and drink whenever they fancied.

But it was a mystery as to who the woman was whom she had seen. A gate-crasher perhaps? She hardly thought so. But where could she have gone in the little time it had taken to speak to the Eldreds?

Twenty-Seven

Throughout the rest of the evening Eileen kept looking around for the person she had seen, but there was now no sign. Had the young woman – she had looked young, though there had been signs of maturity there – been so lost all on her own that she'd decided to leave? But how far had she to go to get home?

Eileen racked her brains to think of anyone new in Wadely, but there hadn't been anyone new since she and David had come to live here as far as she knew.

The whole business began to nag at her so that rather than enjoying the rest of her evening, she grew more and more eager to see the departure of their guests, even her old colleagues whom she had yearned to meet again.

Saying goodbye and thanking everyone for coming, promising those she'd known best from the school to keep in touch, she noted that the fair-haired woman wasn't among them – definitely a gate-crasher then. It happened sometimes, cheeky devils looking for a free evening's eating and drinking, sneaking away well before everyone else left. And who would notice their going or even think to question it? Nor would anyone query who the stranger was, many of them not knowing half the people present anyway. So easy!

'Did you see that woman who was here?' she asked David when they had closed the door on their last departing guests, those living round about with not far to go.

'What woman?' he asked as they went back into the big room to begin gathering up empty glasses, plates, paper napkins and some of the more perishable remains of her spread. The rest of the clearing up could wait until morning, both too tired to worry about it now.

Having borne what they'd collected to the kitchen, they decided to wash everything up in bulk after a night's sleep. It was midnight after all.

'I don't know who she was, standing all on her own,' Eileen said wearily as they went upstairs. 'She was dressed funny, sort of old-fashioned.'

'Who?' David asked as he mounted the stairs ahead of her.

'The woman I told you about. I don't think she had anyone with her. I thought you might know her – someone from your company perhaps?'

'I only asked one or two who work closest to me,' he said absently as he opened their bedroom door for her. 'My accountant John Worthington and his wife, and my company secretary, Bill Summers and his wife. But I didn't invite any young woman.'

She leapt instantly on that last remark. 'How did you know she was a young woman?'

He frowned as he began taking off his tie. 'I thought you said she was.'

'No I didn't.'

He wasn't looking at her. He was concentrating on unbuttoning his shirt. 'I just took it she probably was young, whoever she was you saw.'

'I didn't say a young woman. I merely said a woman. She could have been elderly for all you knew.'

His frown had deepened. He paused in undressing to look sharply at her. 'Well, I never saw her. I just assumed she was young.'

His tone too was sharp. Seldom short with her, she felt her concern heighten. Why had he become so edgy, he of such a placid temperament?

Every day for ten hours or more he was away from her. She had no idea what went on in his business, apart from knowing that he would often attend quite a few meetings to do with its everyday running.

He never brought his work or problems home. When she happened to ask about his work he'd say he was just glad to be home and forget it for a while. She never pushed him, believing in her old-fashioned way that unless a man needed help or advice from a wife, her only role was to look after her husband and be with him when he came home to relax.

Now she was querying what else went on during those hours he was away from her. Yet she couldn't start probing, accusing him of hiding things from her. Nevertheless, it now bothered her so strongly that she could hardly keep herself from asking. But if she were to, it would raise all sorts of nasty feelings and she couldn't have that, especially if those foolish thoughts that came to

322

her now were quite wrong. David wasn't a philanderer, she was dead sure of that.

Shrugging off the thought, she gave him a goodnight peck on the cheek and turned over, his deep sigh and sleepy remark that the party had been a thorough success thanks to her, calming her stupid thoughts. She heard him yawn and whisper sleepily, 'It'd be nice to do it again soon.'

Immediately her mind flew to that next time and a vow to keep a lookout for that woman he'd so glibly told her he hadn't noticed. If she was at the next social evening which she was quietly planning for the Easter, she'd know then, wouldn't she?

The thought made her heart thud and her mind whirl until finally it melted into a nonsensical dream in which she was following him endlessly across fields and Jennifer Wainwright of all people was at her elbow saying, 'I said there was a woman ... He's in love with another, prettier woman...'

Next morning, things having a totally different look to them, she could laugh at such a silly dream, even as she cringed to have thought David could be unfaithful – steady, dependable David. What a fool she was!

Sunday, the piles of dishes and the need to clear away the debris of twenty-five or so people and restore the place to tidiness helped all the more to take away the previous evening's needless concern. She was sure now that whoever the woman was, she'd been someone who'd trespassed on an interesting party, easy in a place like this; someone driving by, irresponsible enough to see an opportunity to enjoy a bit of fun and free food. It now came to her that perhaps the woman might have had a friend with her who'd kept a lower profile so he or she hadn't been noticed.

Whatever, it was over and she would forget all about it and enjoy the day with David, who'd decided that instead of her cooking again they'd drive to Brentwood and have Sunday lunch in an old and very popular inn they'd found there.

Indeed she hadn't looked forward to cooking Sunday lunch and was now seriously thinking of acting on Jennifer Wainwright's suggestion that she employ someone to cook and clean. Not to live in, but someone from the village who'd come daily or at least three or four times a week. She spoke to David about it while they were enjoying their meal and he seemed all for it.

'But let's get Christmas over, then we can sort it all out,' he said, to which she readily agreed.

She'd have to pick carefully, but it would be nice to have someone around to talk to when he was away. One couldn't always be running off to local meetings and groups, sometimes in wet weather and soon maybe in the snow, just to while away the hours until David came home.

'Maybe I'll begin looking around once we get New Year over,' she said, to which David seemed happy enough.

'You need to find someone reliable and that might take time,' was his parting shot.

To her surprise it didn't take as long as she had

expected. Five days on from the New Year, she was in the village shop, its only customer at that moment and with a few minutes to herself, Mrs Evans asked how she and her husband were finding life here?'

Encouraged, Eileen smiled. 'We're settling in very well, thank you, and we like the village. At least I do. Mr Burnley doesn't see much of it, working in London, but I hope when the better weather comes he might get out a little more.'

'Well, there are plenty of social activities, we've a good cricket club, and there's a well-attended bowling green and a tennis club.'

'I'm afraid he might be a little too old for tennis.'

Florrie Evans laughed. 'You should see some of *our* players!' she quipped easily, making Eileen chuckle a little, becoming suddenly talkative.

'David is something of a cricket person and bowls would be nice for both of us. As to myself, I'm enjoying the clubs I've joined here and seem to be fitting in. Someone mentioned I might help out at the infant school, perhaps standing in for any teacher who might be absent through sickness. I was a schoolteacher before I was married, you know.'

'So I heard. It must be a very absorbing profession.'

'Yes. I was sorry to give it up, but a wife's duty is to her husband first and foremost and my school were disinclined to have married teachers—'

'I'm sure a tiny village school wouldn't let that

bother them,' the woman broke in. 'I think they'd be pleased to have you, should—'

'The trouble is,' Eileen interrupted in her turn, 'if I were to take up such an offer, with a big place like Crossways, I couldn't manage all the housework that needs to be done, cook meals and help out in a school.'

Mrs Evans was thoughtful for a second then her brow cleared.

'Why don't you pay someone to do the cooking for you? In fact I know someone who'd be more than eager to take on something like that. She's a widow, lost her husband before the war. She lives next door to this shop, just a hop from you.'

Florrie Evans's eyes almost danced at her good idea as she rushed on. 'Her husband left her quite comfortably off but she's often said she'd like to do a little job that doesn't entail full working hours. She'd be just right for you. Her name is Edna Calder. She has a daughter of fifteen who left school last year and hasn't yet found work. Well, she isn't the brightest of girls...'

She broke off to lower her voice. 'I don't mean she's silly, just that she's not clever enough for a clerical job and her mother doesn't want her working in a factory. But she'd make a good housemaid and it might be the making of her, help get her started in the job world. And what with you being a schoolteacher, you might be able to help her along, some tuition perhaps.'

For a moment, Eileen felt herself draw back mentally. Here was the catch – free tuition on top of wages. Certainly not! But the very next moment her interest was awakened. Her teaching instincts had always been strong, so strong that her blood surged at the idea. Instead of charging a fee, as one should, the girl could work off the cost of tuition by taking a much lesser wage. It was a perfect arrangement, but more it was something to which she was warming by the minute. She'd be teaching again.

'Perhaps your neighbour and her daughter would like to come over, maybe tomorrow or Friday,' she suggested, 'so that we can discuss it.'

Edna Calder was a small, dumpy woman, plainly dressed, no trimmings. She indeed looked every inch a cook, about Eileen's own age. She instantly felt a rapport with the woman.

The daughter Evelyn, however, was a surprise, in fact a shock. Totally different to what she had expected and so unlike her mother as to hardly seem her daughter at all.

Eileen had expected her to be of short stature, a tendency towards plumpness like her mother, maybe round-faced with straight, straggly dark hair and that slightly vacant expression of un-interest some young people tended to bear these days.

Instead she was tall, almost willowy, a young woman looking much older than her fifteen years. Short fair hair curled about her ears, framing a stunningly pretty face and wide blue eyes. She probably took after the father she'd lost.

But it was her mode of dress that shook Eileen. Her mother had obviously spoiled her daughter dreadfully, allowing her to wear such clothes, far too mature for a girl of her age – heels too high for any fifteen-year-old, the blue jacket with its nipped-in waist and tremendously full skirt making her look eighteen at least.

Introduced by her mother, her response, 'I'm fine, thanks,' to Eileen's 'How-do-you-do?' rather gave her a start. High-pitched, breathless, almost seductive; with a voice like that she could land herself in trouble came the thought. How was she expected to tutor such a girl, whom she now saw as more wilful than dim, one used to having her own way – rather than being unsuitable for any job, she no doubt saw herself as being too good.

Recovering herself, Eileen led them into the lounge where they'd be more comfortable. Edna Calder seemed to be perfect, but she needed to scrutinise the daughter a deal more closely. Could she take one without the other or would Mrs Calder say that she couldn't really come here without her daughter?

To Evelyn she said, 'It certainly won't be heavy work. The house was completely redecorated when we moved in, so there'll be little to do other than keeping it tidy, dusting, vacuuming, on odd occasions cleaning a few windows, and also giving your mother a bit of help in the kitchen by clearing and putting things away, general matters, you know.'

To her relief, the girl listened quietly to all she said, both mother and daughter nodding occasionally as each chore was explained.

'I'm sure she'll be more than happy with that,'

Mrs Calder finally said, speaking on her daughter's behalf, at the same time bending her eye upon her with an emphatic, 'won't you, dear?'

It was said with a deal of firmness, to which Evelyn nodded silently. Instantly Eileen saw where the problem lay. Allowing her daughter to dress so precociously, maybe the plump, dowdy mother wanted to see the person she wished she'd been, in her own meek way ruling the girl?

Blessed are the meek for they shall be obeyed, she misquoted to herself, and fell to wondering what this girl might have been like had she been left to be herself. Her every thought taken care of for her, no wonder she looked to others as being somewhat dim.

Often a mother hanging on to her only offspring would do her best to keep that child a child for as long as possible. This woman was doing the opposite, and Eileen found herself wondering what the girl would be like when finally her mother let go of her. She had a good idea that the moment she found her feet she'd kick over the traces without ever looking back, even becoming quite unmanageable. The poor woman was in for a shock one day.

'So do you think Evelyn will be able to do the work needing to be done here?' Mrs Calder was saying, bringing Eileen's thoughts back to the present.

'I can't see any reason why not.' She'd have preferred to address Evelyn personally, but found herself discussing the girl as if she wasn't there. 'I think she will be fine.'

The woman's relief appeared immense. 'I'm so

glad. And I'll make sure she does all she's told.'

'I'm sure she will,' Eileen said, then collecting herself looked directly at the girl, adding, 'I'm sure you will, won't you?'

To which Evelyn nodded vigorously, which actually did seem to make her appear dim-witted. Yet Eileen had a sneaking suspicion that she'd prove as sharp as any, maybe too sharp.

She turned to the mother. 'So when do you feel you could start?'

'We could start any time you wish, Mrs Burnley,' came the ready reply.

'Would Tuesday do you?'

'That would be fine with us,' said Mrs Calder, giving her daughter a light tap on the arm to prompt the girl into adding her nod of consent.

Evelyn had kept very quiet during all this, though Eileen had a feeling that out of her mother's earshot she could prove quite vocal, wasting time talking instead of working. But it was best to see how it went before jumping to any conclusion.

Twenty-Eight

Sitting in the lounge chatting over coffee, this was the first time Jennifer Wainwright had been invited to Crossways Lodge since the Christmas party a few months ago, but she'd only seen the old ballroom then. Until now they'd always gone to the tea shop, but Eileen was eager to show her the improvements they'd done to the house since moving in.

Jennifer Wainwright stole a furtive glance around the lounge. It was quite different from the last time she'd sat here. That had been before the war. She'd quickly dropped Joyce Johns-Pitman after that awful incident, when in a jealous frenzy the woman had plunged a knife into her husband's neck. Whether intentional or accidental was never really proved, except that she'd been committed to an asylum for treatment.

Where she was now, Jennifer had no interest in finding out. But she could still remember how the house had looked when they'd been friends – elegant and beautiful, with delicate spindly-legged furniture in the style of the 1930s, with pictures and photographs on all the walls. All that had been replaced by the more robust, chunkier look still surviving from the utility days of wartime, which five years on still filled the house, the Burnleys having obviously chosen to overlook the introduction of a gentler, 1950s' style.

Had Joyce and Arnold Johns-Pitman still been here and all been well between them, they'd have kept up with the times. But they'd been younger people, eager to follow all that was fashionable. Eileen and David Burnley, twenty years older, were more set in their ways. Preferring to keep to what they knew rather then go ultra-modern, they had opted for darker, plainer, longer lasting colours where once everything had been bright and flowery.

She noticed it very strongly as Eileen conducted her proudly around the house. In every room the wallpapers were subdued, the soft furnishings plain, every bed, wardrobe, cupboard and sideboard, table and chairs, settee and armchair had that utility look about it, completely characterless.

She suspected this was Eileen's choice rather than her husband's. She had come to recognise that Eileen was old-fashioned in her ways, a person naturally very sure of herself, an erstwhile schoolteacher who guided rather than followed. Her husband was obviously the easier going of the two, despite being the breadwinner, and was no doubt wrapped up in his business, she supposed.

Despite its present lack of character she had to admit the house was very warm and cosy. Only in the big room, as Eileen now preferred to call it, the chandelier that had been so talked about in the past still in place, did she instantly feel a chill as they stepped inside, despite the bulky radiators being on. Maybe it was only in her mind, but the room didn't feel at all natural. The chill could have come from it being such a vast room, or the bleak March air tending to infiltrate through the French windows at the far end. But from what she could recall, it had always been said to have possessed a certain peculiar coldness, ever since the man who'd moved here from the East End of London had killed two people then drowned himself.

Today it felt as chilly as ever. The high ceiling probably contributed to it, though a recently added wide picture rail from which hung quite a few large, framed watercolours of country views gave it a feeling of being lived in. Yet the huge chandelier gracing the centre once more worried her.

'It wasn't there when we first moved in,' Eileen told her, seeing her gazing up at it. 'Doesn't it look stupendous? I found it in one of our outbuildings. David doesn't like it much but I think it's beautiful. Let's go back into the lounge. I'll make us some more coffee then tell you all about it.'

Sitting in the cosy lounge while Eileen went off to make the coffee, Jennifer wondered why her friend, so prim and proper in her ways, should have become so animated as she spoke about the chandelier.

Seated opposite each other across the small, highly polished round table, nibbling at their shortbread biscuits, Eileen looked almost smug as she told her of her discovery, like a child telling of a holiday by the sea. It was unusual for her to talk so passionately as she told her the tale, so much so that Jennifer experienced a tinge of concern for her friend.

'It's the one you told me about that day we first had coffee together,' Eileen said. 'It was such a surprise finding it. No one mentioned it when we bought the place. Maybe the agent didn't even know about it. The army must have had it taken down when they were first billeted here and thought it best to put it in storage in case it got damaged. It's probably quite valuable now, and to think it was sitting there under some old tarpaulin all that time until I found it. I had it cleaned and restored and put back in the big room.' Gabbling on, she'd hardly come up for breath. 'Now it's been restored it looks as new as the day it was bought, don't you think?'

'I wouldn't know,' Jennifer said cautiously. 'I never came here when the Butterfields lived here. But I heard about it of course. The first time I saw it was when the Johns-Pitmans came here to live and I became quite friendly with the wife for a time.' She didn't go any further into it, preferring not to get involved in more uncomfortable reminiscences on the tragedy that had happened between those two people. Finishing her coffee she glanced at her watch and said that she really must be going. She had to get home to prepare lunch and do a bit of shopping.

After Jennifer had said goodbye, Eileen suddenly felt the emptiness left at her going. David had gone out to play golf with those of the club he'd joined. He had wanted her to join too, but she had declined, preferring the more gentle company of her ladies' groups.

Why David wanted to traipse around a wet golf course on a chilly day like this was beyond her. But he would be home in a couple of hours and she looked forward to that. They'd have a nice lunch which she would now take herself off to the kitchen to prepare, having given Mrs Calder this Saturday off to see a sister-in-law. This afternoon David would read the paper, probably going into the library while she came back into the lounge and read her book. Each in separate rooms but with the knowledge that he was nearby and that was comforting; she wouldn't feel this unusual loneliness that seemed to have descended on her lately.

It was so odd. She had never felt lonely when she had lived alone, in fact had rather enjoyed her own company. So it was strange to feel this way now she was married.

After a while, tiring of reading, she'd go up to her sewing room which she'd had converted from one of the bedrooms, and finish the patchwork quilt she was making for the WI charity bring-and-buy sale in April. Later she'd go to prepare dinner and afterwards they'd both go into the lounge and sit by the fire together, curtains drawn cosily against the balmy night winds of March, and listen to the radio before going off to bed.

They had separate beds. Used to sleeping alone all her spinster years, she'd not found it at all comfortable sleeping next to someone. He for his own part seemed quite happy with that arrangement.

Sunday morning he'd be going off to enjoy another round of golf, but she wouldn't mind then because she would go to church and he'd be home for lunch and share the rest of the day with her.

Monday he'd be in London, but there was the WI in the afternoon and Mrs Calder would be here, as would Evelyn, doing what little tidying there was, with an hour off to be taught how to add faster than she now did.

To Eileen's surprise, Evelyn was proving a willing learner, far quicker on the uptake than she'd first imagined. So what had gone so wrong with her schooling? But she knew what. She'd come across children like her before, influenced by others into lazy ways, a couldn't-care-less-about-the-future attitude, seeing it all as a bore. Maybe a result of the war with its many distractions, air raids interrupting what should have been the smooth flow of learning, kids evacuated, sent to isolated parts of the country, breaking the steady rhythm of education – so many things.

But this one-to-one tutoring, although spasmodic, was proving quite beneficial for the girl, at the same time filling up her own days while David was at work. It did her heart good, hoping Evelyn would develop into a worthwhile person, and at the same time gave her pleasure.

Taking on Mrs Calder was one of the best things she'd ever done. Her only concern was that local people still indulging from time to time in talk of past violence connected to this house and curious goings on that were said to have emanated from it might worry the woman when she came here.

For weeks she wrestled with the idea of asking her if she believed the creepy stories, but never did. It did occur to her that Mrs Calder never went into the big room, although she'd have no cause to, but still it made her wonder.

Evelyn, on the other hand, would go in there regularly to dust, vacuum and wash the long windows at the front of the house. She'd catch herself watching her closely, but she seemed quite at ease in there, even singing in her flat little voice as she worked. Eileen would find her up on a set of steps dusting the chandelier while she hummed little snatches of those modern repetitious songs youngsters these days called music. Without any accompaniment it sometimes sounded almost like a sort of incantation. She didn't like it, but how could she upset her by ordering her to stop singing?

'You don't object to cleaning such a big room?' she probed on one occasion. 'It is a lot to do.'

'No, it's fine with me,' Evelyn told her in her casual way.

'It doesn't bother you at all?'

'I don't think so.' The pretty face had adopted a questioning look.

'Just that...' Unable to explain her need to enquire, Eileen broke off, saying instead, 'It's a large room and can be a bit chilly in here.'

'Sometimes,' Evelyn muttered dispassionately and went on dusting.

It was best not to press her further. She must have heard the stories about this house, but it probably went over her head, as did most things with the young except what affected them personally. They lived for today and their own pleasures and nothing else mattered.

Trying to fathom it she asked Edna Calder one day, 'What do you think of what they say in the village about this house?'

The woman laughed. 'Oh, things like that don't bother me. People love making mountains out of molehills.'

'So you do believe there have been a few ... *molehills*,' Eileen probed, and again Mrs Calder laughed.

'Well, there were those crimes that were committed, but spooks and hauntings if that's what you're referring to, Mrs Burnley, no, I don't. But I am the down-to-earth sort. And naturally an old house like this has a history.'

'You mean they say it's always been haunted.' She hadn't meant to say it like that, but Edna Calder gave an easy shrug.

'Nothing anyone knows of, not until that chap from East London got here and did in his fancy woman and her lover. I think that started it off.'

She turned back to rolling out the suet dough for the delicious meat pudding she was doing for that evening's meal, happy now to just chat. 'You know the back of this house has been here since the early 1800s. It was quite a big house then. I was told that it was sold around 1910 to people called ... I think it was Darnell, or something like that. It was them that built this part on to it and made it even bigger and renamed it Crossways Lodge. Then it was bought in the late twenties, early thirties, after the Wall Street Crash, by that couple from the East End of London. I remember him well when I was young, trying to turn himself into a country gentleman – made that big room too by knocking three rooms and the hallway into one.' She gave a chuckle as she moulded her dough around the inside of a basin to be filled with pieces of beef.

'People saw him as a silly old fool trying to be what he wasn't. Some reckoned he was a bit of a rogue in London but he seemed harmless enough here. That was until he took up with his fancy bit and his wife left him. He drowned himself, you know, dead drunk. But he wasn't as harmless as people thought, not after finding those two bodies. Could only have been him who'd done it. I don't suppose we'll ever know the rights of that. But from then on, the place does seem to have been curs—'

She broke off sharply, the word unfinished, and Eileen felt a shiver ripple along her spine recalling Jennifer Wainwright telling of someone she'd known having seen something that had caused her to go mad and kill her husband, at her trial raving on about a ghostly visitor.

As she left Mrs Calder to her work, she told herself sternly that she wasn't the sort to get carried away by such tales, yet something switched her mind to Evelyn as a sound came from upstairs.

Making as little noise as possible, she crept up the stairs following the sound. It was coming from her and David's bedroom. Bursting into the room she found Evelyn on hands and knees in front of the fire grate. On the dressing table lay a duster, a tin of Silvo and a cloth with which she had been polishing the silver ornaments, now all sparkly clean. The bed had been made, night-dress and pyjamas neatly folded.

As Evelyn turned quickly at the sound of someone coming into the bedroom so abruptly, Eileen experienced a stab of guilt, knowing she'd been half hoping to catch the girl either taking advantage by peeping into places where she had no business to or idling away gazing out of the window. Instead, the room was clean, tidy and as bright as a new pin.

Recovering from the interruption, she smiled brightly up at Eileen, a blackened polishing rag in one hand, a tin of black-lead in the other.

'Everything all right, Mrs Burnley?'

Eileen hesitated. 'Yes.' What could she say? 'I just need a cardigan.' But she was already wearing one. 'A different cardigan,' she corrected.

Evelyn got to her feet. 'It's alright, Mrs Burnley, I've just finished here,' she said almost apologetically. 'It took me a bit longer than usual.'

Eileen said nothing as she took off the cardigan she was wearing and blindly selected another, only to realise that it didn't even match her jumper, blue on pink, ridiculous!

'I like the brown one you was already wearing much better,' ventured Evelyn with no hint of embarrassment.

Eileen hesitated, completely confused. 'I think

340

you're right.'

Evelyn didn't seem to be listening. 'Anyway, I think I'm just about done up here, Mrs Burnley. If there isn't nothing else, I'll go down and see if Mum wants a hand.'

With that she gathered up her cleaning tools and headed from the room, leaving Eileen gazing blankly after her.

After a while, following the girl's course down the back stairs, she paused at the bottom to hear Mrs Calder's rather high, piercing voice. 'Well, I just hope you weren't being cheeky to Mrs Burnley up there, that's all.'

Evelyn's voice was small and meek – 'No, Mum, I wasn't' – so different to the confident voice of a moment ago, one that could have come from any mature woman speaking to an equal. Now she was the child again and Eileen suddenly felt for her.

On impulse she hurried into the kitchen. Evelyn was sitting on a stool looking down at her hands. Her mother standing over her, she might easily have been some ten-year-old, but looking incongruous even for one her age, in blue jeans, jumper with Dolman sleeves and padded shoulders, the front and back different colours, bolero, a heavy necklace and wedge platform shoes.

'Your daughter does a really lovely job of the bedrooms,' Eileen said. 'I'm very pleased with her.'

Edna Calder looked at her employer, her frown vanishing. 'Well, that's all right then,' she said, 'so long as she isn't cheeky.'

'Oh she isn't, not in the least,' Eileen said

readily.

She heard Edna Calder give a small 'humph' as she turned back to heaping pieces of sliced onion on top of the chopped steak, adding seasoned gravy and laying the suet crust on top.

A quiet smile passed between Eileen and Evelyn. Despite wishing the girl wouldn't go in for such unusually mature clothes, she couldn't help being on her side for once.

Twenty-Nine

Winter not far off, they'd been in this house some eighteen months and well settled in. She and David had become part of the local social activities, he a well-entrenched member of both cricket and golf club. She now chaired one of her women's groups and last June had been asked to step in to take a class of seven-year-olds for a while when their teacher had gone down with 'flu.

With so much taking up her time, Eileen was relying on Edna Calder and her daughter more and more, so long as she didn't allow the woman's incessant chat to interfere with her work. Evelyn seemed happy getting on with hers, at the same time her writing and arithmetic improving immensely under Eileen's tutoring.

David had been sceptical of her at first, but had soon changed his mind, and if he happened to be home when she was working about the house he would chat away to her as if they were old friends or she a daughter. He was a lot more relaxed these days, though he seemed to come home tired. Work was stepping up. 1950 now over, the country was at last putting the austerity of the war years behind it. Petrol rationing like most other commodities had finally ended after ten years, and this summer people had begun driving to the seaside for holidays.

Until last summer David had only been able to take the car as far as the station each day, taking the train the rest of the way into London. Now he could go all the way into London by car, and in August they'd driven down to Devon for a holiday, wonderful being in the car instead of on a train.

This evening they'd stayed up until quite late, talking over next year's holidays, abroad this time, and now she lay wide awake thinking about them. David too seemed restless. Finally he sat up.

'It's no good, I can't sleep.'

'Neither can I,' she said. 'But if I don't I'll be fit for nothing in the morning.'

Even so, she turned over and closed her eyes in the need to find sleep. Some ten minutes later she heard him slide out of bed, listened to him going to the bedroom door. Sleepily she asked where he was going.

'I left my book downstairs. Reading might help me sleep. I don't want to disturb you so I might go into the library for a little read.'

For a while after he'd gone, she lay, eyes closed, willing sleep to come, making herself visualise rolling hills and gentle sea lapping on a sandy beach, a cloudless sky, cornflower blue. She could even see the colour behind her tightly closed eyelids. Then without warning the sky began to darken as thunderclouds as black as night crept towards her. She opened her eyes with a start, became wide awake.

344

David hadn't come back to bed. How long had she been asleep? It did seem that she had, as flicking on the bedside lamp the little clock beside it read 11.30. She had been asleep some twenty minutes. It was time he should have tired of reading. Getting up, she slipped her arms into her robe and, quietly opening the bedroom door, made her way to the stairs, making no sound.

Halfway down she glanced over the banister. The hall was dark but there was just enough light to see that the door to the big room was wide open, allowing moonlight to filter through into the hall. She always made sure of keeping it closed against the draught that tended to come from that room. So why was it now open, unless David had gone in there, but why would he? As she stood there she felt rather than saw a movement, her eyes flicking immediately towards it to see what looked like the dim figure of a woman or girl hurrying from the direction of the library to disappear through the open door of the big room.

Springing into action with a cry of surprise, Eileen sped down the rest of the stairs and across the hall to the place she had last seen the figure. She reached the door in time to see the person about to hurry through the now open French windows.

Eileen's voice came loud and piercing. 'Stop!'

The figure turned towards her, standing very still.

'Who are you?' Her mouth had gone dry but she managed to calm herself enough to demand, 'What're you after? What are you doing here at this time of night?'

There was no reply. The woman remained standing quite still. Eileen knew she should go forward, apprehend the interloper whoever she was, but she couldn't move. A strange chill had begun to creep over her. Momentarily she looked down to draw her robe closer around her. It could have taken less than a second but when she looked up the person was gone.

A voice behind her made her jump almost out of her skin. 'What's going on? Who are you talking to?'

For a moment she stared at David, he having come from the library, book still in hand. Quickly she gathered her wits, now with anger rising – anger and a sick feeling of disbelief at what was going through her mind.

'Who's that woman I saw?' she demanded. 'What's she doing here?'

'What woman?'

'I saw her coming out of the library.'

'I don't understand, love. I've been in there reading.'

'I saw her!'

Eileen's heart was pounding. She fought to still the shock, the words 'another woman' pounding inside her head. How long? And who? Someone in his company, a secretary perhaps, the pair of them enjoying their illicit love? Perhaps she was married too. Maybe her husband had no idea, like herself until now. But to bring her here...

'Who is she?' Eileen said, her voice so faint she could hardly hear it herself.

His bewilderment had begun to turn to annoyance. 'For God's sake, Eileen, what are you talking about?'

'You know very well what I'm talking about.' Her voice came stronger now. 'How long has it been going on?'

'How long has what been going on?' He sounded confused.

'You and her, whoever she is. Who is she?'

He was frowning at her now. 'You've been dreaming, love.'

'I've not been dreaming!' Suddenly incensed, her voice had risen even higher. 'I've been lying awake waiting for you to come up to bed!' She was babbling now. 'I came down to see if you were ready to come back upstairs and I saw that woman cross the hall and go in here.' Standing in the doorway she pointed into the room. 'I saw her as clear as I see you. She seemed in a blessed great hurry. Who is she? And what've you both been up to? And how long have you known her? I want to know. How long has it been going on?' Words tumbled from her lips while he stood as though petrified by her outburst.

He had now become annoyed, his voice rising. 'I don't know for the life of me what you're talking about, Eileen! I've been in the library reading. I've not seen any woman. Maybe you saw a ghost? Have a look!' With that he reached past her for the panel of light switches, flooding the room with instant brightness. 'Have a good look! And tell me, can you see anyone now?'

They both stared into the huge room, half dazzled by the power of the chandelier and wall lights together, seldom if ever turned on all at once.

'She'd have been gone by the time we...' Eileen began, but she broke off mid-sentence. At the far end the French windows lay wide open.

David turned to her. 'They were locked when we went to bed. So who unlocked them?'

'I don't know,' she said weakly.

She looked at him, a shudder running through her. Neither of them spoke. Then he put an arm around her.

'Don't worry. I'll close and lock them, then take a quick look around the house, see if anything is missing. Too late now to contact the police. We'll do that in the morning.'

She stood mute as he dealt with the windows, returning to put an arm about her shoulders as he turned off the lights, leading her out into the hall and closing the door behind them. Meekly she let him guide her upstairs, her flesh feeling ice cold even beneath her dressing gown, despite his holding her close as they went back to their bedroom.

There she waited, her mind full of thoughts as he made a brief round of the house, returning to say all seemed in order.

'I'm sorry, the things I said,' she told him as she lay in her bed.

'Don't be,' he said simply, bending to kiss her on the forehead before slipping into his own bed.

Soon he was snoring, but she remained wide awake, still thinking. He wasn't the sort of man to seek out sex. It was ridiculous to think he would bring some woman here to the house, to carry on a clandestine romance. Yet she had definitely seen *something*, had spoken to it, though it hadn't replied ... It? No, *her,* it had to be flesh and blood, an interloper caught in the act of breaking and entering. She told herself this again and again, but next morning, a bright, sunny, early June morning, her mind was no easier.

The police came that following morning but finding nothing missing, more or less dismissed the incident, David was now convinced he'd overlooked locking the French windows, allowing someone easy entrance in the hope of stealing something. Eileen must have disturbed them.

'A *woman* burglar?' Eileen challenged sceptically.

'There could be some,' he said easily, too easily it felt. 'You gave her a fright. She certainly won't be coming back, and nothing was taken.'

Unconvinced, Eileen didn't reply. He seemed far too eager to write the whole thing off as an attempted burglary, or was he covering up for himself?

Several days later that latter suspicion seemed to be founded. In the last glimmer of twilight, David ensconced in the library busy with some office work, something made her come out from the lounge where she'd been reading, in time to see the figure again crossing the hall, again strangely dressed. This time the twilight was just enough for her to recognise the figure. Evelyn Calder!

She and her mother had gone home long before, so what was she doing back here? Even as she called out for her to stop right where she was, Eileen's mind was racing.

David and Evelyn! The husband she had thought so fine and upright, cheating on her, no better than any other man, prey to temptation, and with a girl hardly more than a schoolgirl. She felt suddenly sick even as she yelled out a challenge to her.

The girl turned at her cry and for a split second seemed to pause. The eyes were narrowed, the painted mouth fixed in a derisive smile. Even as Eileen blinked, she disappeared through the open door to the big room.

Shocked and furious, Eileen bounded after her, her voice rising to a shriek. 'Come back here! You, come back!'

This time she would catch her, demand to know what she was doing here. It took less than a second to reach the room. But there was no sign of her. Even in the dim twilight she'd have seen her, caught her before ever she reached the French windows, this time definitely closed and locked. Yet there was no trace of her.

Running across to the French windows, Eileen fumbled with the key, managing to turn it and fling open the doors to the conservatory. They were also locked. Turning that key with one swift movement, she leapt out to the garden. There was no one to be seen, no movement, no sound. In sudden alarm, she backed away, through the conservatory and back into the room. It was deadly cold, despite having been a warm day. Elsewhere the house still retained the lingering warmth of a fine day, but not here. She could feel it penetrating her skin.

A voice behind her made her swing round to see David standing there. 'What on earth are you doing?' he asked. 'Why are you shouting?'

She made towards him in a fury at his feigned innocence. 'I saw her this time – as clear as I see you. Don't lie to me, David. I know what you've been up to. But a child! How could you – a mere kid!'

'What *are* you talking about?' he began, his tone that of someone who was feeling his patience being tried, but seconds later stepped back as the palm of her hand caught him a stinging smack across his cheek.

'You know what I'm talking about,' she continued to yell. 'Living across the road makes it so easy for the two of you! Take advantage of stupid tales of ghosts and spirits so you can fool me. You disgust me!'

She broke off as he caught her by the shoulders in a grip that hurt. 'What are you implying?' he burst out, his tone grating sharply.

'You and that Calder girl, you and her...'

He shook her almost savagely. 'What do you think I am? How can you think I'd be interested in anyone but you, much less a child of that age? Is that what you've been imagining, Eileen? Have you such little trust in me to even dream I'd look at anyone else? But if that's so, that you feel you cannot trust me, our marriage might as well be over. Is that what you want?'

'No...' The word tore itself from her. She felt near to collapse had he not been holding her. She wanted to cry, 'Swear you've not been unfaithful,' but all she could say was, 'Then who was that girl I saw? What was she doing here?' her voice weak and faint.

He was holding her tightly against him, his voice gentle now. 'There was no girl. You must have been having a dream.'

'I wasn't,' she said feebly. 'I was awake. I was in the lounge, reading. I just felt ... something made me go out into the hall. I don't know why.' Tears began to fill her eyes. She looked up into his face. 'What was it, David? What's happening here?'

'I don't know,' he said quietly. 'Something's going on, but it's not a ghost, there are no such things. If you start to believe that there are, you'll end up going off your head.'

She fell silent, letting him hold on to her. What he said did make sense, but in that case, what was wrong with her? Maybe she *was* going off her head, letting herself be affected by local superstition.

The thought was discomforting and comforting at the same time, for no one in their right mind would have themselves believe in ghosts. Yet she *had* seen something. Local rumours played in her head: some oddly dressed woman seen at Crossways Lodge, said to speak warnings of betrayal, those she spoke to suddenly behaving irrationally with dire consequences. But then, people loved making the most of hearsay. True there had been some drastic acts here in the past, but that wasn't to say it had prompted ghostly appearances.

Even so, it didn't explain away what she'd seen. Yes it could have been Evelyn with a mind to help herself to one or two things lying about. She knew the layout of the house and had seen some nice things. A little more clear-headed now, she let David continue to hold her close. Tomorrow she would ask Evelyn where she was last night. Or better still, first have a word with the girl's mother, who she felt she could trust to answer truthfully rather than Evelyn.

Thirty

The following morning they were their usual selves, Edna Calder talkative as ever, Evelyn too completely at ease as she went about her work.

When they stopped for their usual cup of tea, Eileen sat with them, Mrs Calder busy nattering away concerning every little thing that went on in Wadely. Evelyn, however, had begun to seem just a little on edge. Put on the alert, Eileen hardly heard what Mrs Calder was saying, and it wasn't long before she burst out, 'Did you have a nice time last night, Evelyn?'

The girl looked startled and Eileen felt she had to justify the question. 'I thought you mentioned yesterday you were going out last night?'

She'd tried to make it sound casual but it felt more as though she was interrogating her, like some detective.

'Last night?' Evelyn queried uncertainly, then pulled herself together noticeably. 'Oh, yes, last night – I went to the pictures – in Brentwood.'

Eileen hadn't meant her inquiry to be so direct and Evelyn's mother was looking protective of her. 'Why d'you ask, Mrs Burnley?'

She'd intended to go on to enquire what film Evelyn had seen, but that would have appeared even more like an interrogation.

'I just ... I thought I saw her here last night,' she stumbled on, now feeling somewhat ridiculous.

'Here?' Edna Calder echoed, her tone one of bewilderment.

'I just thought...' She stopped, aware that she was making an utter ass of herself.

Moments later came a wave of relief that she hadn't continued as Mrs Calder said, still bewildered, 'Me and Evelyn always go to the pictures on Thursday night. I hate going on my own. I suppose one day when she meets a nice young man to take her, I'll probably stop going, unless of course I find a friend to go with.'

Eileen let the woman ramble on, glad to have the matter dropped. But who was it she had seen two nights running? The question continued to plague her for days.

At least the person, whoever it was, hadn't come back, leaving her to wonder if it was some unidentified intruder, or even Evelyn, her mother lying on her daughter's behalf. For surely it couldn't have been anything more sinister. That thought was ludicrous.

The only thing she could think was to tell Jennifer Wainwright about it, who said, 'Who in their right mind would return to the scene after almost being caught the first time?' adding darkly, 'I think, deep down, Eileen, you know what you saw.'

It wasn't the advice she'd been looking for. Had she merely come upon some flesh and blood intruder or had she actually seen an apparition? Neither thought sat easy with her. Unable to help herself, she told David how she felt. He gave a somewhat patronising chuckle.

'You probably didn't see anyone, love, real or unreal. Maybe just some reflection or other, some trick of the light, like when we're sure we see a movement or something out of the corner of our eye and it turns out there's nothing there.'

It sounded a limp excuse and somehow put her on her guard. What if it had been Evelyn, crossing the hall from the library at that time of night? If that didn't point to something going on, what did?

Her senses sharpened, she was sure she'd noticed a hesitation in his explanation, seen him catch his lower lip briefly between his teeth, like someone checking over what he'd said. Even his laugh sounded false now.

'Although who can say if there is something in it ... you know, not of this world. I suppose there could be such things?' It sounded an excuse, he even willing to grab at straws to cover his tracks, his conduct more parrying than patronising. 'Whatever it was, love, it's done us no harm. Old houses can be full of strange things. Just don't let yourself dwell on it too much.'

Her mind was working. The idea of a ghost would suit him down to the ground if he was trying to cover something up. For a second she wanted to leap at him, reach out and smack him across his lying face. The next, sanity had returned. She trusted him. He'd never deceive her. Not David.

Yet doubt continued to linger. She couldn't believe his explanation of some trick of the light or seeing things out of the corner of one's eye. She'd definitely seen a young woman crossing the hall from the library and he had been in there. It could only have been Evelyn, in those silly clothes far too old for her. She had to be sure.

The next two weeks she watched but nothing more happened. Either he was keeping a low profile or she'd truly not seen what she thought she had. In any case, the passing of time was starting to dull the memory, she even a little angry with herself for having doubted him.

More and more it seemed akin to a bad dream. She wasn't given to a fanciful imagination. She might have interrupted someone bent on burgling the house, or maybe someone not quite right in the head. Although to come back a second time was cheeky. And locking the conservatory door to the garden could have been overlooked on both occasions. She'd always left it to David to lock up at night but it might be better to go round after him to check in future. But since there'd been no more disturbances, it didn't matter any more.

Despite telling herself all was well, she watched Evelyn as she worked, and although the girl appeared utterly tranquil, Eileen couldn't avoid the suspicion that continually hovered inside her.

This evening David was in the library, these days calling it his office, going over some work he'd brought home. In the cosy lounge Eileen sat before a still, bright fire, a cup of cocoa beside her, a historical novel open on her lap.

357

Her eyes grown weary, she finished her bed-time drink and laid the book aside to go and see if David was ready for bed, first raking down the fire and switching off the light. As she went out into the unlit hall, a movement caught her eye, a shadowy form flitting across it from the direction of the library. Startled, she let out a gasp.

For that split second the figure paused before disappearing through the door to the big room. But in that brief glimpse she was again sure it had been Evelyn, dressed as always to look ten years older. She could only have been with David.

An overwhelming flood of fury engulfed her. He must know she was only a couple of rooms away, could have burst in on them at any time. Or was that part of the thrill?

Rage exploded inside her such as she'd never felt in her whole life. In that split second it took to spring into action, she bounded for the room into which the figure had disappeared.

Already there came visions of plunging a carving knife into David's traitorous heart, but first she'd overtake her quarry and tear her face apart with her own bare hands.

She was screaming out in blind fury, 'You bitch ... you bloody little bitch ... it *was* you ... it was you all along!'

It had taken less than a second to gain the room, yet already the girl was at the far end. How had she got so far in so short a time? The question brought Eileen to a halt, as if caught by some unseen hand as the figure now turned without haste to look straight at her.

'We are ever deceived...'

The voice seemed to come from a distance, trailing off, sounding so sad. Nor did the figure look at all like Evelyn, and all Eileen could do was to whisper, 'Who the devil are you?' even as she felt herself shudder.

'He vowed to love me ... all men lie...' The words faded into silence as though from a dying person's lips.

Rooted to the spot, Eileen watched her turn, go out of sight through the French windows, very slowly, as if without any need of haste.

Coming suddenly to herself, Eileen leapt into action to run after her. The doors were wide open yet she'd seen that they'd been locked earlier. A shiver ran through her despite a vague, almost stupid thought that ghosts didn't open doors, they floated through windows and went through walls.

With an effort she took herself in hand. These windows had been opened by human hands. Who else could it have been but Evelyn? Proof now that Evelyn and her own husband were...

A movement behind her made her turn sharply, heart in her mouth. David was standing there behind her.

'What was that?' he said. His voice sounded strangled.

For a moment she glared at him, wanting to scream the word adultery at him, but the look on his face stopped her. He was staring past her, his voice husky, filled with disbelief.

'She just vanished. Those doors were locked. I locked them myself, both doors. I took the key out. Now they're open. She just disappeared.'

He looked so genuinely scared that she hurried to him, strangely convinced that whoever it was who'd been here tonight had nothing to do with him. He would never have deceived her. She was a fool ever to have believed he would. What she'd seen or thought she'd seen had been induced by the tales of people wrapped up in superstition.

But David wasn't a superstitious man. He was the sanest man anyone could wish to meet. So what had he seen? With her, it might have been her own self-induced visions, but he was a different matter. The all-consuming, murderous rage she'd experienced earlier made her shudder. If he had seen something unnatural, then something unnatural it must have been. In a moment she had thrown herself into his arms, wanting to say how sorry she was for doubting him, for feeling so near to hatred as to even think such an evil thing as plunging a knife into him.

'If it's that interloper again we'll have to talk to the police tomorrow,' she said, trying to reassure, but he made no reply, except that his hold tightened ever more, like someone who'd been thoroughly scared.

Throughout Christmas he remained quiet, her parents spending it with them wondering what was wrong, something she couldn't answer, leaving them bewildered, her mother remarking that he could be sickening for something and to keep an eye on him.

A week after New Year he came home from

London, a determined expression on his face: 'I've been wondering that we ought to do away with that chandelier,' he said, surprising her. 'It's far too large and ostentatious. It might have been okay in the thirties but it's so very old-fashioned now.' It was the most he'd said in one go in a long time, in fact since that incident before Christmas, still a paradox.

The sudden statement shook her. In her mind the chandelier would hang there for as long as the house stood. It was somehow part of it. Why she should think this she didn't know. She could still recall the sheer excitement that had swept through her the first time she had seen it lying in that outbuilding. Maybe because she discovered it, she actually felt a deep affinity with it and to see it go would be like saying goodbye to an old friend she'd never see again. Yet common sense asked what the attraction was exactly? She couldn't say. Suddenly she was feeling mesmerised by it and for some odd reason the words 'chandelier room' played in her brain.

'The whole room needs modernising,' he was saying, suddenly so emphatic that she found herself almost being forced to agree, even as her mind cried out 'No!'

It was after they'd had tea and retired to the comfortable lounge with its cheerful fire and the curtains closed against the January cold that he said, 'I am thinking too that it might be a nice idea to separate that room back into the three. I'm told it used to be three. Or maybe just two. They'll still be quite big. This is a big house, almost too big for just us. Maybe we should find something smaller...'

'Oh, no!' Eileen burst out, wondering why she should feel so against that idea. 'No,' she said in a more controlled tone. 'It's a lovely house. It feels like home and anything smaller would feel cramped after this. And I've made so many friends here. Having to make new friends somewhere else, I couldn't bear it.'

He nodded sombrely and understandingly. 'Maybe you're right. But as regards the big room...'

'The chandelier room,' she interrupted, wondering why she needed to have made the distinction.

'Yes,' he said, and fell quiet for a moment before continuing. 'People who've come here tell me they don't feel comfortable in that room as it is at present.' He gave a little laugh then again fell silent. Finally, speaking slowly, he said, 'I've often wondered why. So I decided to look into it and make some enquiries and in the process found out some of the history of the house. But it's what I learned about that chandelier that's made me decide to get rid of it.'

He sounded strangely concerned and looking at him she noticed he'd seemed to be faintly embarrassed by what he was saying, he who had scoffed so many times at her own over-active imagination. And when she pushed him on it, he became even more uneasy in front of her.

Finally she managed to get from him what he had learned: his enquiries had led him to the wife of the man who had bought the house back in the early thirties.

'Her name is still Butterfield and she told me a lot. She's getting on in years and a bit rambling, but what she told me was quite a story concerning that blessed chandelier.'

Going on in a low voice, he repeated what she'd told him, the reputed suicide of a once-wealthy woman said to have lost everything in the Wall Street Crash of the late twenties.

'She told me her husband was a bit of a crook in the old days but that wasn't part of the story. What she said was that he became fascinated by what the antique dealer told him about the chandelier. She told me that her husband became almost obsessed by it, whatever that meant.'

Repeating the rest of what the woman had told him, it was almost as if he himself was coming to believe the story that had been wound around it.

'It's not a comfortable story,' he said finally, 'and I suppose it does make one wonder. So you see, darling, if only for our peace of mind it might be as well to get rid of it. I'm not being gullible,' he added a little too quickly, as though needing to negate the effect the tale had indeed had on him. 'Just that we could do with modernising the place, don't you agree?'

Eileen's reluctant nod was interrupted by the telephone in the hall, he hurrying out to answer it, already confident that she'd agreed with him.

Eileen herself wandered into the big room and gazed up at the chandelier. Maybe he was right, the room needed modernising and, beautiful though the thing was, it did look rather out of date. Yet without it the room wouldn't be the same, would somehow feel wrong. She now wished she hadn't agreed to get rid of it. She would come to terms with the strange presence she'd seen, or thought she'd seen. But there was David. He'd seen it too and maybe reasoned that with the chandelier gone there'd be no more odd disturbances.

What was really disturbing was that all-consuming rage that for a moment had taken total control of her, nothing to do with what she'd seen or heard, but some other evil lurking deep inside her. Would she really have taken a knife and plunged it into him in a blind fury? She would never know, even though she told herself she'd never in her life succumbed to mindless rage; it wasn't in her nature.

Yet the thought had been there, more an omen than a thought. What if it still lurked, hidden here inside her? Maybe it lay hidden inside everyone, they not even aware of it until suddenly ... Is that what had happened to those others who'd killed the ones they'd loved? Until then they had probably been the nicest of people.

What if on some other occasion, outraged beyond endurance, she did give way to the ferocity that had reared up inside her? The thought made her feel suddenly sick and with an effort she cast it from mind. She mustn't allow herself to think of it ever again.

Making an effort to put it from mind, she made to follow David back into the lounge, where he'd gone after his telephone call, but again the chandelier caught her eye and she hesitated. Gazing up at it, it felt she was being gently mesmerised.

It was a wonderful sensation and, without taking her eyes from it, she backed slowly towards the main switch, pressing it. The delicate festoons of crystals glittering in the instant brilliance of light suddenly took her breath away and she caught her lip between her teeth, the movement distorting her features as she continued to gaze.

Could she really allow such a lovely thing to go, to be lost forever? A slow, determined smile began to spread across Eileen Burnley's face as she walked from the big room back to find her husband.